Cold Enemies

Jake Adams International Espionage Thriller #19

by
Trevor Scott

Calabria Publishing
United States of America

Also by Trevor Scott

Jake Adams International Espionage Thriller Series
Fatal Network (#1)
Extreme Faction (#2)
The Dolomite Solution (#3)
Vital Force (#4)
Rise of the Order (#5)
The Cold Edge (#6)
Without Options (#7)
The Stone of Archimedes (#8)
Lethal Force (#9)
Rising Tiger (#10)
Counter Caliphate (#11)
Gates of Dawn (#12)
Counter Terror (#13)
Covert Network (#14)
Shadow Warrior (#15)
Sedition (#16)
Choke Points (#17)
Deadly Cabal (#18)
Cold Enemies (#19)
Terminal Force (#20)

Lake Superior Mystery Series
The Fall
Winter Kill
Killer Spring

Max & Robin Kane Mystery Series
Truth or Justice (#1)
Stolen Honor (#2)
Relative Impact (#3)
Without Virtue (#4)
Sweet Home Betrayal (#5)
Powder Keg (#6)
No Retreat (#7)
Deadly Crossing (#8)
Abusive Power (#9)

Dystopian Novel
Liberty Lost

Karl Adams Espionage Thriller Series
The Man from Murmansk (#1)
Siberian Protocol (#2)
The Spy Within (#3)
Double Impact (#4)
Ratchet Up (#5)
Into the Darkness (#6)
Endless Resolve #7
Supreme Power #8

Tony Caruso Mystery Series
Boom Town (#1)
Burst of Sound (#2)
Running Game (#3)

Chad Hunter Espionage Thriller Series

Keenan Fitzpatrick Mystery Series

Mysteries, Thrillers & Fiction

Non Fiction

COLD ENEMIES
Copyright © 2021 by Trevor Scott
Calabria Publishing
United States of America

Author's Note:

Most of my works of fiction are based on elements of my personal experience. This novel brought me back to my Cold War days as an Air Force captain working in West Germany during the last years of the 80s and the first part of the 90s. During the fall of Communism and the Berlin Wall, I was a commander in a Ground-Launched Cruise Missile squadron. Under the direction of the INF Treaty signed by Reagan and Gorbachev, I was part of a team that hosted and escorted members of the Soviet military and intelligence community (KGB), as they observed the drawdown and destruction of these intermediate-range nuclear cruise missiles. This experience eventually led to my writing career as an international thriller author. Thank you for reading my novels through the years. I hope you enjoy them.

1

Jake Adams stood on the covered deck of his Montana ranch with his eyes focused on a group of horses frolicking in the nearest pasture. His dapple-gray mare had dropped an off-white colt in the spring, and the lanky young one kicked his legs as he tried his best to keep up with his mother.

A warm June breeze drifted up the Bitterroot Valley, the smell of fresh grass and manure reminding Jake that this was a real ranch in cowboy country.

Sirena came out wearing sweats and a T-shirt, a cup of coffee in her left hand and a SAT phone in her right hand. "You have a call from an old friend."

Jake finished his own coffee and set his empty mug on the log post. He accepted the SAT phone and Sirena took a seat, gazing out at the horses. Then she picked up her own phone and started tapping away at the screen.

"Yeah," Jake said into his SAT phone.

"Hey, Buddy, are you bored yet on that ranch of yours?"

The voice came from his old CIA friend, Kurt Jenkins. Back in the day, Jake had trained Kurt in Germany. Then Jake had left the CIA and Kurt had worked his way up the chain, until he eventually took over the Agency for a number of years. Kurt was now officially retired, but Jake knew his old friend still had many contacts in the Agency and other intelligence groups in D.C.

"I figured you would have eaten your gun by now," Jake said. He glanced at Sirena and shrugged. She shook her head disapprovingly.

"My wife would kill me first," Kurt assured Jake. Then, after a brief pause, he continued, "Listen, I'm calling with some bad news."

"I didn't guess you'd call to ask me to tea," Jake said.

"Maybe a beer," Kurt said. "Anyway, an old friend of yours has died."

Jake waited for the answer. He had been losing old friends for the past few years, and the intensity of his own mortality seemed to be slapping him in the face monthly.

"Your old Icelandic girlfriend, Hildur Hilmarsdóttir," Kurt said.

Kurt had butchered Hildur's last name, but Jake could forgive him for that. Icelandic words were hard for Jake as well. Despite this, Jake's mind reeled as to how this woman, a few years his junior, could have died.

"How?" Jake asked.

"Something about an accident on a glacier. She fell deep into a fissure."

Jake tried to visualize Hildur's fate, but his mind wouldn't allow it. Jake had met Hildur back in Nineteen

Eighty-Six, when he was a young CIA officer and Hildur was a Varðstjóri or Inspector with Icelandic Police. The two of them had hooked up for a while. Then Jake had lived with Hildur in her remote family cabin in the hinterland of Iceland following the death of Alexandra, Emma's mother. At that point, Hildur had risen to the top of the heap, where she had been appointed the head of the force that controlled all law enforcement in Iceland—the FBI of the land of fire and ice.

"That's terrible," Jake said. "I heard Hildur had retired."

Sirena sat forward in her chair with Jake's words.

"She had," Kurt said. "About a year ago."

"She was an expert on those glaciers," Jake said.

Kurt said nothing.

Jake continued, "Did they recover her body?"

"Just this morning," Kurt said. "It took them a couple of days to get down to her."

Jake knew that sometimes the glaciers never gave up those that fell deep into the fissures. It could be too dangerous to go down after victims. "How did you find out?" Jake asked.

"That's why I'm calling. She left an encrypted note with her former colleague, saying if anything strange happened to her to give me a call."

Jake wasn't hurt that she had not mentioned him. Kurt had always been Jake's point of contact. His new satellite number provided by his private organization was known only by a select group of people. This phone could no longer be traced by the CIA, NSA or any other intelligence agency in the world. And that was the way Jake needed it.

"Do those in Iceland think her death was anything other than an accident?"

"Honestly, I don't know. Based on the man's voice alone, I think there's some concern."

Jake glanced at Sirena, who seemed to understand what he was talking about without hearing the other end of the conversation.

After careful consideration, Jake said, "When's her funeral?"

"Memorial service," Kurt said. "It's in Reykjavik in two days." Then Jake's old CIA friend gave him the location and time for the service.

"Thanks for the info," Jake said.

"Are you going?"

Jake glanced at Sirena again, and wondered how she would feel about him going to the memorial service for one of his old girlfriends.

"We'll see," Jake said, and then thanked Kurt again before hanging up.

Jake turned to Sirena, who waited patiently.

Finally, Sirena asked, "Who died this time?"

He explained the death of his old Icelandic friend.

"We met once, remember?"

Yeah, he remembered. Sirena had flown Kurt out to Hildur's remote cabin to fetch him for an operation in South America. Jake had been a mess after the death of Alexandra, drinking himself to near death, and contemplating eating his own gun out on the tundra. Sirena had saved him from that fate. Had given him purpose in life.

"I think I should go to her memorial service," Jake reasoned.

"We should go," she corrected.

"You wouldn't mind?"

"Things are heating up here in Montana," she said. "It's not Vegas, but this is my least favorite time of year on the ranch. Don't get me wrong, I love this place. It couldn't be any more serene."

Jake waved his hand at her. He knew what she meant. She was bored. "Then it's settled. We head to Iceland. You think there's any chance to get the company jet?"

She turned her SAT phone toward Jake and said, "I asked and they said it could be here by this afternoon." Sirena hesitated as she stood up. Then she added, "You don't think this was an accident."

Jake shrugged. "I won't know until we get there. I do know that Hildur was an experienced glacier hiker."

"Guns?" she asked.

"Standard Go Bag. Pack warm clothes. June is not exactly balmy in Iceland."

"So, no bikini," she said, smiling.

"Bring it in case we want to sauna."

"I thought those were done in the nude."

He pulled her against his body, grasping her tight butt. "Not unless we're alone."

"Jake Adams. Since when have you become a prude?"

"About the same time I became a grandfather."

"You are getting old," she said, and turned to leave.

He slapped her butt and said, "I'm still functional in all areas."

"I know that." She smirked and left him alone on the wide porch.

He glanced at the horses again, his mind shifting back to the task at hand. Iceland was an interesting place, but he wasn't sure he would be able to find the truth about Hildur's death without busting a few heads. The people of Iceland were some of the nicest folks in the world. Murder wasn't something that happened every day there. In fact, the last time Jake operated there in 1986, they had to put an asterisk in the official records that tracked murders. Although those who had died were not officially murdered, their deaths were not of natural causes.

He grabbed his mug and went inside to pack his bags.

2

Reykjavik, Iceland

The Carlos Gomez organization jet flew over Canada and Greenland, getting Jake and Sirena into Iceland with a day to spare before Hildur's memorial service.

Jake rented a Land Rover SUV and the two of them headed down the road 50 kilometers from the international airport to Reykjavik.

Jake's first stop was Icelandic Police headquarters in downtown. En route Jake had arranged a meeting with National Police Commissioner Lars Jonasson.

The two of them were escorted into the commissioner's office, which overlooked the harbor and the mountains to the northwest. The commissioner wore his dark blue uniform with four gold stars on his epaulets. He was a man in his mid-fifties with a combover blond hairstyle and a paunch gained through overconsumption of food and drink.

"I understand you are here for Hildur's memorial service," Lars said, taking a seat behind his unimpressive Ikea desk. His accent was nearly indiscernible.

"Yes," Jake said. Both he and Sirena decided to stand.

"Please," Lars said. "Sit. I'm sure your flight was long."

"We slept on the flight," Jake said. "I understand you spoke with Kurt Jenkins."

The commissioner folded his hands in front of him and nodded. "I did."

"You don't think Hildur's death was an accident," Jake surmised.

Getting up from his desk, the commissioner went to a large map that covered most of one wall. He pointed to an area inland covered in ice. "Are you familiar with the Langjokull Glacier?"

"I've been there," Jake said. "The second largest glacier in Iceland."

"That's correct," the police commissioner said. "Then you know it's not the most difficult glacier to travers."

"You can slip in the bathtub and die," Jake said.

"True. But you knew Hildur, I understand. She was always prepared for the worst."

"What were the conditions?" Jake asked.

"That could have contributed," Lars said. "I understand a squall came through, with near white out conditions."

"In June?" Sirena asked.

Lars studied Sirena for the first time. "Yes. The Arctic Circle runs across the top of our country here." He pointed to the dotted line on the map that barely touched the northernmost sections of Iceland. "We can get snow at any time of year. Especially on our glaciers. It could rain here in the city and snow out there."

"Why do you suspect something other than a simple accident?" Jake asked.

"She was hiking alone," Lars said. Then he went to his desk and picked up a piece of paper, handing it to Jake.

"What is this?" Jake asked.

"A text sequence from someone with Hildur," the commissioner said.

Jake read the cryptic texts. The first thing he noticed was that both sides of the conversation were written in English. The second was the fact that Hildur was set to meet someone at the glacier. The third, and perhaps most damning thing, was that the other person on the texts was identified clearly: Jake Adams.

"I didn't text her," Jake said, handing the paper to Sirena.

"I understand," Lars said. "I discovered you were in America. Also, the phone was a prepaid cell phone purchased at a store here in Reykjavik."

"Video of the purchase?" Jake asked.

Lars shook his head. "Afraid not. We have many cameras in the tourist areas. But this was purchased in a small store out by the university. No cameras."

This was disturbing. Someone using Jake's name had lured Hildur out to the glacier. But she had to be skeptical. Jake would have simply gone to her house if he wanted to talk with her. She had lived in the same place for years.

"This is bullshit," Jake finally said. "Hildur was obviously lured to that glacier and murdered. Why aren't you simply investigating?"

"It's complicated," Lars said.

"Deconstruct it for me," Jake demanded.

Lars let out a deep breath. "When your name came up, we looked over past associations with Hildur. This led to a highly classified, sealed file from the time of the Reagan and Gorbachev summit in Nineteen Eighty-Six."

"Surely you can access that file," Jake said.

"Unfortunately, no. Only the prime minister can access this. And she won't do so."

This didn't matter to Jake. He knew what happened back then intimately. In fact, he knew much more than anything Hildur could have reported in her account. Could her death be related to Jake's old operation in Iceland? That's something he would have to find out.

Jake was feeling hot, so he unzipped his leather jacket.

The police commissioner's eyes grew large. "You are armed? This is not allowed in Iceland."

"According to the Schengen Agreement of Eighty-Five," Jake said, "I am authorized reciprocity."

"But you are American," Lars stated.

"I am also an Austrian citizen, authorized by its president to carry concealed for life," Jake said.

"I see," Lars said. "And your lady friend?"

Sirena said, "Spanish government authorization."

The commissioner gave them both a skeptical glare. But he said, "I understand. You know that our police officers do not regularly carry handguns. They have a lock box in their vehicles."

"Good to know if I'm an armed criminal," Jake said. "I could kill your police before they get to their weapons."

"We don't have many gun-related incidents here in Iceland."

"Right," Jake said. "You just throw people into glacial fissures. End result is the same. People always find a way to kill."

This brought a grimace to the commissioner's face and Jake felt a little bad for being so harsh. After all, the man had alerted Jake through Kurt that Hildur had died. If he was a bad guy, he would have kept his mouth shut.

"The Italians have a term," Jake said. "*Mi dispiace molto*."

"Meaning?" Lars asked.

"I'm so sorry," Jake said. "I understand this is a different country with your own set of laws and rules. I know you're only trying to help. And I appreciate any help you can provide."

"Thank you, sir," Lars said. "I hope to see you at Hildur's memorial service."

"That's why we're here," Jake said. Then he excused himself and wandered out of police headquarters.

Once Jake got behind the wheel of the rental Land Rover, he turned to Sirena and she seemed to want to say something to him. He could always tell when she wanted to chastise him for something.

"What?" he asked.

"You don't apologize much," she said.

"That's because I usually say things for a reason. Even if it's harsh or wrong. I'm doing so to get a response."

"And the police commissioner?" she asked.

"He seemed really hurt that Hildur was dead," Jake said. "Maybe they had something going once. Maybe he simply admired Hildur and was sad for her death."

Jake started the engine and took off, driving toward the ocean.

Sirena said, "You were right to push him. I'll do a background on him and see what his relationship was to Hildur."

"Thanks."

Jake pulled into the parking lot of a tall hotel along the waterfront. They took their Go Bags into the hotel, checked in, and went to their room overlooking the harbor on the eighth floor.

He stood before the large window checking out the ocean and the mountains beyond.

Sirena came up behind Jake and wrapped her arms around him. "You like this place."

"I do. I love the people here and the physical structure is amazing. Especially when you get out into the hinterland and see all the waterfalls. It's very striking."

"You forget that I flew a chopper out to get you a number of years ago," she said.

"I didn't forget," he said. "I was a mess back then. But I'm thinking about the first time I met Hildur back in eighty-six."

"You never told me that story."

He turned to face her and said, "There's a lot I haven't told you."

"I can see your mind churning, Jake. Your name came up and you want to know why. Does it have something to do with that old mission?"

Honestly, Jake couldn't say. But he didn't believe in coincidences. "I'm afraid so. Let me tell you the story and you tell me what you think."

She nodded agreement.

"As I mentioned, it was Nineteen Eighty-Six. The height of the Cold War. Reagan and Gorbachev were about to meet here in Iceland. . . .

3

East Berlin, German Democratic Republic (GDR)
October, 1986

There was a saying in East Germany. Either you worked for Stasi (Ministry for State Security), or you were being watched by Stasi. This wasn't entirely true, since even those within Stasi were watched like pedophiles at a playground by another branch within Stasi.

Jake Adams gripped the steering wheel with his left hand as he shifted the stick with his right, ground a pound, and finally found a gear. He jammed the gas down to the floor and the Trabant sputtered and complained but finally pulled forward in pursuit.

Until a moment ago, Jake had been simply observing a known Stasi officer as part of a CIA operation. The Stasi officer had been watching an East German dissident named Georg Beck. A man who had opened his mouth too much in the past few months in objection of the Communist GDR government.

It was almost midnight when Jake observed the Stasi officer knife Beck a number of times in the chest and stomach and simply walk away. Beck was dead before he hit the sidewalk. Then the Stasi man got into a waiting Trabant and the chase was on.

The car ahead careened around a corner almost on two wheels, and Jake cranked the wheel hard to keep it close. He thought his car would tip over, but the back tires slipped instead and nearly spun him out. He downshifted and hit the gas again. Then he ran through the gears and tried to get closer.

This wasn't normal operating procedure, Jake thought. But he had gotten pissed off when Beck, a man he was working with, met his fate. He had assured the man that everything would work out. Beck just needed to stay the course and eventually the GDR would unite with their prosperous brothers in the west. But Jake knew deep down that a dictatorial regime was most dangerous in the beginning and in the end.

The car ahead slowed some and Jake hit his brakes, pulling over to the curb. There was a check-point ahead, a Stasi and military barricade. Crap! Jake knew what that was. It was the entrance to Berlin Schönefeld Airport. Although his Austrian passport was good, he still needed a reason to be going to the main airport for the GDR. His assignment had brought him from Vienna to Munich and then to West Berlin as a communications businessman. Truthfully, his papers didn't even allow him to be in East Berlin.

So, he waited and watched, as the car ahead went through the checkpoint as if the man inside was General Secretary Erich Honecker himself. Stasi had the real power in the GDR. Everyone else picked for scraps.

Jake was dead in the water and he knew it. He pondered his options. Although he was relatively new to the Agency, he had spent nearly his entire stint in Air Force intelligence in West Germany. He was not only fluent in German, he could speak in most of the regional dialects, as well as Austrian and Swiss variations. But that only got him so far. Beyond the Soviet Union, East Germany was the most closed society on the planet. You needed papers to take a crap. And Jake had nothing that could get him through the checkpoint.

His eyes scanned the street and he saw the phone booth to the right of his car. He left the engine running, not sure if it would start again, and he got out to make a call. He found a number of East German coins in his pocket and shoved them into the slot. Then he punched in his contact's number and waited. He had to assume every public phone was bugged in East Berlin, so he would need to be prepared for that.

The phone clicked until a man answered groggily on the other end with his last name: "Schumer."

"Would you like to go out for a beer?" Jake asked in German. In other words, this conversation concerned Beck.

"Isn't it too late?" his contact asked.

"Perhaps for some," Jake said. "It's too late for beer, but maybe we could have some schnapps."

Hesitation on the other end as Jake saw his time from the East German coins was almost up, and he didn't have any more to feed the phone.

"Thirty minutes," Jake said, and then he slammed down the phone just as his time ran out.

While Jake had been on the phone, he had observed two men walking up the sidewalk toward him. Now they were closing in faster.

Jake was an everyman. With his clothing and language skills, he could blend like a local. He quickly assessed these men. They were not Stasi, but they could have been off-duty GDR military.

Before Jake could round the front of his sputtering Trabant, the men rushed him. Jake shifted his body to the left and forward. He kicked the closest man in the knee and the big guy's body collapsed to his knees. With a swift move to the side, Jake struck the man with a fist in his right ear, knocking him to the pavement.

Now the second man came with a haymaker. Jake parried that and chopped this man in the throat. Then he shifted around him and punched the guy in his right kidney, dropping him to one knee. Now Jake had the guy dazed and confused and struggling for air. Without wanting to hurt him too much, Jake simply planted a short kick to the guy's chin, knocking him out.

Jake looked around for any other danger, but there was none. Now, he simply got into the warn-out car, ground the gears again, and did a U-turn, heading back toward Checkpoint Charlie.

4

Jake dropped off the acquired Trabant a few blocks from Checkpoint Charlie, breezed through the U.S. Army guards, and then walked a few blocks before picking up a taxi.

He always felt relieved after getting back to western civilization. In East Berlin he could have been jailed for spitting on the sidewalk and not get out until the new millennium. It was a brutal regime. The Stasi made the KGB look like a cub scout pack. They were like the Gestapo without the ornate uniforms. Well, there were uniformed Stasi, some ten thousand of them, but they were those who the GDR didn't think were big enough assholes to become the 90,000 strong regulars.

Jake took a taxi to downtown West Berlin, where the drunken revelers and hookers allowed in from the east were just starting to get their shine on. He paid the driver in Deutsche Marks and got out a couple of blocks from the

Schwarzwald Bar. It was almost as dark inside the bar as it was on the street. Jake wandered to the bar and bought himself a large beer from the tap. While he waited for his beer, he checked out the room with his peripheral vision and in the large mirror behind the multitude of liquor bottles against the back of the bar.

There. His contact sat in the far back booth on his left. Tactically it was the perfect location, with full view of the bar and a possible escape route out the back door with easy access.

Jake paid for his beer, giving the bartender only a modest tip. Anything bigger and he would be remembered. Tips were the guilt of Americans.

He took his beer and walked directly to the last booth. His contact was an older man from the U.S. Embassy, dressed in a casual wool suit that made him look like a professor. His hair was gray and he had an equally gray beard—all fake of course. He was really a senior Agency officer and second in command at the Berlin CIA station. A man in his early forties. They had met only once before-two days ago at Tempelhof, where Jake had been briefed on his target.

Jake stopped at the table and considered his options. He really wanted the seat where the other officer sat, but it wasn't like he could force a senior Agency officer out of his chair. So, reluctantly, he took a seat against the wall opposite his contact.

"Is our man dead?" the fake older man asked in German. Their entire conversation would be in German.

"Yes," Jake said. "It looked like a normal meeting."

Georg Beck had been working both sides of the wall. At least intellectually if not physically.

"Are you sure?"

"I didn't stick around and check his pulse. But I saw the Stasi officer stab him multiple times. Our man dropped like a sack of flour. Now what?"

"Now you go back to Munich and continue with your job there."

Jake had been tasked with setting up a front company dealing with communications equipment that catered to businesses in Bavaria and Tyrol, Austria. Really the company tracked foreign intelligence officers interested in stealing western technology, along with counter espionage from nearby East Bloc countries and the Soviet Union.

"So, that's it?" Jake asked.

"Until further notice."

Jake took a sip of his beer and then leaned across the table. "Then we let those Stasi bastards murder our asset?"

The senior Agency man shrugged. "That's the game we play. Everybody knows the risks."

"He went to the airport."

"Who?"

"The damn assassin," Jake said. "The Wolf."

"He was a dead man walking."

Jake shook his head and sucked down a third of his beer. "That's bullshit. Why can't we track the guy?"

The bearded man got up from his side of the booth and stood at the end of the table. Then he leaned in and whispered, "Who said we couldn't? Just let us deal with it. Go back to your hotel. I'll call you tomorrow."

Jake's contact hobbled like an old man out the front door.

This was frustrating, Jake thought. His contact was killed and the Agency simply shrugs. Would they do the same with his own death? It made him consider his own worth to the Agency.

Screw it. He picked up his beer and finished it off. Then he went to the bar and got another. This would be at least a three-beer night.

5

The first understanding Jake had of his peace being disturbed was the annoying ring from the hotel phone. He opened his eyes and saw a tall blonde woman, entirely naked, pointing at the ringing phone.

"Should I get this for you?" the woman asked in German.

Jake sat up and studied the naked woman, trying his best to remember picking her up. It wasn't the first bar, he thought. No, she was at the hotel bar on the ground floor. Now it came to him. She was a Lufthansa stewardess.

She picked up the phone and greeted the caller. Then she handed to phone to Jake. "He says he's your father from Vienna."

Great. Jake took the phone from the naked woman, who pointed toward the bathroom. He checked out her perfect ass as she walked away. In fact, she looked even better in the morning light than she had in the dark bar the night before. That was a rarity.

When the woman closed the bathroom door and started the shower, Jake finally said, "So, my father. What can I do for you?"

"Who was that?" his Agency contact asked.

"Just a friend from last night. We had a slumber party."

"How much did she cost? You know the East German hookers need to be back across the wall by zero six hundred."

Jake checked his watch. It was ten to six now. "She's not a hooker. She's a stewardess."

"About the same thing. Can she hear you?"

"She's in the shower. I'm thinking of joining her."

"Well, you better hurry. You have a meeting at Tempelhof at seven. Check out and get your ass over there." The Deputy Station Chief hung up.

Jake set the phone back down. Then he checked under the sheets. He too was naked and interested. He hurried into the bathroom and joined the woman whose name had escaped his waking brain in the hot shower. When he was done, Jake left her to rinse alone, while he dried off and gathered his things in his small duffle bag. He found the woman's purse and checked out her credentials— memorizing her specifics. For all he knew she could have been KGB or Stasi.

As Jake was about to leave the room, the stewardess came out of the bathroom, still naked, with a towel wrapped over her head.

"Are you leaving?" she asked.

"Afraid so, Ingrid. There was a death in my family."

"I'm so sorry."

Jake waved her off. "It was a second cousin. And we don't really like that side of the family. But we still have to make appearances."

She nodded agreement.

He went to her and gave her a quick kiss on the lips. Then he slapped her lightly on the bare ass as he headed to the door.

Jake stopped and said, "Have a good flight. Where are you heading?"

"Paris."

He smiled and left her there, naked and uncertain. He could have used at least one more round with her.

After checking out, he found a taxi out front and told the driver to take him to the airport. He got to Tempelhof Air Base a few minutes before seven and walked to a secure meeting room at the Air Force Office of Special Investigations, arriving a few minutes late.

This inner conference room was simply a sound-proof room with no electronics—not even a phone or computer or slide projector. It was meant for frank discussions by the intelligence community, from Air Force Intelligence to the CIA and State Department officials. Diplomats could fly into Tempelhof, brief or be briefed, and fly out within an hour.

The meeting was already in progress, with the deputy director of the Berlin station at the head of the table. Jake quietly took a seat and listened. The deputy had gotten rid of his fake beard and now looked like a rosy-cheeked boy in his father's suit.

Jake scanned the room and noticed it was mostly military officers. He had worked for the colonel across from him in his early years as an officer in Air Force intelligence.

The CIA officer was explaining the current situation in Berlin. Finally, he got into the death of the dissident the night before, and how the Stasi seemed desperate. Maybe even cornered. Which made them even more dangerous.

After a short while, Jake began to wonder why he was at this briefing.

Finally, the CIA deputy turned to Jake and said, "We were able to track the Stasi officer. He got on a Soviet flight to Tallinn. From there he took a night ferry on the *MS Georg Ots* to Helsinki." He hesitated.

Jake gave the CIA deputy a critical glare. "And?" Jake asked.

"We just got a call a half hour ago. He got onto an Iceland Air flight to Reykjavik."

Letting that settle in for a moment, Jake said, "Are you serious?" He checked his watch and continued, "The Reykjavik Summit between Reagan and Gorbachev is in four days."

Now the CIA deputy wiped sweat from his brow. "I understand."

"He's a known Stasi assassin," Jake reminded him.

"I know. We've already informed the Secret Service advance team. They'll put him under surveillance from the time he steps off that flight."

"They better do more than that," Jake said. "President Reagan is in danger. No offense, but the Secret Service is not equipped to follow this man. He's a chameleon."

The CIA deputy cleared his throat. "You mean like you?"

"Better," Jake said. "He's been doing this for a long time. He only has a couple of subtle tells. And I know those."

"Outstanding. That's why you're going there immediately."

Great. Jake envisioned another flight in a C-130 web seat, freezing his ass off over the north Atlantic. He glanced around the table and saw the colonel smile.

"Get down to ops and get into your flight suit," the CIA deputy said. Then he slid a small envelope across the table to Jake. "Everything you need is in here. You can read it en route."

"Flight suit?" Jake asked.

"You'll be flying back seat in an F-15D. A KC-135 is in the air now and you'll slow just to take a drink."

Jake smiled at the thought of cruising at Mach 2. He got up and said, "Is that all, sir?"

"That's it. Unless you think you've been compromised in some way."

"Negative," Jake said. He smiled and nodded to the colonel on his way out of the room, knowing that his old friend had probably made his sexy ride possible.

Fifteen minutes later and he was in his flight suit and strapped into the back seat of one of the fastest jets in flight history. Jake had said nothing at all to the young captain pilot to this point—only the specifics of how to punch out, if necessary, and to follow his orders.

Finally, Jake turned on his mic and said, "Listen, Captain Cox, I want to let you know that until a couple years ago I was an Air Force intelligence officer. A captain just like you. So don't try to make me puke with fancy maneuvers. Just get me to Iceland in one piece."

"Roger that," the pilot said. "The last thing I want you to do is spew in my cockpit. I'll try to keep the Gs to a minimum. But we will be going full afterburner for a while, so strap in tight."

"Understood," Jake said. But he couldn't synch himself any tighter.

Moments later and the F-15D was taxiing down to the runway and they sat for a moment at the end of the runway waiting for clearance. Then, while Jake fully expected a damn near vertical ascent, they powered down the runway and lifted off with minimum effort.

"I thought you were going to slap me back into my seat," Jake said.

"This is a tight urban area, sir," the pilot said. "That really pisses off the locals."

Now they rose in a steady climb, up through the clouds and toward the northwest.

Ten minutes later and the pilot said, "Hang on. Going to afterburner."

Seconds after the pilot said that and Jake felt like the skin would peel from his face as the Gs planted him back into his seat. Holy crap, Jake thought. Now he was in for a ride.

6

Naval Air Station, Keflavik, Iceland

After a quick aerial refueling over the north Atlantic, they had continued on to Iceland. As a former intelligence officer, he knew that the F-15 could have made the flight without refueling, but they would have had to fly a lot slower. As it was, they were able to cut down their flight to about an hour and a half.

Jake got down the ladder to the tarmac and shook the pilot's hand. "Nice job, captain. Sweet ride."

"No problem. We should do a beer some time."

"Roger that."

A navy plane captain handed Jake his small duffel bag from a garment pod on the right wing.

"What else do you have in there?" Jake asked the pilot.

The pilot smiled. "Some good German beer. We're gonna trade it for smoked Icelandic salmon. All they can get is weak beer here."

"Fair trade."

Jake wandered to the operations building, where he changed from his flight suit to civilian clothes—black slacks, long sleeve black shirt, and his black leather jacket. Then he found his issue Beretta M9 and slid it into the leather holster under his left arm.

When Jake came out of the ops dressing room, two men in dark suits were waiting for him. "Let me guess," Jake said. "Secret Service?" How secret were they if he could spot them from a satellite image?

"Please come with us, Mister Konrad," the biggest of the two said.

It wasn't a question. Thankfully, they had used his persona name.

They took Jake to a secure area where a briefing was in progress with various American alphabet agencies, the Secret Service, and a few local police officers. On a projection screen was a blurry photo of the Stasi officer, which looked like it could have been an image of Bigfoot. There was no way in hell anyone would be able to identify the man from that image.

Without any warning, the briefer from the Secret Service waved his hand for Jake to come to the front of the room. This was awkward and disconcerting for Jake, since he was supposed to be working in the shadows on this operation. Every op, he thought.

Jake could play this game. He went to the front of the room and introduced himself by his Austrian persona, Jacob Konrad. When Jake established a persona, it was the personification of a lie that anyone must believe. The persona was so good, in fact, the Jake himself came to believe he was that person. Most, even those in the Agency, didn't know his entire real history.

"I'm sorry to say we don't have a better image of this man," Jake said. "But we'll try to get a better image soon."

One of the FBI agents in the front row asked, "How do we know he's here to kill President Reagan?"

Expecting that question, Jake said, "We don't. He might be here to kill Gorbachev. The hardliners in East Germany and the Soviet Union aren't exactly happy with their leader right now. Or, maybe he's here to visit the volcanoes and waterfalls."

A few in the room snickered.

The FBI agent relented. "And you know this man, this killer?"

"We're not on a first-name basis. But I saw him kill our asset in Berlin last night. This man is dangerous. Do not attempt to take him alone. He is known only as The Wolf."

"Which agency are you with?" another man asked.

Jake started walking back to the main door, but he said from the side of his mouth, "The Boy Scouts."

That got a full round of laughter.

He was stopped at the main door by another man in a suit, who introduced himself as the lead Secret Service agent with this presidential protection detail.

"How may I help you?" Jake asked.

The large man turned to the side revealing a slight woman in an unfamiliar uniform. She might have been five four and weighed perhaps a buck ten. The Secret Service man introduced her as Hildur Hilmarsdóttir. Jake would have guessed Icelandic women would have been blonde and sturdier, like their Viking ancestors. But this police officer, despite her high cheek bones, had more delicate features.

"She's a Varðstjóri," the Secret Service man said.

"Varðstjóri," the woman corrected the pronunciation. "Inspector with the Icelandic Police."

Jake shook the woman's hand trying not to crush it, but she came back with remarkable strength. "Inspector." He looked at her name tag. "Hildur? Isn't that your first name?"

"We use first names in Iceland," she said. "My brothers and my mother and father all have different last names."

Jake was confused, but even more so by the introduction. "What can I do for you?"

Secret Service man said bluntly, "She'll be your partner while you're in Iceland."

"Seriously?" Jake said. "A strong breeze will knock her over."

The woman smiled and said, "I wear heavy boots."

"I don't need a partner," Jake said.

"The locals insist."

"I'll have to clear this with my boss," Jake said. "Do you have someone sitting on my assassin?"

"He's in room two-fifteen at the Reykjavik Marina Hotel. We've got it covered."

"Don't bet on it."

"Our people are good."

Jake shook his head and went out the door, mumbling under his breath. By the time he got outside, the woman had caught up to him.

"Mister Konrad," she said. "Please stop."

He stopped and turned to her. "What?"

"Do you have a car?" she asked him.

"Are you old enough to drive?"

"Of course. I'm twenty-five."

"Wonderful. Do you have a car?"

"Yes, of course, Mister Konrad."

"Just call me Jake."

"Okay. You can call me Hildur." She smiled at him. "My police car is there."

Jake laughed. "Seriously? I can't go driving around in a police cruiser."

"No, just until we get back to the station. Then I can change to my private car."

He looked her up and down more carefully. She was tiny, but filled out the uniform in all the right places. More importantly, she had an intensity in her eyes.

"Swell," Jake said, and walked to her car.

7

Jake stood out on the street while the Icelandic police officer turned in her colorful cruiser, which looked more like a clown car than a law enforcement vehicle. He took in the crisp morning air, which smelled of the sea, and wondered what had convinced the Vikings to settle here. On the 50-kilometer drive from the military installation adjacent to the international airport in Keflavik to downtown Reykjavik, the landscape had more resembled the surface of another planet, with the jagged volcanic rocks and sparse vegetation. He could easily understand how this island had been influenced by volcanic activity.

When a new silver Toyota Celica GT pulled up to the curb next to him, Jake leaned down and looked inside the open window. Hildur was still in her uniform.

"Nice car," Jake said. "But I thought you were going to lose your uniform."

"I will," she said. "But my clothes are at my apartment."

Jake threw his bag in the back seat and got in to the front passenger side. He leaned back and yawned.

"Please buckle up. It's the law here."

He strapped himself in and she pulled away. She drove a few blocks before pointing out a building near the sea, indicating that was the hotel where the Stasi man was staying. Then she drove a couple miles into the hills overlooking the downtown area and parked on the street in front of what looked like a large white house, but it was built from concrete. The surface of the structure was streaked with green mold.

Jake followed her inside to the second of three floors and she opened the door for them.

"I have just one bedroom," she said, "but you are welcome to stay on my sofa. It folds out to a bed."

"I can check into a hotel," he said.

She shook her head. "You could, but that might be difficult. With the summit coming, all of the rooms are filled with media and people like you."

"People like me?"

Hildur started unbuttoning her uniform shirt and smiled. "You know. Security types. Boy Scouts."

He was sure she had no clue he was with the Agency, which was a good thing. Jake always did his best to maintain his cover.

By now she was down to her bra, which revealed rather nice breasts.

"Would you rather change in your bedroom?" Jake asked.

"I'm sorry. We don't worry about these things in Iceland. I'm used to dressing in front of my colleagues."

"It doesn't bother me. But I am a man with better than twenty-twenty vision."

She lifted her chin and shrugged. Then she went into her bedroom but left her door open. She took off her pants and then turned her head to see that Jake was still watching. He turned his head and set his small bag on the wooden floor next to the sofa. Then he unzipped his leather jacket and took it off.

Moments later she returned to the living room wearing black slacks and a gray sweater. She looked at him like he had just taken a dump on her wool throw rug.

"What?" he asked.

"You have a gun."

"No shit!"

"That's not allowed in Iceland. Even our police don't carry guns."

"That's nice, Hildur. But I assure you our Stasi assassin will be armed. And he won't drop his gun if you ask pretty please." He hesitated and considered the prospect of cops not carrying weapons. That prospect was incomprehensible to him. "This makes police officers vulnerable."

"No police officer has ever been killed on duty in Iceland," she assured him.

"Not yet. But when that happens, you will have to change your mind. I won't give up my gun. Are you going to tell your boss?"

She thought for a long minute. "That won't be necessary." Hildur looked him in the eye and said, "Would you like some coffee? Or maybe a nap. You must be tired from your travel. I could give you one of my sleeping pills."

He laughed. "It was less than two hours from Germany."

"No way. What did you fly in, a fighter jet?"

Jake sat on the sofa. "Let's just say I didn't fly commercial." He didn't mention that she was the only official in Iceland that knew he was in country, and even she didn't know his real name or organization. "You said something about coffee. Do we go out for that?"

"Out. Would you like to change?"

He got up and took off his leather holster. Then he quickly pulled off his T-shirt, revealing his muscular chest. He caught her looking as well. Inside his bag he found a stick of deodorant, which he rubbed under his arms. Then he pulled out a rolled up black T-shirt, almost identical to the one he had just removed, and he put it on and tucked it into his pants. Finally, he swung his gun and holster over his shoulders before putting his leather jacket on again to hide his weapon.

"Let's go," Jake said.

She smiled and opened the door for him. Then she locked the door behind them and they went back out front to her car.

They drove downtown again, neither of them saying a word, and she parked a block from the Reykjavik Marina Hotel.

"There's a good coffee shop and café on the first floor," she said. "You must be hungry."

He was. They found a spot in a booth with a view of the front lobby, where Jake sat observing the scene while he sipped his strong, black coffee. He shook his head when he saw obvious security types watching the elevators and common corridors. Maybe that was all right. The Stasi man would see them and not him. And it wasn't out of the ordinary, since most would know about increased security leading up to the summit.

"Is everything all right?" she asked.

"Just peachy," he said.

A waitress brought him his food, an omelet and hash browns, supposedly. But it looked more like a frittata and fries.

"Are you sure you're not hungry?" Jake asked.

She shook her head.

Suddenly, Jake reached across the table and took her hand in his. But his eyes were focused to the side of her head at the man who just entered the restaurant. Like Jake, this man wore black from top to bottom, including a black leather jacket. His blond hair was longer than average, and it flowed down into his eyes until he shifted his head to the right. That was one of his tells. The other was a very slight limp that the man desperately tried to hide. It was definitely the Stasi assassin. And this was the closest Jake had ever been to the man.

The Stasi man glanced at Jake for a microsecond. But by now Jake's eyes were set deep into his lover's gaze across from him.

Going with the flow, Hildur pulled her body across the table and kissed Jake on the lips. A quick loving gesture from girlfriend to boyfriend. Then she sat back and squeezed his hand tighter.

"You're a natural at this," Jake whispered.

"Maybe that wasn't an act," she said. "Perhaps I wanted to do that all along."

He ignored her while he observed the Stasi man sit down across the room with his own view of the lobby. That would have been Jake's second choice of seats. Now he wished he had a camera to capture that asshole's image.

"The man is here?" she asked.

"Yeah. He just sat to your right across the room."

She pulled her hand away and pretended to look into her purse on the seat to the right of her, but instead took a quick look at the man. Then she pulled out some Icelandic Kronur and set it on the table.

"I'm guessing you don't have any of our money," she said.

Jake tried to remember what he had for cash. A few useless East German Marks, less than a hundred Deutsche Marks, and maybe a thousand Austrian Shillings. None of which could probably be used in Iceland.

"All right," Jake said. "Get me to a bank to convert some money and I'll pay you back."

"I didn't mean that."

He got up and took her hand, pulling her to her feet. Then he put his arm around her as they left the café.

Once they got to the car, Jake sat for a moment in the passenger seat, considering what to do next.

"Where now?" she asked as she started the car.

"The bank. You're right. I need some cash."

"Then where?"

"Back to your place to hang low. I'll need to make a call on your phone."

•

The Stasi man ate and went right back up to his room on the second floor. When he turned the key and opened the door, two men pulled guns and pointed his way until they saw it was him. KGB assholes, he thought. Too quick with their guns.

"What did you see?" the older of the KGB officers asked.

There were no names here. They only knew him by his most recent cover name, as well as the code name used by the CIA and the BND, the Federal Intelligence Service of Germany.

Stasi man sat down on the end of the bed and lit a cigarette. "The lobby is crawling with agents of some kind. Probably American Secret Service. They were too obvious for CIA."

"What about FBI?"

"No. They usually don't work overseas. I'm guessing they're with the advance team."

"Any from our side?" the younger KGB man asked.

The Stasi man lifted his chin and took in a long draw on his cigarette, his eyes squinting against the rising smoke. "Is this a test?" Then he swore at them in German.

"I don't think that's physically possible," the older KGB said with a smirk.

The German flicked some ash onto the low-pile carpet. "Did you get me the rifle I requested?"

"You will have it by this evening."

"Good. I'll need to test it in the morning to make sure it zeros properly." Then he considered his own test. "Is it a CZ three-O-eight with a Zeiss scope?"

The older KGB man turned to his young partner and then back to the Stasi man. "No. It is a Remington seven hundred in seven millimeter, with a Leupold scope. It was purchased over the counter in Virginia last week. Bore sighted and zeroed to two hundred meters by a former Olympic shooter from the Soviet Union. It should be right on."

"These scopes can move when shipped," the Stasi man said.

After some internal calculus, the senior KGB officer said, "All right. You can take the rifle out into the wilderness to test the sights yourself."

The Stasi man sucked down the last of his cigarette and looked around for an ash tray. When he didn't find one, he simply wet his fingers and put out the last of the fire. Then he threw the butt toward the garbage can but missed by two feet. The younger KGB officer picked up the butt and brought it to the bathroom, flushing it down the toilet.

"We will bring you a car this evening with the gun in the trunk," the older man said. Then the two KGB officers left him alone.

He walked to the door and looked out through the peep hole. Then he locked the door and put up the chain.

Sitting back on the bed, he considered his options. Truthfully, he hated working for those Soviet bastards. They had really fucked up his country, pitting cousins against cousins. The only way to make this whole prospect work was to take down one of these world leaders. He knew what his contract said, but he was beginning to think that he might need to deviate a bit. With that thought, he lit another cigarette.

•

Just before his Icelandic partner pulled from the curb, Jake glanced into the side mirror and noticed two men coming out of the front of the hotel.

"Crap," Jake said.

Hildur hit the brake. "What?"

"Behind us. See those two men?"

She looked into the rearview mirror. "Black slacks and leather jackets. One older than the other. Getting into a Volvo. What about them?"

"How are you at tailing someone?"

"I've never done it. Why?"

He leaned across, put his hand behind her neck and pulled her to him, kissing her long and seemingly passionately on the lips. When he saw the Volvo pass, he finally got back into his seat.

"Whoa," she said.

"Follow them," Jake said. "But stay back."

She did as Jake said. "Who are they?"

"KGB."

Hildur turned to him swiftly and then concentrated again on her driving. "How do you know?"

"They're wearing the uniform. Their leather jackets have a distinctive cut." He thought about the Stasi assassin and who might be running them, and now he knew for sure. But that still didn't tell him who they were planning to kill. If he had the authorization, the prudent thing to do would be to simply take out the assassin. Not leave the guy on the loose. But he was already beginning to believe that his government had been short-sighted when they decided not to continue with those types of operations. Jake memorized the license plate number.

"Break off," Jake said.

"What? Why? Did I do something wrong?"

"No, you're fine. We know who they are. It's just better if they don't know we know."

She turned left on the next road and drove up a hill toward her apartment.

"Take me to your place," he said.

8

They got to Hildur's apartment and Jake immediately got on her phone, calling his station in Bonn, Germany. Although he worked out of the U.S. Consulate in Munich, he reported through the U.S. Embassy in Bonn. The Agency didn't want him seen coming and going from the consulate, since he was supposed to be a business owner.

It took him moments to go through surreptitious authentication before Jake actually got on the line with the deputy station chief.

"Jake, what do you have to report?" the deputy asked.

Jake glanced at his new Icelandic friend and said, "Our Stasi friend has settled into his hotel. We just tracked two KGB officers coming from there and getting into a Volvo." Jake gave the man the license plate details and the line went blank for a moment. A secure phone only worked if each party was using one, but Jake didn't have that option at this time.

Hildur said, "I could have run the plate for you."

"I know," Jake said. "But I hate to get the police involved now. Besides, I'm sure the KGB men are part of an advance team for Gorbachev."

The deputy came back on the line. "The Volvo is a rental by the Soviet government."

"I thought so. That's why we backed off. But the East Germans don't have a stake in this summit. What can we do to take out the threat?"

The deputy in Bonn cleared his throat. "You're not sanctioned for that."

"I'm not talking about killing him and dumping his body in the ocean," Jake said, although that would work. "But we should be able to have the Icelandic government expel him."

"I don't know about that. His passport was copied upon entry. It looks legit. He also has press credentials."

"That's bullshit," Jake said. "What name is he using this time?"

"Karl Wolf."

Interesting, Jake thought, since the man was known as The Wolf. "He flew commercial. Which means he won't have a rifle. Any idea where he might get that?"

The deputy let out a heavy sigh. "Probably from his KGB handlers. The Soviets will be armed just like our snipers. It wouldn't take much for them to slip an additional rifle into Iceland."

"Good point. What do you suggest?"

Short of killing the Stasi bastard? "When the Soviets fly in, we could track them. But that would be almost impossible. Our advance team flew in with armored vehicles and weapons, and are in the process of setting up superior positions for snipers, if they haven't already done so. For all we know, the Soviets already have the gun in place." He thought about The Wolf for a moment, and what Jake had read about the man.

"What are you thinking, Jake?" the deputy asked.

"The Wolf is a control freak. He won't just trust any gun. He'll want to make damn sure it's zeroed properly."

"What are you saying? He'll need to shoot the rifle?"

"Exactly. I know I would."

Hildur chimed in. "We have a police range north of the city."

"Who was that?" the deputy asked.

"My liaison officer. An Icelandic police inspector."

"Who authorized that?"

"The Secret Service said the Icelandic government insisted."

"It never went through our office."

Jake stretched the phone cord and turned away from Hildur. "That's because nobody knows who I am," he whispered.

"Good point."

He turned back and smiled at Hildur. "Yes, she's very pretty."

"I didn't ask that."

"I know. There's something else you can do for me."

"What's that?"

"I need some communications equipment."

"All right. I'll make a call to the Secret Service. Where should I have them drop it off?"

"The police station downtown," Jake said. "Two sets. One for me and one for my Icelandic friend. Have them mark it for Inspector Hildur."

"Will do. Anything else?"

"Yeah. Approve the sanction of The Wolf."

Hesitation on the other end. "I'll see if we can make that happen."

Jake hung up the phone and took a seat in the living room on his future bed.

Hildur paced the room, her arms across her chest. "I don't understand. What is a sanction?"

"It's just the elimination of a threat."

"You mean like deportation?"

"Something like that." Jake's mind drifted for a second as he considered his options. "I hope you don't mind if I send that comm equipment to your office. I didn't want anyone knowing about your apartment."

She shook her head. "That's fine. But we have radios."

Jake smiled. "These are a little more discreet. And we want to make sure we'll be able to talk with everyone. I'm sure your tactical teams will get these as well."

Hildur shook her head. "We don't really have a military in Iceland. We have a coast guard. And our Icelandic Police force has less than 800 personnel for the entire country."

"And you're unarmed. How in the hell do you maintain the peace like that?"

She tightened her jaw. "Because not every Tom, Dick and Bjorn has a gun. We are a peaceful nation of some three hundred thousand citizens."

"That's fantastic," Jake said. "But it just takes one asshole with a gun to break that peace. And your cops better be ready to shoot to kill. Because the only way to stop a bad guy with a gun is with a good guy with a gun. Or good girl."

Hildur paced again, obviously disturbed by Jake's brashness. Finally, she turned to him and said, "Do you really think I'm pretty?"

"Seriously? You could stand close to a glacier and melt it."

She looked uncertain, but her face turned crimson.

"You're hot as hell," he explained.

Now she tried her best to hold back a smile.

9

After hanging out at Hildur's apartment through the afternoon, Jake and the Icelandic cop drove to her station and found the communications equipment left by the Secret Service. They were to use one frequency for their individual communications, and eventually shift to another to contact the Secret Service and the other members of the advance team. These were the newest and smallest devices Jake had ever seen, but were still too large to wear covertly, he thought. The radio was as large as his hand and the headset cords were intended to slide up through the back of his shirt or jacket and lead to both of his ears. Although his hair was fairly long by Agency standards, anyone with marginal observational skills would see the wires.

"This is crazy," Jake said, sitting in the front passenger seat of Hildur's car. He shook his head and shoved the headset into the glove box.

"What's the matter?" she asked, playing with the headset. "These are amazing."

"Hopefully, someday, these will by invisible to the most astute observer. But I can't wear it. I'll be spotted from a mile away. We can still use the radios for contact with our people, though."

Jake gazed out at the sea. Clouds swirled above, and darkness was threatening to take hold. "When does it get dark this time of year?"

"About six-thirty," she said. She looked at her watch. "Half an hour."

"Let's get something to eat. I'm hungry enough to eat a horse."

She laughed.

"What?"

"That's on the menu. So is whale."

"Amazing. You don't carry guns, but you eat horse and whale. I guess you still have some Viking blood."

"Don't judge us so harshly." She started the car and pulled away.

She looked pissed, he thought.

An hour later, darkness now enveloping the downtown of Reykjavik, the two of them strolled down the main pedestrian street of the capital.

"Did you like the whale?" she asked him.

Jake stopped at the window of a clothing store, glancing at wool sweaters. But really he was observing various people on the street behind them.

"What?"

"The whale. Is something wrong?"

"Don't turn around. We have a tail." He put his arm around her like they were boyfriend and girlfriend.

"Seriously?" she whispered.

He turned her, keeping her on his left side with his gun, in case he needed to draw it with his right hand. Then he unzipped his leather jacket.

"What do we do?" she asked, somewhat nervously.

"If the shit hits the fan, you need to run."

"I can't leave you alone."

"Just do what I say," he said sternly.

They continued slowly down the sidewalk until Jake stopped suddenly again, turning to Hildur so he could get a peripheral view of the man walking behind them. Now he could see that it was the older of the two KGB officers who had left the marina hotel earlier in the day. The KGB man stopped also and lit a cigarette.

"Go ahead and get the car," Jake said. "Pick me up on the cross street a block down the hill."

"Are you sure?"

"Yeah." He smiled and kissed her on the lips quickly.

Reluctantly, she turned and walked ahead of Jake, looking back only briefly and trying to smile at him.

Jake continued down the sidewalk at a slower pace. When Hildur had gotten a half a block ahead, she suddenly disappeared. Shit! He ran after her.

As Jake rounded the corner, down an isolated, narrow alley, he found Hildur scuffling with the younger KGB officer. The Soviet had her in a bear hug and was trying to drag her to the other end of the alley.

Jake considered pulling his gun, but instead he rushed the man, slamming his body into both of them and crashing the KGB officer against the brick wall, stunning him long enough to make him loosen his grip on Hildur.

She took the opportunity to break free and back fist the man in the groin. Now she was free as the KGB officer leaned over in pain.

Jake grasped the man behind his head and shoved his knee up into the guy's face, knocking him out.

Hearing a scream, Jake turned to see the older KGB officer with his gun drawn and pointed at Jake's head. Without hesitation, Jake moved closer to the KGB officer.

"You shoot me and the summit will be off," Jake said.

The KGB officer smiled. "And that's a bad thing?"

Jake hadn't considered that possibility. But now his face was just six inches from the barrel of the gun. He smiled at the Soviet man as he tried to understand the goal these two men were trying to achieve. Why would they do this? It didn't matter now.

With one swift move to his right, and a parry of the Soviet's arm, Jake was able to draw his own gun and point it at the KGB officer's head.

"Now," Jake said. "I think you need to reconsider your position."

"This is not a chess board, Mister C-I-A." The KGB man spelled out the Agency name with disdain.

Jake ignored the man as he circled the guy and headed toward the main street again, keeping Hildur behind him at all times, as he maintained his gun on the Soviet's skull.

"This might be check, but it is not checkmate," the KGB officer said. "You are only alive because I allow it. You're a rat and I'm an alley cat."

"More like a little pussy," Jake said.

Hildur finally let out a slight giggle.

Pushing her ahead of him, they rounded the corner and Jake put his gun at the side of his right leg while they hurried to her car.

Finally feeling safe, Jake put his gun back in its holster under his leather jacket.

They got to her car and she immediately started the engine and pulled away from the curb, slapping through the gears, and she sped twice the speed limit to get some distance away from the downtown.

"I should have arrested those men," she said, her voice shaking.

"It wouldn't matter. The Soviet government would have simply gotten them out on diplomatic immunity and shipped them back to Moscow."

"That's crazy. They tried to kill us." She slowed the Toyota slightly as she approached a red light. But the light changed to green and they continued toward the hills away from downtown.

"I don't think they were trying to kill either of us," Jake said. "The older KGB officer had the jump on me and could have blown my head off."

"Why didn't he?"

"Those aren't his orders." Then Jake tried to comprehend why they would even confront them. It made no sense. He pulled out the radio and switched it to the Secret Service frequency. All kinds of chatter about confrontations around the capital city came across the comm. So, it wasn't just these rogue KGB officers. Their colleagues were doing the same thing all over town. But why?

"This is crazy," Hildur said. "I need to go in to work."

"No," Jake said. "That's what they want."

Sirens sounded from nearly every direction.

"Where do we go?" she asked.

"Turn around," Jake ordered.

Without hesitation, Hildur cranked the wheel and made a U-turn. Then she downshifted and powered up again, running through the gears.

"Where to?"

"The Reykjavik Marina Hotel."

She turned and stared at him for a bit too long. "Why?"

"Because I have a feeling our Stasi friend, The Wolf, is up to something. Let's hope we're not too late."

As they got closer to the ocean, sirens continued to echo through the night air.

Finally, she said, "The KGB officer said you were with the CIA. Was he right?"

How could he answer that? Did she have a right to know? Did she have a need to know? "He was fishing," Jake said. "That's all."

10

Hildur parked a block from the hotel where The Wolf was staying. Then Jake got out and replaced her behind the wheel.

"Why do you need to drive?" Hildur asked Jake.

Jake adjusted the rearview mirror. "I've been trained in covert surveillance by car."

"So, you are CIA," she stated.

He reached into the glove box and retrieved one of the Secret Service radios. Then he called the man in charge of the advance detail.

Once the Secret Service man was on the radio, Jake relayed his experience with two Soviet nationals—that's all he called them, and that was enough. Despite the security of these radios, Jake still wasn't entirely sure that their signal couldn't be intercepted.

"What can you tell me about the German hotel?" Jake asked.

"All secure," Secret Service responded.

"No activity?"

"Negative." Pause. "Well, about five minutes ago there was a scuffle in the lobby. But our men held tight."

Shit, Jake thought. He turned to Hildur. "Is there another exit from this hotel?"

"There's a loading dock on the other side," she said.

Jake turned over the engine. Into the radio he said, "I'm on the move. We suspect our man is heading out."

"Roger that. I'll inform my men."

He handed the radio back to Hildur and pulled forward slowly, his eyes keen to anything out of the ordinary. Just as he was about to turn left and go around the back of the building, a dark blue Volvo came out from the back and passed them. Without mistake, the driver was the Stasi man, The Wolf. Luckily, they were not under a street light, and the only reason Jake could recognize the assassin was from the light of the cigarette hanging from the guy's mouth.

Jake looped into the back road and quickly pulled a U-turn, heading after the Volvo.

"Is that him?" Hildur asked.

"Yes. But we'll need to stay way back."

The Volvo headed along the marina and a few blocks later turned left toward the regional airport situated right within the downtown region of Reykjavik, two kilometers from the city center.

"Where do flights go from the downtown airport?" Jake asked her.

"Regional flights within Iceland," she said, "along with a few to Greenland and the Faroe Islands."

In a few minutes none of that mattered, since The Wolf drove right past the airport and then into the darkness away from the city lights.

"What's out this way?" he asked.

She shrugged. "The country."

What in the hell was the Stasi man up to? Jake was able to stay far back, keeping the German's headlights visible in the stark terrain ahead. The road eventually started to rise into the mountains, and then the guy's lights would fade around corners and rises in the road. They were some fifty kilometers out of town when, just after dropping over a sharp rise in the road, Jake was forced to hit his brakes, nearly running over a small herd of sheep. Once the sheep cleared the road, Jake noticed stationary lights in the distance. The Stasi man had turned right onto a side road.

Jake shut off his lights and pulled the car over to a small gravel patch on the side of the road. "What the hell is he up to?"

The Wolf was almost a mile off in the distance, but Jake could still see a dark figure moving out in front of the lights, stepping in a methodical way away from the car.

"What's he doing?" Hildur asked.

By now The Wolf had reached nearly to the edge of his headlights.

Jake got out and Hildur followed him.

Now, The Wolf was heading back to the car.

Smiling, Jake said, "Target practice."

"Seriously?"

Seconds later and the German clearly pulled out a long rifle. Then, with measured patience, the first shot rang out into the cool night air. Hesitation. Then another. And a third. Finally, two quicker shots.

Hildur glanced at Jake. "Sniper rifle?"

"Bolt action with five-round magazine. Probably internal. As I mentioned, someone would provide a rifle and he wouldn't trust it. He would need to make sure it was properly zeroed."

"I understand," she said. "Maybe I should just go arrest him."

"On what charge?"

"He's a foreign national with a high-powered rifle. A third of our population owns guns, but only shotguns and rifles. No handguns. We go through a medical exam and take a test to own guns."

Jake shook his head. "If you bust him, the Soviet government will just ship him off."

"But you said he was East German," she reminded him.

"True. But the Soviets won't let anyone question this man. They'll just put a bullet in his brain. Or make him disappear." Jake paused and watched the man in the distance rummage around the ground. He was collecting his brass and would probably wipe it clean, throwing one out the window every ten kilometers on his way back to Reykjavik.

"What do we do?" she asked with exasperation.

"If we stop him now, the Soviets will replace him," Jake reasoned. "In fact, they might have another shooter already assigned."

"Why?"

"Back up. Or to kill the shooter after he assassinates one of the leaders." Jake watched the man in the distance and tried his best to come up with a plan.

"You have a devious mind, Jake," she said.

No kidding. "I try to think like the bad guys. You must always stay a few steps ahead."

"Like chess."

"Right. With deadly stakes. Let's go. He's heading out."

They got back into the car and Jake quickly turned the car around and powered up, heading back toward Reykjavik.

"We're not waiting for the German?" she asked.

"No. We can't let him know that we know."

Once they got within radio range, Jake called in what he'd just observed to the Secret Service. He was disturbed that Jake hadn't taken some sort of action, but when Jake asked him what action that might be, he had no good answer. There wasn't a good answer.

Jake drove to Hildur's apartment in the hills above Reykjavik. Once inside, Jake took off his leather jacket and sat down on the sofa.

"Would you like a drink?" Hildur asked.

"Sure."

She went into the kitchen and came back with two shots of vodka. Then she took a seat across from Jake and said, "Is your work always that exciting?"

He shook his head. "It's usually more intense than that."

Her thin eyebrows scrunched downward. "Really? We just got into a fight with two Soviet spies. Then we followed a hitman into the country and watched him prepare to assassinate one of the most powerful leaders in the world."

"Well, when you put it that way, I guess it could be considered exciting."

She drank down about a third of her vodka, but kept her eyes on Jake. After she set her glass on the coffee table, she said, "Would you like to have sex with me?"

Jake startled somewhat. "Just like that?"

"Yes, of course. We're very open with our sexuality here in Iceland."

He wasn't sure if he believed her, but he decided to play along anyway. "In that case, the obvious answer is yes. I'd have to be a blind monk to not even consider it."

She smiled and got up. "Good."

Then she wandered to her bedroom and Jake watched her every step. In the light from the living room, Jake watched her slowly strip down until she was entirely naked. Now she turned to him, revealing a remarkable body. He didn't hesitate now as he downed the last of his vodka and accompanied her in her bed.

11

Jake got up the next day and got on the radio to the Secret Service, setting up a meeting with the director of the advance team.

Hildur dropped Jake off at the waterfront pier where fishing boats would normally dock, but were still out on their morning expeditions.

"Are you sure you want me to wait here?" she asked Jake.

He leaned back into the car. "Yeah. Our government still has a lot of secrets. Cooperation only goes so far."

She smiled and nodded her head.

Jake closed the door and then walked down the pier toward the end. The morning was cold with clouds swirling in the sky, but at least the rain or snow was holding off, he thought.

As he got closer to the end of the pier, a man in a suit with a long wool overcoat stepped out from behind a pile of fishing nets.

"What's so important?" the Secret Service man asked. "And why did you want to meet like this?"

Moving to within a few feet, Jake said, "I didn't like the answer I got last night. And I don't like the possible outing that nearly happened at our last briefing. We're supposed to work in the shadows."

The Secret Service man lowered his chin toward his chest and shook his head. "This comes from beyond my pay grade."

This was crazy. It was this man's job to protect the president of the United States. Unless. . .

"You want the assassin to make the attempt," Jake said. He glanced back down the pier and saw two other men close in from the far end, heading their way. They too were obviously Secret Service.

"That's absurd."

"Not really. You just keep track of the man and take him out while he's in the process of shooting at Reagan or Gorbachev. Or maybe you let him kill the Soviet. Then our government doesn't have to make a crappy deal with those Communist bastards."

"You're crazy," the man said, but his non-verbal reaction was belying his words. This guy actually believed they could control a brutal assassin.

"I can't believe my Agency would go along with this," Jake surmised. "I'm guessing the KGB has set up this whole scheme to placate the hardliners in Moscow."

The Secret Service man tightened his jaw. "Your Agency will do as it's told. And so will you."

"What if the German decides for himself that Reagan would be a better target?"

"It'll never get that far."

"How do you know?"

"We're all over him."

"You mean like last night?"

"Reagan and Gorbachev are not even in country yet. We'll tighten our control of the man when they get here in two days."

"I've seen this man kill first-hand. He might be a professional, but he's also Stasi."

"He's hired help."

"You don't understand the Stasi. Pretend you took the KGB, the Nazi Gestapo and the worst SS officer you could find, shove their sperm in a blender, and inseminate Mata Hari. The spawn, cloned thousands of times, would be the Stasi."

The Secret Service man stood blank, like a man without a concern in the world. "You've done your job here, Jake. You've identified the potential threat, and we've got images of the man distributed to our people. You're being recalled to Germany."

"Bullshit."

"Call your boss in Bonn. He'll confirm it."

Jake turned to leave and took just a couple of steps, but he was stopped with a quick call from the Secret Service man.

He stopped and turned but said nothing.

"My men will escort you to a military transport at Keflavik."

"Not until I talk with my boss," Jake said. "And I can find my own way to Keflavik."

"I don't think so. The Soviet delegation complained about you to the Icelandic Police this morning. They're the ones who initiated the recall."

"That's a bunch of crap," Jake said. "They attacked an Icelandic Police Inspector. I was only helping her."

"That's not the way they heard the story," he said. "Just go back to Germany and drink a few real beers. Let us handle this."

They never wanted him here in the first place, Jake realized. It was possible that they already knew about the assassin before Jake even arrived. God, he hoped not.

"Hey, I'm more than happy to get the hell off this frozen rock," Jake said. "What time is my flight?"

"Fourteen hundred."

"Awesome. Just let me take another shot at that hot Icelandic cop."

Secret Service nodded approval. "You're sleeping with her? Nice."

"Not much sleeping going on, partner." Jake smiled and left him with that image.

Damn it! Now he had just hours to come up with a viable plan to stop this assassination attempt. And everyone wanted him to vacate the country. Conspiracy was only a crazy notion when there was no possibility of something nefarious happening. That wasn't the case now, Jake knew.

When Jake got to the two other Secret Service agents, he hoped like hell they would try to stop him so he could kick their asses. But instead, the two stern-looking men simply parted like the Red Sea for him. Jake simply looked at them with a derisive glare and continued down the pier.

12

Jake got into the passenger seat of Hildur's Toyota and said, "Let's go."

She put the car in gear and pulled away from the curb. "Is everything all right?"

How much should he tell her? How much did she need to know? He had learned quickly in this game that trust was earned over time, and they had not reached that level yet. Still, perhaps she could help him.

"We've got a problem," Jake said. He quickly told her that he was being expelled from Iceland because of the incident the night before, leaving out the real reason.

"That's crazy," she said, shifting the car into third gear and heading toward a roundabout. "I can explain it to my boss."

"It won't matter." He saw a line of buildings on the other side of the roundabout and said, "Go through the roundabout and get me to that pay phone. How much change do you have?"

"There's a plastic bag full of change in the glove box," she said.

Jake found the bag and then had Hildur pull up to the curb by the pay phone. He filled the phone with coins and dialed the long international number to his boss in Bonn. It took him a good chunk of that change to get authenticated through to the deputy station chief.

The deputy sounded like a wounded animal on the other end, apologizing for having to recall Jake.

"This is bullshit," Jake said. Then he explained what had really happened, including his theory on the potential assassination. About halfway through the conversation, Jake was prompted to insert more coins. He put in everything he had left and continued talking.

"It's beyond me," Jake's boss said. "The Secret Service wants you gone. So you're gone. Besides that, we've got word that protesters are planning a huge protest at Wueschheim Air Station on the eleventh of October."

Wueschheim Air Station was the new location for Ground-Launched Cruise Missiles in Germany. This intermediate-range nuclear missile deployment was widely disliked by what had become pacifistic Germans. Protests were common at the U.S. Air Force GLCM site in the Hunsrück region west of Frankfurt.

"That's the first day of the summit," Jake said. "They're trying to influence the results before it even starts."

"That's right."

"All right," Jake said. "I don't know where the flight will drop me, so it might take a while to get back to Germany."

"No problem. But we need you at Wueschheim to linger in the crowd and make sure nothing crazy happens. They're expecting tens of thousands."

"I'd watch out for the Baader-Meinhof Gang," Jake said.

"That's why I want you there. You already know some of the players."

"I'll be there." He hung up just as the phone was prompting him to add more coins.

Jake got back in to Hildur's car and he considered his options. He was used to following orders as an Air Force officer and as an Agency officer, but he also had a brain. Orders were much clearer in the military, as were the consequences of non-compliance. He was learning that the Agency was a little different. There were orders and then there were real orders. The last thing Jake had heard his boss say was to get to Wueschheim, Germany by the eleventh. He would take the last order first.

"Is everything all right?" she asked.

"Yeah, it's cleared up." He hesitated and smiled at her. "What would you be doing if you weren't babysitting me?"

"Many of us have been ordered to flex our time before the world leaders get here, since we won't have any time off once the summit begins. We will all be working at least twelve-hour shifts. Why do you ask?"

He sure as hell didn't want her going in to work and finding out that Jake was to be deported. That would put her in an awkward position. No, he needed to keep her away for a while.

"I have a flight to catch tomorrow," he lied. "What do you say you show me a little of your country?"

"Like what?"

"The natural beauty."

She smiled. "Didn't you see that last night?"

"That too. But I was thinking about waterfalls. I heard you had some nice ones here."

She put her car in gear and got into the roundabout, turning away from the ocean and toward the road leading out of the city. "You're gonna love this. We can get lunch out in the country."

It took them about two hours to drive the 115 kilometers to the Gullfoss Waterfall, the most famous in Iceland. But they had first stopped along the way to see less impressive geysers. They were in no hurry, Jake knew, since he was just wasting time and staying out of reach of the Secret Service, the Icelandic Police, and the KGB. The last thing he wanted was for Hildur to get in trouble, so he kept her in the blind.

Gullfoss was the most beautiful waterfall Jake had ever seen, and he had been to Niagara. The two of them parked at the lower parking lot and hiked up to the top edge of the falls. With the freezing temperatures this was probably a mistake, since the spray from the falls had gotten them both quite wet. But the cold had also kept away most tourists. Only a few hardy souls braved the cold, the wind, and the spray.

When they had experienced enough of the falls, they hurried out of there and found a nearby restaurant to warm up.

They both ordered lamb soup and shots of vodka, which warmed them almost instantly. So they ordered a second vodka.

"Are you trying to get me drunk, Jake?" she asked.

"No. Just trying to warm you up."

She smiled. "We usually don't come to Gullfoss this time of year. Spring and summer are much better. The water is flowing stronger and you don't freeze as much."

"I can imagine that water is glacial run-off and is always cold."

"That's right." She raised her second glass of vodka and he did the same.

Both of them downed the second vodka.

She put her hand on his and said, "What is going on, Jake?"

"Nothing. Why?"

"You're really not into this. Is this too boring for you?"

"God, no. I've just got a lot on my mind." They had discussed the direction the U.S. government was taking with this assassin, along with the position of the KGB and the Soviets. She was not used to thinking about geopolitical implications, he could tell. And that was understandable in this placid land, where they might have just one murder per year on the entire island.

"What will you do?" she asked.

That's what he had been contemplating when she busted him. "I don't know," he lied. "The smart thing to do is just go back to Germany."

She laughed. "But not until tomorrow. We have one more night together."

"So, you still want me to stay with you?" he asked.

"I'm looking forward to it." She squeezed down on his hand.

He stood up. "All right. Give me your keys."

"Why?"

"Because two shots might put that tiny body of yours over the limit."

"Good point."

"Besides," Jake said. "They're already kicking me out of the country."

13

Jake and Hildur got back to her apartment in late afternoon. They didn't wait until night to make love. It capped the most restful day Jake had experienced in years.

Shortly after five p.m. Hildur got a call from her supervisor at the Icelandic Police. She talked in her language, her eyes concerned and darting from side to side and trying not to concentrate on Jake. Then she slowly set her phone back in its cradle.

"Are they looking for me?" Jake asked.

She wrapped herself in her arms and nodded. Her eyes seemed to be sinking. "They said you were supposed to be on a plane this afternoon."

He wanted to come clean with her. They had bonded in the past couple of days. "I couldn't tell you," Jake said. "They just want to shut me up and get me out of Iceland."

Tears streaked down both of her high cheek bones. "If they find you here, I can lose my job. Or worse." Her stance became more uncertain as she rocked on her heels.

Jake went to her and took her in his arms, hugging her tight to his chest. "I'm sorry, Hildur. I'll leave."

"I just lied to my boss. What if they send someone here?" Now her words started to slur, as if she were in the early stages of inebriation.

He let her go and rounded up his clothes into his small bag. He was never more than a minute away from departing at any given time. Then he picked up his leather jacket and turned back to her. "Tell your boss the truth. I lied to you."

"What will you do?" she asked, moving closer to him, her stocking feet nearly tripping on nothing.

He shrugged. "I'll take a taxi to Keflavik and stay there until I can get out on another flight." He stepped closer to her just in case she fell.

"I can give you a ride," she said.

"No. If they catch me with you, that would get you in trouble."

"Let me at least call you a taxi," she offered.

He checked his watch and knew that the end was near for her. "I could use the walk," he said.

"It's a couple of kilometers to downtown." She shook her head. "I'm really tired."

"It's all the fresh air. I feel it as well." He took her in his arms just as she sunk toward the floor. Then he lifted her in his arms and carried her to her bed, setting her down gently. He pulled her pants off and tucked her under the covers.

Jake hated himself for drugging her with her own sleeping pills, but he really didn't have a choice. It was better for her.

Now that his Icelandic partner was safely tucked away, Jake found her car keys, locked the door behind him, and got into her car down on the street out front.

Darkness was hard over the city now, with clouds swirling overhead and threatening to rain or snow. It was cold enough for the latter, Jake thought.

He drove Hildur's car toward downtown Reykjavik and stopped at one of those large stores with everything from food to hardware, picking up a few items and paying with cash he had gotten from Hildur's purse. He would have to get some of his own cash and pay her back before leaving Iceland. Next, he filled up her gas tank, which just about took the last of his cash.

Now Jake drove downtown and parked Hildur's car a block from the Iceland Police station, locking her keys in the center console. He slung his bag over his shoulder and walked toward the sea.

When Jake got to the Reykjavik Marina Hotel, it took him only a few minutes to find the dark blue Volvo in a remote area of the parking lot. He smiled and considered his approach, which he had plotted out in his mind all afternoon on the drive to and from the Gullfoss Waterfall.

Jake found the back entrance to the hotel next to the single loading dock. He noticed there were no cameras in this area. In fact, the only cameras he had seen in the hotel were in the front lobby. He wasn't sure about the corridors, though, since he had not been in that area.

With deliveries obviously over for the day, Jake was relieved to see the loading area empty of personnel. He guessed as much.

He got into the main part of the hotel and walked up to the second floor, where he hesitated for a moment to let his eyes adjust to the darker corridor. He considered how to get the man to open his door. What would make Jake do so? It wasn't like Jake could just kick the door in. In Iceland most of the hotel doors opened outward into the corridor. No, he needed to get the man out another way. A woman might work, but the Stasi man might be expecting that. The Wolf was good but he was also arrogant—he was a legend in his own mind, yet much of his bravado could be backed up by his resume.

When Jake heard footsteps coming from the staircase, he drew his gun and stepped to the side of the door. The gun and man's hand appeared first, but Jake put his gun at the man's head as he came out.

"Put the gun down," Jake said quietly in German.

It was the young KGB officer. When the man set his gun on the carpet, Jake made sure the guy was alone.

"Where's your old partner?" Jake asked in English with a German accent, using his foot to slide the man's gun away from the KGB officer.

"Where's your beautiful girlfriend?" KGB asked, his English not close to perfect.

Jake ignored the question. A brilliant thought came to him. "You're gonna help me out."

The young man smiled through crooked teeth. "Why would I do that?"

"Because if The Wolf kills Gorbachev the whole world will think America did it."

The KGB officer couldn't hide his surprise. "I don't know what you're talking about."

"You'd make a bad poker player," Jake said with a smirk. Then Jake thought for a moment. What did this man really know? The KGB liked to keep its people in the blind, only giving them enough information to complete single tasks. The big picture was generally only known by those high up the food chain.

"What do you want from me?" KGB asked.

"I want to have a little talk with our Stasi friend."

The Soviet smiled. "And you need me to get you in to his room."

"In theory. I could just shoot up the damn hotel, break into the man's room, and kill the bastard."

"Why don't you?"

The KGB officer shifted his head down the corridor toward The Wolf's room and then back to Jake. "You don't have the authority." Now the synapses in the man's brain seemed to go off in the proper direction. "You know about a hired assassin, yet you do nothing to stop him. Why?"

"That's a good question. Why do you think?" Jake needed this guy to come to the proper conclusion on his own.

Finally, the KGB officer said, "Your people want Gorbachev dead as well."

"Not my people," Jake assured the guy. "Perhaps some people. Just like the hardliners in your government. They don't want him signing any deals with America. Especially not with a cowboy."

"I just follow orders," KGB said.

"So did the SS guards at Auschwitz. And they ended up hanging. Do you really think your bosses can let you live knowing what you know?" Nothing like playing with a young KGB officer's mind, considering they were always one step away from Siberia or worse.

"You really think they will kill me?"

"That's the first rule of assassination," Jake said. "You take out the assassin and anyone else close to the assassin."

The KGB officer said something in Russian, but Jake wasn't up on that language entirely yet. He could guess what the guy was saying based on his non-verbal expressions, though.

Finally, the Soviet said, "What do you plan to do with this man?"

Jake shrugged. "If we take him out your people will just hire someone else." Now something came to Jake. "Why are you here?"

Hesitation. "I was watching our asset."

That was crap, Jake guessed. "Where's your partner?"

"I am alone."

Now Jake had to call this guy out. "The KGB does nothing alone. They believe in the two-man rule. That way nobody gets an idea they can defect."

"That's how your leaders brainwash you."

Maybe so, Jake thought, but he also saw a chink in this guy's armor. "Let's just go have a talk with your Stasi friend. See what he thinks."

Jake waved his gun for the guy to move down the corridor. Once the KGB officer got a few feet away, Jake picked up the guy's gun and shoved it into a side pouch on his bag.

When they got to room 215, Jake kept his gun behind his leg while the young KGB officer knocked lightly with his knuckles on the wooden door.

As the door opened into the hallway, Jake shoved the KGB officer into the Stasi man and then pointed his gun at both men. Before the Stasi could respond, Jake had The Wolf drop his gun to the floor.

"What the hell is this?" The Wolf said in German.

The KGB officer was about to say something, when Jake smacked him in the back of his head with the butt of his gun, knocking him out, the man hitting the floor hard and subsequently busting his skull open when he hit the edge of the furniture.

"Sit on the bed," Jake said in German. In fact, he planned to keep everything in German for now.

The Wolf reluctantly sat on the bed, but he was clearly looking for a way to kill Jake.

Part of Jake wanted to just put a damn bullet in this man's head. He had killed their asset, the East German dissident, for no good reason. Yes, the man was writing the truth about the East German government, and that was harmful to their security, but he didn't deserve what he got from The Wolf.

"Who are you? What do you want from me?" the Stasi man asked.

"You are a smart man. Guess."

The German's mind tried to calculate and answer. Finally, he said, "My West German brother in BND."

That worked for Jake, letting the man think he was in the Federal Intelligence Service of the Bundesrepublik Deutschland.

"Roll onto your stomach," Jake demanded.

The German called him a disparaging name, but he reluctantly complied. Once the guy got to his belly, Jake smacked him on the back of his head. He didn't go out with the first strike, so Jake hit him again.

Now Jake had the guy right where he wanted him. He quickly pulled out some items from his bag. Then he zip-tied the man's wrists behind his back. He did the same to the guy's ankles. Then he duct-taped the man's mouth. Not just the mouth, though. He wrapped the tape all the way around The Wolf's neck. When he was done, he did the same thing to the young KGB officer. The Soviet's head had already stopped bleeding, but he'd have one hell of a bruise. With this guy Jake also zip-tied him to the bed frame.

Searching the knocked-out Stasi man, Jake found the keys to the Volvo. Then Jake put a Do Not Disturb sign on the outside door handle. With some difficulty, Jake hoisted The Wolf over his shoulder and headed out into the hallway.

He hurried down the staircase to the loading dock and set the limp body onto the cold, concrete floor.

Jake went to the Volvo and backed it up to the loading dock. Then he opened the trunk and retrieved the limp body, packing The Wolf into the trunk. He made sure there was nothing the man could do to escape, and even removed the hard rifle case and put it in the back seat.

Once he got behind the wheel of the Volvo, he considered his options again. None of this was authorized. But he had learned in his days as an Air Force officer to never ask for permission, but to ask for forgiveness.

He drove off into the dark night, quickly leaving the city lights behind him.

14

This time it took Jake only an hour and fifteen minutes to drive the 115 kilometers from Reykjavik to the Gullfoss Waterfall. The road was a bit more challenging in the dark, with the occasional sheep wandering out onto the pavement. By the time Jake got there, he was hearing pounding from the trunk.

He opened the trunk and pointed his gun at the German.

Jake switched to English. "Are you ready to take a little walk?"

As Jake guessed, the parking lot was empty. Not an Icelandic soul would come to this place at night. There was nothing to see at this hour. Darkness shrouded the area completely. But the sound of the massive waterfall roared in the distance.

The Wolf said nothing. Of course, his mouth was duct taped. As Jake pulled the man from the trunk, the Stasi man struggled with all his power. But he would never get those zip ties to budge, Jake knew.

Jake propped the man against the back of the car and closed the trunk behind him. Then he put his gun in his right hand and punched the German in the stomach, buckling the man over to his knees. Now Jake pulled out a knife and cut the duct tape. He ripped it away from the man's mouth.

"I'm going to fucking kill you," The Wolf spit out.

"I knew you could speak English. Get up."

"You don't make it easy," the man said. "Untie my feet."

Jake knew the man was quite adept in the martial arts, and his feet were his most dangerous weapon. Instead of letting the man's legs loose, Jake found three more zip ties. Then he kneeled on the man's legs as he changed the ties from a tight fit to a looser arrangement, which would give the guy the ability to shuffle like a prisoner in shackles. When he was done, Jake helped the man to his feet.

Pointing up the hill, Jake said, "Start heading up there."

"Why should I?"

"Because if you don't, I'll put a bullet in your Stasi brain right now."

Reluctantly, the man started to shuffle up the path. Jake glanced down the road and smiled. Then he pulled the rifle out of the case in the back seat and checked it out in the light from the dome. Just as he thought, everything about this rifle was American, from the rifle itself to the scope mounted on top. He opened the bolt and slid the rounds from the inner magazine. Five rounds. Any good assassin would need just one, since a reasonably decent security detail would be all over their protected asset before he could get a second round chambered.

Jake closed the Volvo door and slung the rifle over his right shoulder. Then he easily caught up with the Stasi officer.

"You could make this a lot easier if you cut my legs free," The Wolf said.

"Yeah, well I don't trust you as far as I can throw you," Jake said.

"So, that's the plan?"

Jake shoved the man forward. It took them fifteen minutes to climb up the edge of the waterfall, the spray soaking the both of them and the cold wind chilling Jake to the bone. He kept looking back to the car, hoping he was making the right choice. But only time would tell.

When they reached the top, just as Jake had done earlier in the day with Hildur, the spray was actually less intense, since they were now almost even with the top tier of the waterfall. He could see the water periodically when the partial moon poked through the swirling clouds. They were in the center of a rock precipice with a sharp cliff to the water.

"Now what, chief?" the German asked Jake.

"Now you tell me your plan. If you tell me the truth, I might let you go."

The Wolf laughed aloud. "Now who's not telling the truth?"

"Just spit it out," Jake said, losing patience.

"You don't get it, do you?"

Jake thought he did, but he needed to hear it directly. "Enlighten me."

"You've been part of this since day one. Since you first stepped foot in Berlin and started following me around. There was no dissident. He was a Stasi plant who betrayed his country."

"You're saying he was a double agent? We knew that."

"Do you know that he's still alive?"

"Bullshit."

"It's true. It was part of the whole plan. We pretend to kill him, pissing off a young CIA officer, and then we leave a bunch of bread crumbs leading you here to Iceland. You would naturally fill in the blanks, guessing I was here to kill Reagan."

This guy was a total liar, Jake thought. "Why would you do that?"

"Because every assassination needs a patsy to blame," the Stasi man said. "You are that patsy."

Jake glanced down toward the car and finally saw what he expected to see—a car driving slowly up the road toward the parking lot with its lights off.

"I know that the real target is Gorbachev," Jake said. "Hardliners in your country and the Soviet Union don't like the direction he's taking."

"Ding, ding, ding. Give the man a stuffed animal. You finally figured out part of the plan."

Jake tapped the butt of the rifle. "And you bought a Remington rifle with a Leupold scope. More than likely somewhere in America. But that's a flaw in your reasoning. I couldn't have possibly purchased that rifle. I've been in Europe."

The Wolf smiled. "It was purchased for you by someone else, who will commit suicide in the next few days."

Interesting concept, Jake thought, as he saw the car down the hill park next to the Volvo. It was too dark to see the type of car.

"Why should I believe anything you say?" Jake asked.

"I've got no reason to lie."

What if this man was telling him the truth? Could the KGB have orchestrated this whole thing, pulling his strings like a puppet? "How did you plan to set me up? I won't even be in the country when you take the shot."

"Travel plans can be changed. You still don't get it."

Yes, he did. "So, you take the shot and kill Gorbachev. I just happen to be laying around, drugged I'm guessing, and you take off, leaving me there to hold my dick. Somehow you have my fingerprints on the rifle and the shell casings."

"That's easy enough to do. In fact, they're on there right now."

Good point. But he had plans for this rifle that didn't include killing the Soviet leader. Jake pulled the rifle from his back and took the scope covers off before aiming it down the hill toward the cars. He could barely make out the vision of a person in dark clothes moving up the hill toward them.

15

Jake shouldered the rifle again and pulled out his knife. He had no choice now. These people were crazy. They had actually set him up from the beginning. Had he been that stupid? Or perhaps just naïve?

Then a better thought came to him. He pocketed his knife and took the rifle from his shoulder again. Now he slipped each bullet from the magazine, throwing each of them into the Gullfoss Waterfall. When he was done, he grasped the rifle by the butt and flung it as hard as he could out into the river. No rifle, no problem.

"That was stupid," The Wolf said.

"Maybe," Jake said. "But you can't pin an assassination on me. And you can't kill Gorbachev with that rifle."

"You don't think these people have a backup plan?"

Jake was sure of it. But he could only handle what was in front of him. He glanced down the hill again, but he couldn't even see the dark figure anymore. The waterfall spray was obscuring his view.

Pulling his knife out again, Jake knew what he needed to do. Now he took out his 9mm handgun from inside his jacket with his right hand.

"Get on the ground," Jake demanded.

"Why should I?"

"Because if you don't, you're going for a swim. It might be hard to swim with your hands and feet tied." Of course, the man would never survive the first drop of the waterfall.

Reluctantly, the man sat on his butt.

"Roll onto your belly," Jake said.

The Stasi man did this, putting his feet up in the air. Jake cut the man's ties from his feet and threw the plastic ties into the water below.

"What about the hands?" The Wolf asked.

Before Jake could answer, the first bullet cracked through the darkness, and he thought he heard the bullet pass by his head. He twisted to his right bringing his gun up and looking for a target. Nothing.

Jake vectored away from the waterfall, his gun waiting to fire at the shooter. Finally, Jake saw movement and he shot once.

Two shots came back at him and Jake dove to the ground. Now the black figure moved to the left, crouching low to the ground. Just then the clouds let through some moonlight and Jake could see his target. Jake shot twice and the man dropped to the ground.

Rushing down the hill, Jake found the man lying in the pathway. He kicked the gun away and rolled the man over. It was the older KGB officer. One bullet had hit the man in the center of his chest and the other had entered his face next to his nose. Jake found the man's gun and threw it over the cliff into the waterfall.

Then suddenly Jake remembered the Stasi officer. He had released the man's feet. Jake methodically pushed up the hill toward the top ledge. He aimed his gun around, but didn't see The Wolf anywhere. How the hell could he have escaped? There was nowhere for him to go, Jake thought.

He walked slowly toward the edge of the ledge, his gun still guiding his way. When he sensed movement, he turned and almost fired, but then hesitated, knowing he needed to take this man alive.

Somehow the Wolf had released his plastic tie from his hands, and he tackled Jake in the chest, knocking both of them onto the ground, with Jake's gun flying from his right hand down the precipice.

They struggled on the ground, with each landing punches. Jake was able to break free and jump to his feet. So did the Stasi officer.

Now they each kicked and punched, and each blow was blocked by the other.

The Wolf backed off and wiped blood from his mouth. "Not bad for a young CIA officer," the Stasi man said. "But some things get better with age."

The Stasi rushed toward Jake and instead of stepping to the side Jake took the man's rush by grasping his shirt, falling with the flow to his back, and catching the man in the groin with his right foot. Jake continued his backward roll and shoved up with his foot, sending the man careening through the air behind him.

Hitting the rock with a thud, the Stasi officer bounced a couple of times and finally caught hold of a rock before plunging into the abyss of the waterfall.

Jake got to his feet and searched for his gun. But it was clearly gone over the edge. Then he stepped lightly toward the edge of the cliff, finding the Stasi man holding on to the rocks like a cat on a tree.

"I suppose you want me to save your sorry ass," Jake said.

The man gave a grunt and said, "That would be nice."

Sitting down onto the rocks a few feet from his opponent, Jake said, "First, tell me the truth."

"I told you the truth," the Stasi man said.

"Maybe. Who gave the old KGB officer his orders?"

The Stasi man shook his head. "I don't know. You've got to believe me."

Jake guessed he might never know the answers to these questions. "Is there a backup shooter?"

Reluctantly, the man said, "No. They didn't want a wide conspiracy."

"What about the young KGB officer? What does he know?"

The Stasi laughed. "We couldn't trust him. His father works for Gorbachev."

Interesting, Jake thought. "So, the conspiracy will die with you."

The man's fingers seemed to be getting tired, Jake could see.

"Come on," the Stasi man said. "How about some professional courtesy?"

"Your people were about to let me take the fall for the assassination of Gorbachev," Jake said. "They would have probably put a bullet in my head first."

"I had nothing to do with that plan."

When the Stasi started to swear in German, Jake knew the man could not hold on much longer. He started to scoot down toward the man, got within a few feet, and then The Wolf lost his grip with his left hand.

He screamed now for Jake to grab his hand. But Jake considered his options. The rocks were wet and slippery. He wasn't sure he could take the entire weight of that man without the both of them tumbling down into the waterfall.

Before Jake could decide what to do, the man's grasp with his right hand came free, and the Stasi man fell backward into the darkness. With the heavy noise from the falls, Jake didn't even hear a splash. But without a doubt there was no way that man could survive the fall or the subsequent plunges through the other tiers of the waterfall.

Jake let out a heavy sigh and backed his way to the top of the cliff.

Now what? His head swiveled around, trying to see if there was anything left behind. Brass. How many shots had he taken? He went to the place where he had fired his gun and found the spent brass. He threw them over the cliff, certain that he had gotten all of them.

Then he made his way down to the dead KGB officer. He couldn't just leave the man here for some tourist to find. But first he searched in the darkness for that man's spent brass. He found only four. Not enough, but that would have to do. Jake threw the brass over the cliff.

That left the dead KGB officer.

The task was obvious, but the man was not small. Jake dragged the older KGB officer to the edge of the cliff and was finally able to send the man over into the waterfall.

Jake was exhausted. He slowly made his way down the path to the parking lot. But now he had another problem. Two cars. It wasn't like he could drive both of them away from Gullfoss. The easiest choice was the most obvious for Jake. He found his knife and slit both front tires of the car brought there by the old KGB officer. Then he got into the Volvo and pulled out. He would drive very slowly back to Reykjavik now.

16

It was past midnight when Jake finally got back to Reykjavik. He had stopped along the way and dumped the rifle case and anything else that could have been associated with The Wolf in a river. He wiped down the Volvo of all prints before dropping off the car in the parking lot of the Reykjavik Marina Hotel.

Then Jake put his bag over his shoulder and started off toward the downtown area. Eventually he found a bar still open and made his way to the bathroom, where he washed up and changed his clothes. He disposed of his old pants and shirt in the garbage can, covering them with used paper towels. With a nearly empty bag, Jake went back into the bar and drank a quick shot of whiskey.

A police officer came into the bar and Jake kept his eye on the man in the mirror behind the line of bottles. Once the officer left, Jake did the same.

Outside in the cold, Jake turned and started hiking out of town toward the downtown regional airport. Once he got there he was forced to simply wait until just before five a.m. for the doors to open. Then he found a flight that would work for him and paid with a credit card associated with his Austrian passport. His flight would leave before seven a.m.

A week later

Hildur woke up in her bed to the ringing of her phone. She had been off for a couple of days following the Summit between Reagan and Gorbachev, which had gone off without incident from a security perspective.

"Hildur," she said into the phone.

"I still can't get used to calling everyone by first names," came a man's voice.

"Jake?"

"Afraid so."

"You're all right."

"Of course. Why?"

"I don't know. You left without. . .I'm not sure what happened. I just woke up the next morning in my shirt, bra and panties. And, as you know, I sleep naked."

"Yes, and I appreciated that."

"Where are you?"

"Back at work," Jake said. "Looks like the summit went off without a problem."

"I'm guessing you had something to do with that. That morning you left I got a visit from your Secret Service. They were not very happy."

Jake laughed. "They rarely are, Hildur."

Neither said a word for nearly a minute.

Finally, Hildur said, "That afternoon the police were called out to the Reykjavik Marina Hotel. Would you like to guess what they found?"

"I have no idea. Do tell."

"A man tied up in room two-fifteen. A Soviet man. The same young man who tried to attack me in the alley."

"KGB? Really. Now that's interesting."

"Of course, the Soviet government just called him a member of their delegation. It was called a robbery."

"Well, that makes sense. Since crime in Iceland is out of control."

"Are you laughing?"

"No, not at all. I love your country, and would like to come back soon for a visit."

"Really?"

"Of course."

Another hesitation.

She didn't want to do this, but she had no choice. "The man who was staying at the Marina Hotel is missing."

"I thought you said he was tied up in his room."

"No, that was the young Soviet KGB officer."

"What about the older KGB officer?"

"The Soviets didn't mention him."

Jake said, "They probably recalled the older man, since he couldn't even keep his partner safe. My guess is he's been sent to Siberia."

"And the German Stasi man you were tracking? He never checked out of his room."

"I'm guessing they saw the folly of their plot and he was sent back to East Berlin," Jake said. "Maybe he tied up the young KGB officer and left."

She considered what Jake was telling her, but was having a hard time believing any of it. Regardless of what really happened, the two world leaders had left Iceland safely.

"It was great working with you, Jake," she said. "I do hope we can see each other again."

"We will," he assured her.

Then they both hung up and she gently set the phone back in its cradle. Maybe some things were never meant to see the light of day, she thought. Her final report would be filled with holes. But that didn't bother her. Nor did the fact that Jake wasn't telling her the truth about the fate of the KGB and Stasi officers. Something deep inside her knew that these men would never leave Iceland.

17

Now
Reykjavik, Iceland

Jake and Sirena talked late into the evening, trying their best to stay awake to fend off jet lag. The next morning, they woke up late and Jake saw that the famous Iceland weather was in full display out his hotel window. Marine fog had drifted in and obscured his view of the mountains across the water. A light rain filled the damp air. Good, Jake thought. A memorial service should not be held on a perfectly sunny day.

The two of them went to the top floor of the hotel for breakfast and then headed back to their room to wait for Hildur's service.

Sirena came to Jake and put her hand on his shoulder. "Are you alright?" she asked.

"I don't know. It seems that anyone I had once dated dies. And not by natural causes."

"That's not true."

He shook his head and said, "Anna, Toni, Alexandra, and now Hildur. I rest my case."

"But I'm still here," she reasoned.

"Maybe you shouldn't be," he said. Then he regretted saying it. "I didn't mean it that way. I really appreciate what we have."

She sat on the end of their bed. "Listen. They were all big girls in the intelligence game. They knew the risks. As do I."

"But they were with me when they were killed."

"Technically, only Anna was with you when she was killed."

He knew she was right, but it didn't help his pain. "Maybe I'm cursed."

"No. You've had some bad luck," she said. "This is true. But this is over a long, distinguished career. You have been put into many positions of danger. Think of all the good you have done in this world. Think about how many people are alive because of your actions. That's how we should be judged."

Jake had to admit that he didn't linger much on the past, because those days were over. And he couldn't think about the future, since that always led him to his own death. No, he lived for the present. Nothing else really mattered. But the past seemed to linger in his mind now. Something wasn't right.

"I'm bothered by someone using my name to contact Hildur," Jake said.

"I've been thinking the same thing," Sirena said, rising from the bed and meeting Jake at the window overlooking the wet city. "It makes no sense."

"As I mentioned last night, I was forced to kill two men in Iceland—a KGB officer and a Stasi assassin."

"Forced," she reiterated. "They didn't give you much of a choice."

"Well, I could have followed orders and simply left Iceland."

"True. And then either Reagan or Gorbachev could have been killed."

She had a point, he thought. "Maybe our people can help us," Jake said.

"What do you have in mind?"

Jake took out his phone and sent a text to his team in Portugal. Within seconds, Jake got a return text from Sancho Eneko, their computer whiz. Because Jake and Sirena had taken the company jet to Iceland, Sancho was one of the only people who knew where they were at this time.

"Sancho?" Sirena asked.

"Yep. Seeing if he can track down some names from my past."

"If anyone can do it, he can."

They lingered for a while until it was time to head out to the memorial service. Then Jake drove them in their rental Land Rover up the hill to the largest church in Iceland. Besides the obvious phallic symbolism of the

Hallgrimskirkja Church that loomed over the capital city, the church itself was not much to look at from the inside. It appeared more like a nuclear bunker than a place of worship.

Jake expected to find the church packed, but instead the front rows were filled with uniformed officers and a few more rows contained people modestly dressed in civilian clothes.

The two of them found a place back quite a distance from the others on the right side of the church.

The ceremony itself was very short and without much in the way of emotion, Jake thought. He expected to see a coffin up front, but there was only a number of large pictures of Hildur from her past—mostly in uniform.

Once the words were said, folks got up and went to glance at the photos. Some left. The current National Police Commissioner Lars Jonasson, recognized Jake and Sirena and came over to them in his dress uniform.

"Thank you for coming," Lars said, shaking both of their hands. "Hildur died too young."

"That she did," Jake said. "Are you investigating her death as a homicide yet?"

The commissioner shrugged. "Other than the texts, we have nothing to go on."

For the third time, Jake's phone buzzed in his pocket. But he ignored it. As they talked, Jake's eyes instinctively scanned the crowd.

"I thought there would be more people," Jake said.

Lars shook his head. "She had no family left. Her parents had already died. She was an only child."

"She had cousins," Jake said.

"Yes. They were here. But her family was really the police department."

"Then you have an obligation to discover the truth behind her death," Jake said.

Sirena grasped Jake's left arm and then took his hand in hers.

As Jake glanced at Sirena sideways, he noticed movement from the front of the church heading in their direction. He immediately recognized the gun when it came out from the man's jacket.

With one quick motion, Jake swung Sirena behind him and drew his Glock from inside his leather jacket.

The first shot came from the other man's gun, the blast echoing through the cavernous interior of the church. Before the man could fire again, Jake shot three times, dropping the man to the hard surface.

Jake swiveled his gun around looking for another target, but all he found were shocked faces from unarmed police officers in uniform.

He checked on Sirena and said, "Are you hit?"

"No," she said.

Then Jake checked on the police commissioner. "What about you?"

"I'm fine," Lars said.

"No, you're not," Jake said. He could see blood dripping down the man's left arm and a hole in the man's uniform.

The commissioner put pressure on his wound and Sirena helped him into a chair.

Jake moved quickly to the man he had just shot, kicking the gun away from his hand. All three of Jake's shots had hit the man center mass. But the man was still conscious.

Kneeling down to the man, Jake said, "Who are you? And why'd you try to kill us?"

The gunman gnashed his teeth and swore at Jake in German. Jake patted the man down for any other weapons, but found none.

In German, Jake said, "Who hired you to kill us?"

More swearing from the man in pain.

Jake continued, "Did you kill Hildur?"

In English, the man said, "Proudly. You are a dead man, Jake Adams."

Now that the man had admitted to killing Hildur, Jake felt like putting a bullet into the man's face. Instead, he holstered his gun and searched the man for identification. He found a German passport, which he photographed quickly, along with an image of the man's face. By now the man had closed his eyes. If he wasn't dead, he would be within seconds. Jake knew that breathing from others he had killed over the years. It was the man's last gasps for life.

The police commissioner and Sirena came over and stood by the shooter.

"Has he said anything?" Lars asked.

Jake handed Lars the man's passport and stood up. "Yeah. He admitted to killing Hildur. The bullet that hit you was meant for me."

"If you hadn't reacted so quickly, who knows what would have happened," the commissioner said.

"That's why I'm always armed," Jake said.

"I see that now," Lars said. "Old enemies from your past?"

"Something like that."

Just then, a group of police in full tactical gear came rushing into the church. Not a terribly slow response time, Jake thought. But not fast enough. All of the uniformed officers in attendance should have been packing.

The police commissioner calmed down the tactical team while Jake and Sirena slipped to the side of the church. Finally, Jake pulled out his phone and read the texts. They were from his man in Portugal, Sancho.

"What is it?" Sirena asked.

Before answering, Jake sent a photo of the man he had just shot, along with an image of the man's passport.

Jake turned to Sirena and said, "The names I gave Sancho set off a flag. He was able to stop the flag from going back to the source, but just barely."

Another text came in and Jake looked at the screen. "That's what I was afraid of," Jake said.

"The shooter was German," Sirena said. "Since his name set off a flag, he had to be BND."

Jake disagreed with a head shake and said, "More likely former. Otherwise, he wouldn't have been carrying a normal German passport."

The BND was the Federal Intelligence Service of Germany. Their version of the CIA. The same agency that his old girlfriend Alexandra had retired from before being killed in Italy.

"We should keep this to ourselves," Sirena said.

"Agreed."

Lars came over to the two of them, his hand still over his wound on his left arm. "We will have to get a statement from both of you, including the man's final words."

"He mostly swore at me in German," Jake confessed. "But, as I mentioned, he did admit to killing Hildur."

"What was his motive?" Lars asked.

"We might never know," Jake lied.

The police commissioner gave Jake a suspicious glare and said, "Something tells me you know more than you're saying."

That would always be the case, Jake thought. He said, "Some things are still classified Top Secret."

"Even from the old days?" Lars asked.

"Especially from those times," Jake assured the commissioner.

Sirena pulled at Jake's arm for them to depart the scene.

Just as a medical woman arrived to help the commissioner, Lars said, "I'll need a report from both of you on what happened here."

Jake gave the man a thumbs up as he departed the church.

They got to the rental Land Rover and Jake got behind the wheel.

Sirena put her hand on his leg and said, "Are you alright?"

"Some things come full circle, Sirena."

"What do you mean?" she asked.

"Before one of the files was flagged, Sancho had tracked down the man code named The Wolf, finding his real name.

The man I just shot was the Stasi officer's son, a former BND officer."

"You think he found out you killed his father?" Sirena asked.

"It's the only logical explanation. Probably through his BND contacts."

"How can you be sure?"

"When he was dying and swearing at me, he called me Shadow Warrior."

"Your code name in Germany?"

"And elsewhere. Because of my association with Alexandra, the BND became aware of parts of my past. The German must have linked Hildur with my operation in Iceland back in Eighty-Six."

"Then she gave you up?" Sirena asked.

"No. He already had my name. He killed Hildur to lure me here so he could avenge his father's death."

"But there was no official report as to what happened to The Wolf."

"I know. But the Stasi and the KGB had to know they were killed. Remember, the KGB also lost one of their officers. And I was forced to leave that man's car at the waterfall."

"Did you ever get any blowback from the death of that KGB officer?" she asked.

Jake checked his watch. "That's another story. I didn't find out until later that the man's name was Alexi Sokolov. I had a run-in with his brother in Italy."

He started the engine and pulled out onto the street, heading down the hill toward their hotel.

"Could you call the flight crew and tell them we need to be wheels up within the hour?" Jake asked.

"Sure. Where are we going?"

"We'll let them know once we get airborne," Jake said.

She gave him a pissed-off stare.

"We're going to Bergen, Norway."

"Seriously? Why?"

"Because if our dead German didn't get my name and code name from the BND, then he got it from someone in the old KGB or the current SVR."

"You can't involve your son in this," she said.

"I know. I had Sancho look into Alexi Sokolov, including relatives and associates. One of them retired in Bergen."

"Good enough," she said, and then texted their flight crew.

•

The dark-haired woman kept her distance behind the Land Rover, knowing how dangerous their target could be. She should have never allowed the German to go after the American alone. Especially with his Jewish whore at his side. Her intel indicated that this woman was as dangerous as Jake Adams.

As she hung back, she tapped her phone and made a call. Her contact answered with a code phrase and she gave her response.

"The German is dead," she said. Then she listened carefully. Not for instructions, but for intel.

The man on the other end said, "Someone tried to access our database."

"Tried?" she asked.

Hesitation on the other end of the call. Then, he said, "We don't know for sure what they got. But they were good."

"CIA?"

"Probably not. We can trace them back through our normal channels. This person was better."

She had heard that Jake Adams was involved with a private security entity with nearly unlimited resources. But she didn't want to bring this up to her people at the headquarters. She needed to handle Jake Adams off the books, with only a little help from her friends.

When the Land Rover pulled back into the hotel parking lot, she pulled her vehicle to the curb but kept the engine running. There was no way to know for sure what the German might have told Adams before he died. Maybe nothing. Maybe everything. After all, he had not stayed with German intelligence long because of his own intellect. But the man had been a useful idiot. At least he had gotten Adams to show his face. That was something.

She glanced at herself in the rearview mirror, touching a speck of black mascara at the edge of her catlike right eye. At this time, she had her black hair pulled back into a bun at the back of her head. Next time she would have to change her look.

18

Keflavik, Iceland

On the drive to the airport Jake's mind drifted back to the earliest days of his CIA life, during the height of the Cold War. While he drove, Sirena was on her regular Carlos Gomez organization cell phone typing something into it. This number was the only one they had given to the Iceland National Police Commissioner Lars Jonasson.

"What's Lars saying?" Jake asked.

Sirena grumbled. "He left the hospital with ten stitches."

"The bullet ripped the edge of his arm," Jake concluded. "Been there."

"Based on the scars on your body, you've been just about everywhere," she said.

"Is he still insisting that we provide a written statement?"

"Not as much," Sirena said. "He said that he would be forced to give a press conference, since the city is so small and rumors fly through it like wildfire. My words, not his. He said to send him our versions as soon as we could."

"You didn't tell him we were leaving Iceland."

"No. As far as he's concerned, Hildur's killer was found and neutralized."

Jake dropped off the rental vehicle and the two of them slung their bags over their shoulders and walked to the private operations section of the international airport.

The company jet was fueled and ready for them on the tarmac. They handed their bags to a crew member, who shoved them into a baggage compartment, and then they climbed aboard the Gulfstream.

Jake stuck his head into the cockpit and said, "How long for our flight to Bergen?"

The co-pilot said, "A little less than two and a half hours."

The pilot said, "Are you in a hurry? We can get there in about two hours if needed."

Jake shook his head. "No, take your time."

"We are here for you," the pilot said. "Mister Gomez told us to stick with you."

"We appreciate that," Jake said. Then he headed into the main cabin and saw that Sirena already had a cold beer.

"It's after noon," Sirena said.

"No judgement here," Jake said, taking his normal seat. "You can drink a beer for breakfast if you want."

"I have."

"Me too."

The Spanish flight attendant who had been with Jake and Sirena many years came to Jake with a glass of amber liquid. "Your special rum," she said, handing the drink to Jake.

"Thanks, dear," Jake said. Then he took in the fine smell of the 25-year-old Nicaraguan Flor de Cana, before taking his first sip. This was rum to be savored, not downed like a shot of cheap whiskey.

Soon the pilots started the engines and taxied toward the runway. Seconds later they were airborne.

"Are you still going back and forth with the police commissioner?" Jake asked Sirena.

"No." She lifted her phone and added, "This is my SAT phone. Sancho sent some more information."

Jake had felt his phone buzz in his pants but he had ignored it. "What's he saying?"

"He verified the address of the Russian in Bergen," she said. "Along with the dossier on his actions in the old KGB and SVR."

He didn't need to ask how Sancho had gotten that information. Jake knew his man could find out just about anything on anyone anywhere in the world.

"What's the plan once we get to Bergen?" Sirena asked.

"Proceed with caution. This man tried to kill me decades ago. I let him live."

"Why?"

"Because I had just killed his brother," Jake said. "Maybe I made a mistake."

"That doesn't sound like you, Jake."

"You had to be there. I don't think he was really trying to kill me. Anyway, this was the first indication that the KGB had started to build a dossier on me. Truthfully, I don't think the man was sanctioned to kill me. He simply put me under surveillance."

"Well, the man married a Norwegian woman years ago," she said. "Just before he retired."

"Was she NIS?" Jake asked.

"She was not with the National Intelligence Service of Norway. That's the first thing I asked Sancho. She was a teacher in Bergen until retiring a couple of years ago."

Jake sipped his rum and then swirled the remaining liquid in his glass. He thought carefully about the man they were going to see in Norway. He had no idea if this man knew anything about the death of Hildur or the attempt on his own life. Not every former intelligence officer went gently into that good night. Many had deep-seeded demons pulling at them to make things right from their past.

"What are you thinking?" she asked.

"I don't know. First, I need to tell you how I met the Russian. I had just finished my operation in Iceland, and was back in Germany for a while. A couple of months later and I was tasked to go to Italy. It was around Christmas of Eighty-Six."

"They needed an outsider?"

"Yeah. Anyway, things never go as planned. Here's what happened. . . ."

19

Rome, Italy
December 1986

Jake Adams took the night train from Munich to Rome, arriving in the eternal city in late afternoon. The relaxing ride had given him time to consider his new assignment. The station chief in Rome had needed an outside Agency officer to work with one of their female officers who was currently undercover with the Red Brigades somewhere in Italy. The Red Brigades, or *Brigate Rosse*, was an ultra-left-wing Marxist-Leninist terrorist organization that had been making trouble in Italy since the early 70s. Most of the intelligence community thought they were on their last legs, but Jake knew that's when organizations like that could be most dangerous. In reality Jake thought they were a bunch of punk criminals using their dislike of the

Italian government to justify their nefarious activities—kidnapping, bank robberies and bombings.

Since he didn't want to just walk in to the American embassy for a briefing, Jake had been given a location to meet an Agency contact at a small café near the base of the Spanish Steps.

Jake got to the Spanish Steps area, a place filled with tourists every day of the year regardless of weather conditions, fifteen minutes before his meeting time of 1800. Darkness was coming and Jake knew this was the best time to see the area, where lights accented the buildings in ethereal hues of sepia and burnt sienna. He carried a small 35mm Leica camera and shot various angles of the steps, but in reality, was scanning for anyone who might look out of place. Slowly he wandered up the steps, occasionally turning around and shooting downward.

When he reached the top of the 135 steps, Jake paused and viewed the scene below. Despite the slight chill in the air, couples sat on the steps nuzzled together, while tourists photographed the famous attraction in a daze of amazement.

Casually, Jake checked his watch and saw that it was nearly time for his meeting. Nothing seemed out of place to him. He had been to these steps a few times in the past few years and nothing had probably changed since they were built in the 1700s.

From the top he could see the café on the far side of the Piazza de Spagna. Slowly now, he wandered down the steps, pretending to photograph more of the scene in front of him.

He saw a man walking with purpose, a local dressed in a nice black suit covered by a long overcoat, slip along the far edge of the square and go into the café. The man was carrying a black leather attaché case in his left hand, meaning he was probably right-handed and kept that hand free to draw his weapon. Jake thought of his own appearance in black slacks and his short black leather jacket, and was glad he didn't have to wear a monkey suit to work every day. He let his left arm rub against the butt of his gun in its holster under his arm, an imperceptible and comforting gesture.

He paused to make sure his contact wasn't being followed. Negative.

Now Jake got to the bottom of the steps and moved around the back side of the fountain in the center of the square, shooting back up toward the steps. Darkness had transformed the steps in the short time it had taken him to travel up and down them. It was now what Ansel Adams, no relation of his that he knew of, would call the 'vital moment' for a proper exposure. This was a time that God was waiting for Jake to take a picture. Although he was here for a singular reason, there was no reason he couldn't also come away with at least one nice image on his roll of 36 frames. Quite often when he used his camera like this, he didn't even have film inside. The camera was only a prop.

Satisfied, Jake wandered along the back side of the square and stopped to gaze at the menu on the window. Actually, he was checking the reflection to see if anyone was following him. He was clear, so he went inside.

He walked directly to the last table on the left and stopped in front of his contact. "The lighting on the steps is beautiful right now," he said, his code phrase.

The man with his back to the wall smiled and answered, "They would look better without all the tourists."

Jake smiled, shook the man's hand briefly, and took a seat across from him. According to Jake's boss in Germany, this guy was being reassigned to a new post, a promotion to a deputy station chief somewhere.

"You had no trouble finding the place," his contact said.

"I've been here before."

"Of course."

The man seemed nervous or reticent to Jake. The good field officers could hide their angst; the bad field officers were promoted to desk jobs.

His contact flipped open his attaché case on the seat next to him and removed a thin manila folder. He slid that across the table to Jake.

"I've heard you have a photographic memory," his contact said. "Remember the data from this page and the woman in the photo."

Jake flipped open the folder and was greeted with the photograph of a beautiful woman with black curly hair and intense eyes. Very exotic looking, Jake thought. She had high cheek bones and a strong yet surprisingly delicate jaw. Resolute perhaps.

"Very beautiful," Jake said.

His contact shook his head. "Don't let that fool you. She's deadly, with brains to boot. She might end up running the Agency if she decides to."

Okay, Jake thought. He flipped to a single page of data on the woman in the picture. Toni Contardo, age somewhere in her mid-twenties, but nothing specific. Born in New York City to first generation Italian immigrants. Top of her class in college. No college or major specified. Fluent in Italian, German and Arabic. Working knowledge of a few more languages, but it didn't give details. At five seven she was a few inches shorter than Jake.

Jake looked up. "No weight or bra size," he quipped.

"That's classified. But I can guarantee she's well equipped and proportioned." He nodded his head knowingly as he flipped the file shut and threw it back into his attaché case.

"And you want me to work with her?"

"That's right. But first you need to find her." He leaned closer to Jake. "For the past month she's worked her way into that commie organization. But we haven't heard from her in a week. You need to go to Naples immediately and track her down. We have an address we set up for her, but we have not sent anyone to check on her."

"Why?" Jake asked.

"She was concerned if someone from our office came down, those in the Red Brigades would know it. During her last call she said they were still following her."

"My Italian is not great," Jake said.

"We know. That's perfect. All of our officers here are probably known. We want you to go down there as a former member of their German counterparts."

"The Baader-Meinhof Gang?" Jake whispered.

"Exactly. We heard you were establishing an angle into that group."

Jake shook his head. "The Red Army Faction is a closely-held gang. It will take months to establish a decent cover into that group."

"We know. We just need someone who will be able to pass as a German long enough to not get killed in the process—by either the Red Brigades or Toni. You're fluent in German. Flawless, from what I've heard."

That he was, Jake thought. But he didn't like going in blind like this. "What's the address?" Jake asked.

His contact said the address and Jake planted it in his memory along with Toni Contardo's other vital stats.

"Anything else?" Jake asked.

The Agency man slid a set of keys across the table. "A maroon VW Golf. It's parked two blocks behind us on Via de Condotti."

Jake shoved the keys back to the man. "I'll find my own way to Naples."

"All right."

"So, where are you going next?"

"Egypt."

"Good luck with that." Jake got up and left the Agency man in the café.

Out on the street, night had finally come to Rome. He adjusted his camera toward his right kidney and headed off toward the Trevi Fountain, but he noticed a man in his early forties paying particular attention to him across the square. And the guy wasn't likely an Italian. He looked more like a Scandinavian, with wispy blond hair and a tightly cropped beard.

As Jake passed by the famous Rome landmark, he noticed that not just tourists seemed to be hanging out around the massive fountain structure. On most days the fountain saw more than three thousand dollars' worth of Lira coins, which attracted a lot of youngsters hoping to fill their pockets, especially at night. This drew a lot of Rome's police to make sure that didn't happen.

Stopping briefly, Jake brought his camera to his eye and shot a number of images. In doing so, he was able to look back and see that the blond man was still tailing him. It could be a coincidence, Jake thought. But he usually didn't believe in those.

Jake slung his camera to his back and wandered down a side street, heading toward the nearest Metro Station. Once he got on a subway train, he would be only a couple of stops from the main Rome train station. From there he could take a late train to Naples, arriving on a direct train in just two hours.

He was having a hard time getting the picture of Toni out of his mind. She would be hard to forget, he knew. Focus, Jake.

The farther he got from the tourist areas the less people he saw. When he noticed a man ahead on the street disappear to his right, Jake considered crossing to the other side of the narrow street, which was lined with parked cars. But Jake had one advantage over the normal tourist—he was armed. Then he heard quickened footsteps coming from behind him.

Jake stopped and turned suddenly, expecting to see the blond man, but instead he caught a young Italian man behind him off guard, stopping the guy in his tracks.

The Italian yelled something, but Jake only picked up a couple of words.

The two of them were now just ten feet apart. Jake swiveled his head to the right for a second, and noticed the second man approaching from behind him. He too was Italian. What about the blond man?

"You picked the wrong mark," Jake said in English with a German accent.

The Italian moved in closer, so Jake made him pay with a right-leg roundhouse kick to the man's left cheek. The Italian hit the pavement on his knees, shaking his head.

Swiveling his hips in a continuation to the right, Jake shoved his left foot back, catching the second man in the groin with his heel. That man went directly into a fetal position on the cobblestone sidewalk, moaning in pain.

The first man recovered somewhat, pulling a switchblade from his pocket and pointing it at Jake as he struggled to his feet.

Jake shook his head. With one swift movement, he drew his 9mm automatic pistol from inside his leather jacket and pointed it at the man's head.

Eyes wide now, the Italian turned and ran down the street, leaving his buddy behind trying to recover from his balls in his throat.

Casually, without saying a word, Jake simply holstered his gun and walked off in the direction of the Metro station.

Where was the blond man? Maybe the guy was just a tourist. Or maybe this was a test for Jake.

20

Jake got on a center car on the Metro line, in case he needed to move in either direction to escape. He remained standing and glanced toward the back cars for any danger.

There. He caught a quick glimpse of the blond man. The guy was two cars back, standing like Jake, his eyes viewing the side of the car as if he were reading the advertisements or the Metro line map. Jake guessed the guy had already caught a glimpse of him and was now simply waiting for Jake to make a move.

His training taught him to not just look at the shiny object, but to look beyond that. This blond man could have simply been like when a chess player moves a bishop out quickly to distract his opponent. The player sees one threat and forgets to look in the direction of the real harm about to come, losing an important piece that would eventually lead to checkmate.

Twisting around the pole, Jake turned his attention to those in his own car. Since it was Friday and moving into the early evening, he guessed the evening commute was nearly over. What remained were people moving about the city heading to their favorite restaurant or bar. Predominantly Italians, he reasoned. But none of them seemed overly interested in him.

In two stops Jake got out onto the platform and tried to blend with the crowd as he moved up toward the main Rome train station. The corridors here were packed with travelers. Maybe the commute wasn't over, he thought. Perhaps some needed to take commuter trains to nearby towns.

As Jake rounded a corner at the top of the stairs, he glanced back briefly and saw that the blond man was still there. Better to know where the guy was, he thought.

Once he got to the main terminal, he went to the ticket counter and glanced behind him in the glass. He paid for a first-class car to Napoli, which was scheduled to leave in fifteen minutes. Trains in Italy were not on time like those in Germany, so he knew it could actually leave in a half hour.

He turned and walked toward the center of the cavernous terminal area with high ceilings, struggling not to glance back for a moment. Finally, he stopped and turned to view the large wall of arrivals and departures. In doing so, he could see through his peripheral vision the blond man at the ticket counter. But the guy made a mistake by glancing sideways to locate Jake's position.

Dozens of trains were leaving for various locations around Italy and beyond, so if the blond got on his train,

Jake would know he was on his tail. Had he made a mistake? Who knew about his meeting with the Agency man? Nobody in his office in Germany. The man must have followed his contact in Rome from the embassy. Perhaps the guy was East German or Soviet from the Baltic region.

Jake grabbed a sandwich and a coke from a kiosk along the edge of the terminal. While he ate, he kept an eye on the blond man, who seemed to be oblivious to Jake's presence. Was he being paranoid? Not likely. This guy was good, he thought, but not good enough.

When his train departure neared, Jake walked with purpose toward the platform. With just seconds to spare, he climbed aboard the first-class car on the direct train to Naples.

Surprisingly, the train slowly pulled out of the terminal only a few minutes late.

He found his first-class cabin and slid the door open. Sitting on the left side were two Italian girls in their late teens or early twenties—either high school or college, Jake guessed. He would have the right side to himself.

If the blond man got on this train, Jake didn't see him do so.

The train picked up speed and slipped through the darkness of the city, the lights of inner Rome falling behind them as they moved through the outer suburbs.

The girls were snuggled together whispering something to each other. Then they giggled. Then the one on the right asked Jake something in Italian, but he didn't understand. Remember, Jake, you are Austrian.

He shrugged and smiled. "I don't understand," Jake said in English with a German accent.

"You are German?" the one on the right asked.

"Austrian. But you speak English?"

"A little."

"And your friend?"

"Not at all."

Jake smiled again and leaned back in his chair. "What do you find so funny?"

The girl looked at her friend and then back to Jake. "My friend thinks you are handsome."

"And you don't?"

"No. I do also." Then she said something to her friend and they giggled again.

"Well, thank you," Jake said. "The two of you are very pretty." And he had no problem saying this, since they both had stunning features, from similar black hair to their flawless olive complexions. Looking a bit closer, he could see that they were well developed in the right areas, and were more likely college aged.

From Jake's peripheral view he saw a flash of movement. By the time he looked, the blond man was past his sliding door window. But it was clear that he had seen Jake. Their eyes connected for a second.

"If you go to Napoli, we can show you around," the girl said to Jake.

He was confused, his attention still on the door. His hand instinctively slid into his leather jacket, touching the butt of his gun.

Jake turned to the girl. "What?"

"We are on Christmas break from university," she said. "We can show you Napoli."

He pulled his hand out from his jacket and smiled at the pretty, young college girl. "Thank you so much for the offer, but I will be on business in Naples."

The girl stuck out her lower lip. Then she turned to her friend and explained what Jake had said. She reached into her backpack and came out with a small notebook and pen. She scribbled something and handed the note to Jake.

He looked at the series of numbers and saw the name Francesca. Following that was a smiley face. Jake had come to know the Italians as open and friendly, and this girl probably meant nothing by this gesture other than what she said to him. In all likelihood, she was not offering to sleep with Jake.

"In case you want to have a drink or pizza," she said.

"Thank you. If I get some free time, we should do this." He folded the paper and slid it into his jacket pocket.

Francesca smiled and told her friend the news. They continued to hold hands like sisters at a park.

But Jake's mind was on the blond man. If he was tailing him, and he was KGB or some other intelligence officer, he was not using the best technique. It was as if he wanted Jake to know he was there following him. He thought back over the past couple of months and considered his actions in Iceland just before the Reagan-Gorbachev summit, where he had encountered a couple of KGB officers while he tracked down the Stasi officer from East Berlin. That mission had not gone well for his adversaries, and perhaps they were seeking retribution.

Jake had not even briefed his bosses in Bonn and Munich entirely about his actions in Iceland. The Agency didn't need to know everything he did on a mission. They could de-brief him all they wanted, but he could beat any lie detector test. The Agency only knew what Jake wanted them to know about his past and his current actions. Part of that, he knew, was his belief that any organization leaked information like drunken high school girls gossiping at a kegger. Given the state of covert operations, he felt much safer knowing that only he knew certain things about his actions.

Jake had two choices. He could let this blond man follow him, or he could confront him in this confined space, where the man would have no escape.

Time to take the initiative, Jake thought.

He got up and said, "I'm going to get a beer. Would you two like something? My treat."

Francesca smiled and nodded her head.

Jake slid the door open and the blond man rushed him immediately, shoving Jake back into the cabin. Before Jake could consider drawing his weapon, the blond man had his gun out and pointed at Jake's chest.

When the girls saw the gun, they both gasped and then shoved themselves against the outer wall of the compartment.

Now the blond man closed the door behind him and then pulled the curtains shut to give them privacy.

"What the hell do you want?" Jake asked in German.

"I don't speak German," the blond man said in broken English with a Russian accent. "What did you do with Alexi Sokolov in Iceland?"

Looking closer, Jake could see that the man's gun was a Makarov with a silencer. Meaning that this would be questions followed by a bullet to the head regardless of the answers.

"I don't know what you are talking about," Jake said, maintaining his German accent.

The Russian pulled out a photograph and extended his arm out toward Jake. Crap. It was an image of the older KGB officer Jake had encountered in Iceland.

Shrugging, Jake said, "I don't know this man. You must have me confused. I am from Austria."

The man let out a frustrating huff and returned the photo to his inside pocket. Then he pulled out another photo and Jake couldn't deny knowing this man. It was an image of him with his Icelandic police partner walking down the street just before they were attacked by two KGB officers.

"That is you," the Russian said.

Thinking fast, Jake said, "I was in Iceland selling communications equipment to their government."

The Russian laughed. "You are a bad liar. You are American spy."

Jake heard the young Italian girl gasp behind him. The train rocked back and forth, clicking along with a steady rhythm. "I don't know what you mean."

"Alexi was my brother," the Russian said, his jaw tightening and his grip on the gun squeezing the handle. The man had his finger on the trigger ready to fire. He wasn't just bluffing. "And I believe you killed him."

Having no choice now, Jake had to simply react. But he couldn't endanger these young girls.

"Let these young girls go," Jake said. "They have nothing to do with this."

Two things happened almost simultaneously. First, the Russian shifted his gun from Jake toward the Italian girls. And then Jake shoved the man's arm toward the back of the train. The Makarov discharged once before it fell from the Russian's hand onto the floor, the bullet striking the wall behind the girls.

Then Jake rushed into the man, sending his right elbow into the guy's jaw, knocking him back into the door. The Russian lifted his knee to strike Jake, but he blocked that with his own knee. In these close quarters, Jake would have to use grappling moves—quick strikes and short punches and elbows. Jake sustained a number of strikes to his chest and stomach, but nothing to incapacitate him. And he got his strikes in to the man's face, throat and pressure points in the Russian's upper torso.

Finally, Jake was able to swivel around the man and put the guy into a sleeper hold around his neck. The Russian struggled and tried to head butt Jake, but these moves were unsuccessful. Within a minute or so the man collapsed toward the ground. But Jake twisted the guy and placed him on the bench where he had been sitting, making it look like he was simply sleeping.

Then Jake found the photos in the man's jacket and he pocketed them. He searched for identification and finally found a Russian passport zipped into an inside pocket. He memorized the man's data, even though he knew it was probably all fake.

He turned to the young girls, who were still huddled together against the far wall.

"Are you alright?" Jake asked the girls.

The one who spoke English nodded her head.

Jake picked up the Makarov, wiped the prints and then threw the gun out the window. He looked at the Russian again and wondered if he should have just killed the man. Although it would have been self-defense, he wasn't sure that he wanted to try to explain this to the Italian authorities—despite having the two girls vouching for him. No, he was doing the right thing. He looked at the photo of the Russian and decided to throw that out the window as well. But he kept the one of him and his Icelandic friend. It was a good photo.

"Is he dead?" Francesca asked.

"No. He's just sleeping," Jake said. "I promised you two a beer. Let's say we let this man sleep."

The girls got up from their seats and slung their packs to their backs.

Jake escorted the two girls to the dining car.

21

Naples, Italy

When the train finally pulled into Naples, Jake had purchased two beers for each of the girls and himself. He guessed there was nothing like a little danger to entice the thirst on those less inclined to encounter a man with a gun. Francesca, the one who spoke English, seemed unusually enthused with the danger, and might have wanted more now than to just show Jake around Naples. But he had no time for relationships outside of his job.

Once they reached the terminal, Jake hugged both girls, kissed them both on each cheek, and sent them on their way.

Despite Jake's best efforts, he didn't see the blond man again on the train or in the Naples terminal. He had a feeling the guy was embarrassed by his failure and had to know that Jake was armed, while his gun had been lost.

Jake knew that making an approach on a covert operative working undercover could be a dangerous proposition.

If Rome was the favorite son of Italy, then Naples was the bastard son, whose father had beat the shit out of his child daily until he finally realized he could do better on his own. Jake had been to Naples before, but mostly just passing through on his way to Capri, or to the south in Calabria. He had gone to the top of Vesuvius and toured Pompeii, but that was about his extent of exposure to this city. He had heard from old Navy friends that it was a cesspool of crime and corruption. Before every sailor hit Naples as a port of call, he was told to avoid certain areas, since that's where all the prostitution and drugs could be purchased. So, essentially, the Navy leaders had given the sailors a road map of where to go to have fun. This area of Naples was called the Gut, and Jake was beginning to see why as the taxi driver took him from the train station to an address a few blocks from the location he had gotten from the Agency man in Rome. Jake thought they could have called the area the rectum.

Jake paid the driver in Lira and got out to the curb. The first thing he noticed was how dark the streets were, as if the Neapolitans had not paid their electric bill. It was hard to find a brick or stone wall without graffiti—a stark contrast to Germany, where Jake was sure that anyone found with a paint can after dark got the death penalty.

He checked the numbers on the buildings and saw that he needed to head up the street to Toni's address. But he wasn't quite sure how to approach her. From what he could tell from her data sheet, she had been with the Agency a year or so longer than Jake, since he had spent a number of years in the Air Force as an intelligence officer.

Looking at his watch, it was closing in on midnight. Not exactly a great time to make a first impression with a beautiful operative, but perhaps a good time to find her at home.

The streets here were narrow, and Jake could tell the buildings were older than America. But most of the structures looked like they still had bullet holes from World War II. Everything was in decay here. If Toni Contardo was trying to blend in with the locals, she was doing a damn good job.

Toni's building had a number on it, but the door to her place looked to be up a dark, narrow set of stairs.

He hesitated for a moment to assess his surroundings. A half a block up her street were three women standing a respectable distance from each other, and Jake knew that meant each had her own territorial cobblestones. It also meant that these prostitutes probably had someone watching them.

Jake couldn't linger any longer. In a neighborhood like this he would stand out too much. So, he slipped into the narrow staircase and moved up to the door at the top.

Out of an abundance of caution he considered pulling his gun, but that would put Toni in a position to kill him.

Instead, he knocked lightly on the metal door, which looked like it had soaked in seawater for a decade and was then splattered with acid. He then stepped back with his hands up.

No answer.

Jake glanced back down the stairs and saw a dark figure pass on the sidewalk. When he turned back, he was staring at the barrel of a 9mm automatic pistol. Behind the pistol was the beautiful woman, his Agency contact.

He scanned her body from top to bottom. She was wearing black stretch pants that showed every beautiful curve. And on top she wore a tight baby blue Italian football club jersey with a V-neck. The Rome Agency officer was correct—Toni's substantial breasts filled out the jersey to distraction. Her feet were bare.

"Toni, I presume," Jake said in English.

She grabbed him by his leather jacket with her left hand, shoved him back a foot to glance around him, and then pulled him into her apartment and quietly shut the door behind them—locking three strong bolts on the door.

"Who the fuck are you?" she asked.

"Could you put the gun away?"

"Answer my question."

Okay, so this was how it would go. "Are you alone?" He pretty much knew she was, since the place was one small room, with a tiny bathroom off to one side, but he could see in there as well.

"Who are you and what are you doing here?" she asked, her voice more disturbed this time.

He spit out what he knew about her, from her real name to her parent's names, her vital stats, and her boss's name in Rome. Then he added, "I think five-seven is stretching the truth a bit. You might be five-six tops."

She lowered her gun and said, "Who the hell are you? And I am five-seven."

Jake wandered around her small apartment, memorizing what he saw. "Right. And I plan on playing in the NBA next season."

Toni set her gun down on the coffee table and sat down onto a beat-up leather sofa. "I didn't know the Agency was now hiring stand-up comedians. What the hell are you doing here?"

"I'm on loan from Germany," he said. Then he reached out his hand to her. "Name is Jake Adams."

Reluctantly, she took his hand and squeezed down like a man. "You already know my name. But I'm going by Toni Borelli. And you?"

He pointed to a chair and she nodded her head yes, so Jake sat in a chair across from her. "I'm building a persona in Germany to get in with the Baader-Meinhof Gang. I'm actually an Austrian named Jacob Konrad, which matches my current passport."

"Outstanding. Where are you really from?" she asked.

"Can you guess?"

Her face contorted with consternation. He guessed she didn't experience that often.

Finally, she said, "I'd have to guess somewhere out west. You are almost devoid of accent. Not the south or Texas. Not east coast. You're too slick to be from the Midwest. If I had a gun to my head, I'd guess Washington or Oregon."

"I've spent some time in Oregon," he admitted. "But I'm originally from Montana. Not bad."

"You want a beer?" she asked. "I've got a Peroni or two in the fridge."

"Sounds good."

She half smiled, got up from the sofa, and went to the attached kitchen alcove. Jake couldn't help watching her butt sway seductively as she slipped toward the refrigerator. She was something special, Jake thought. She looked just as good coming back with the beer. She popped the tops on two beers, handing one to Jake before sitting down again and taking a long drink from her bottle.

After a quick sip of her beer, Toni said, "Drink that and then get the hell out. Tell my overlords in Rome that I'm fine."

Jake laughed. "Nice try. But I've been assigned to assist you here."

"Bullshit. I don't need a babysitter."

"Give them a call in Rome."

"I don't have a phone."

Jake knew that. They both took a drink of beer, staring each other down.

"Tell me about these local communists," Jake said.

"The Red Brigades? A bunch of pot smoking zealots who want everything handed to them by the government. I'm convinced they're descendants of anarchists."

"Are they true believers?"

"I'm not sure ideologically speaking, but they're pretty brutal. And they have big plans."

"Like what?" he asked.

She drank down the last of her beer and set the bottle on the coffee table. "Blowing shit up."

"Are you working with an Italian counterpart?"

Toni shook her head. "The Agency thought it would be better if I worked alone. Until now."

Jake had a feeling why. "They didn't trust the locals."

"Maybe I'd believe that if we were going after the Mafia, but the government has no great affinity for the *Brigate Rosse*." She paused, as if checking for a response by Jake, and then continued, "So, tell me how you can help."

He explained how he was trying to build a relationship with the Red Army Faction in Germany and how he would help her take down those she was currently after in Italy.

"You know these Red asshole organizations are not affiliated in any way," Toni said.

"That we know of," he corrected. "A lot of their members are still in exile in France. Are they coming back and restructuring?"

"That's why I'm here. As you probably know, they split into two factions a few years back. Now political assassination seems to be their major goal."

"I was an Air Force intel officer when General Dozier was kidnapped. The Italians did a good job of freeing him."

She smiled. "The Agency helped with that. If these people stopped with the drugs, they might become really dangerous."

"They do anything heavier than pot?" Jake asked.

"Sure. Why?"

Jake shrugged. "We could set up a party and give them all delayed hot shots."

"You mean kill them all? That's insane. Like something Langley would come up with."

"If you're getting all wet for these people, maybe you need to be recalled."

She stood up and gave Jake a brutal glare. "You asshole. Not all of them are murderers."

"I didn't say we had to kill them all," he clarified. "We just incapacitate them and call it in to the local police."

Toni brushed her long hair back with both of her hands. "Oh. I thought you might have been one of the hardliners."

Jake thought about his recent mission in Iceland, where he was forced to kill. He might not have been one of the old guard hawks, but he also wasn't a dove. "If someone tries to kill me or my partners, I'll put them in an early grave. That's Jake Adams rule number one."

"What's rule number two?"

"See rule number one." He yawned. "Any chance I can crash here tonight?"

Toni stood up and put her hands on her hips. Then she pointed at Jake and said, "You can take the sofa. But remember my rule number one: If you ever think you're gonna get inside me, you can forget about it."

"After you've been with those communist hippies, I wouldn't screw you with double condoms."

"I'm not screwing any of them," she assured him.

He shrugged. "Hey, I'm not here to judge you. Just trying to keep you from getting killed."

She picked up her gun and walked to her bedroom area on the far side of the room, setting the gun on the nightstand. She found a sheet, blanket and spare pillow in the closet and threw them on the sofa.

Wow. Cold as ice, Jake thought. Strange indeed. In Iceland he found a girl hot enough to melt glaciers, and in Italy he found a beautiful girl who could walk by a thermostat and the furnace would kick in.

22

The next morning Jake woke up to the sounds of rumblings in the kitchen area. He glanced over and saw Toni in a pair of shorts and a bulky T-shirt putting dishes away from her dishwasher. He could smell coffee brewing.

Jake looked under the sheet and realized he was wearing only underwear and a black T-shirt. He quickly put on his black slacks and headed for the bathroom.

Toni turned and said, "Did you sleep all right?"

"Yeah," he said. "I'm getting used to sleeping on sofas."

"It was pretty noisy out in the street last night," Toni said. "Friday nights are like that in this area." She waved her hand at him. "Go take care of business."

Jake did just that, relieving himself and then looking at himself in the mirror. He had transitioned in the last couple of years from an Air Force officer to a shaggy Austrian civilian living in Germany, undercover as a communications expert building a new company. But this persona gave him the freedom to travel throughout Europe on special assignments like this. The communications company was a real business employed with unsuspecting Germans on the outskirts of Munich. The only profit he cared about, of course, was the acquisition of information—especially in some of the nearby East Bloc countries like Czechoslovakia, Hungary, Poland and East Germany. Strangely enough, though, the front company was actually starting to show a decent profit. Some of that would end up in his new Luxembourg bank account, after being converted from Deutsche Marks to U.S. dollars.

He ran some warm water over his face and through his longer hair, trying his best to control the bed head without having to shower at this point. Then he scratched the three-day stubble on his face, a ubiquitous condition for him lately. His gruff appearance would let him blend in with the locals.

When he got back out to the main part of Toni's apartment, she was waiting for him with a mug of java, which he accepted eagerly.

"Thank you," Jake said. "The last couple of days have been filled with travel."

They both sat at a small bistro table and sipped coffee.

"This is good," Jake said.

"I'd prefer a cappuccino," she said. "But I can get that later."

"How would you like to use me?" Jake asked.

Staring at him over the top of her mug, she delayed with a long sip. Finally, she said, "I don't know what to do with you. If I were to bring you in to the group, many would be suspicious."

"True. What do you have against them so far?"

Toni shrugged. "They've got something big in the works. I've heard word of their acquisition of explosives, but I'm not sure what kind."

"They've blown stuff up in the past," Jake reminded her.

"I know. But this seems like an escalation. In the past few years, they've been more interested in kidnapping and assassination of politicians who seem to be their biggest threat."

Jake sipped his coffee. "They could have been doing that, along with the bank robberies, to get the money to buy the explosives."

"That's why I was brought in," she said. "The Agency thinks they might be looking for an American target."

"Like the Berlin disco bombing last April?"

"Exactly."

"At first we suspected the Red Army Faction," Jake said, "but then our people in Berlin intercepted a message to the Libyan embassy in East Berlin."

"So, we blew up a few tents in Libya."

"We could have done a lot more damage if the damn French had allowed us fly-over rights from the U.K."

"I agree. Some of our friends in the Red Brigades are French. In fact, there seems to be more influence from foreigners recently."

"It's bad enough that we have these asshole communist groups to deal with, but now we have state-sponsored terrorists. I'll bet the explosives you get here will also be plastic explosives and will probably come from the East Bloc." He considered telling Toni about the KGB man he had put to sleep on the train, but he wasn't sure if he could trust her. Not yet.

Toni finished her mug of coffee and looked to see that Jake was also empty. Without asking she went and got the pot from the burner and refilled each of their mugs. Then she sat down again and said, "That might be our in for you."

"What's that?" he asked.

"Word has not gotten out how the disco bombers got their plastic explosives. I could introduce you as a supplier."

"I thought you said they already have a supply."

"They do. But they're always looking ahead. I overheard the leader say they didn't have enough to make a huge impact."

"What the hell is their target?" he asked.

"I don't know."

"If it's in Naples, it must be the U.S. Navy. The base and the ships in port are heavily guarded. What about a soft target like a favorite club? The problem with the disco was that it was a known location for U.S. servicemen and women. They killed two U.S. Army soldiers and injured seventy-nine more. With a little larger bomb, the number of dead could have been much worse. Is there any place in town like that disco?"

"Not a large congregation," she said. "Besides, after Berlin the military has told its people to avoid large gatherings like that."

"How did you get in with these people?"

"I have ties with the Malavita in Calabria. One of the capos there vouched for me."

"I didn't think the Mafia and the Red groups liked each other."

"They don't. But I was presented as a sort of peace offering."

"What the hell does the Agency have you doing with the Mafia?" Jake wanted to know.

"Good question. The Agency believes they have cooperation with a number of foreign groups from the middle east, especially Palestinians, and north African countries."

"I'm guessing they're concerned after the *Achille Lauro* hijacking last year," Jake surmised.

"Exactly. That was the Palestine Liberation Front."

"Right, but I don't care what Yasser Arafat said, his PLO was also involved."

Toni nodded agreement.

Jake sipped more coffee. "All right. Let's keep this simple. I'm a former Austrian Army officer named Jacob Konrad, with access to large quantities of Semtex."

"How does that jive with your persona?" she asked.

"Not a problem. They're two separate entities. If they check, there was a Jacob Konrad who was a captain in the Austrian Army. He actually went missing four years ago while climbing Mont Blanc in France."

She looked him up and down. "I could see you as a mountain climber."

"Good. Let's go with that. If they push the issue, I'll say I needed to get away from a nasty relationship."

"Okay. But first we need to get you some new clothes."

"That's why I didn't bring a bag," he said. "Italy is the land of clothes."

"Let's start with a good pair of Italian leather shoes," Toni said. "You buy good quality and they'll last."

"I got my leather jacket in Venice a few years ago."

"It looks like it's been through a war."

"I've had a few run-ins with knives."

"I understand that. Nothing stops a knife like sturdy leather. I know a couple of great places within walking distance, but they don't open for a while on Saturdays."

"Well, then I should buy you breakfast."

She set her coffee mug down. "And a cappuccino."

"Deal."

23

The two of them ate like a real couple at a café three blocks from Toni's apartment. Then they ventured out toward a market with a high curved ceiling of glass. Along each side were permanent stores with name brands, but the center was filled with chaotic kiosks with clothes, shoes, cheap jewelry, and tapestries of all sorts, from traditional patterns to dogs playing cards.

First, Toni found Jake a small leather duffle bag. Then they started filling that up with everything he would need, from socks and underwear to shirts and another pair of slacks. Finally, she brought him to a shoe guy, an old man who looked like he might make the shoes in his own shop.

Toni talked to the man in Italian and the guy dug around in a stack of boxes and came out with a nice pair of leather oxfords. Instead of the standard hard soles, these had a more practical soft surface that would hold up during long hours on his feet. They would also be quiet on the cobblestones, Jake guessed.

Jake tried on the shoes and they fit him perfect. "How did you know my size?" Jake asked Toni.

"It's a gift," she said. "Not the shoes. You have to pay the man for those."

"How much?"

She asked the shoe vendor, seemed to haggle for a bit, and then turned to Jake and told him the price.

"Isn't that a little high?" he asked.

"These are hand-made by him. They're worth it."

Jake pulled out his Lira and paid the man. Then he shoved his old shoes into the bag. "Do I look a little more European now?"

"You looked German. I mean, not all-out German, with socks and Birkenstocks. You understand."

Yeah, he did. And she was right. He wasn't much for fashion. He viewed clothes in the practical sense, not for style.

They spent the rest of the day wandering the streets, with Toni showing Jake where those in the Red Brigades were currently hanging out. Most of the local faction lived in a three-story brick structure covered with graffiti. It turned out this apartment building was only five blocks from Toni's apartment.

"We shouldn't get any closer," Toni said, leaning against a wall in front of her building.

"They'll eventually see us together," he said.

"I know. But I think we should proceed carefully. For the next couple of days, I'd like you to tail me."

His eyes instinctively shot down past her midsection, concentrating too long on her butt.

"Hey, eyes up here," she said.

"I'll be happy to follow you around," he admitted.

She shook her head and then looked up to the second-floor window across the narrow street. Toni smiled and waved. By the time Jake looked, nobody was there.

"Listen," Toni said. "You can't stay with me."

"You have a boyfriend."

"Please. I wouldn't sleep with these communist bastards if they were the last pricks on earth. I just don't want them to get the wrong idea. We can't appear that close."

"But we're not screwing," Jake complained.

"They don't know that."

A young woman came out and crossed the street. She was poured into jeans and wore a faux fur coat with puffy sleeves. She walked with precision on high heels across the cobblestones. Toni went over and met the pretty girl about ten feet away. Jake could hear the two of them talking in Italian, but with the speed of their language he didn't understand a word.

Finally, the two women came over to Jake. Toni introduced the young woman as Maria.

"Just Maria?" Jake asked.

"Si," the Italian woman said.

Toni pulled Jake aside and said, "She said you can stay with her for two nights. That's when she suspects she'll be back in action."

"She's a . . ."

"Friend," Toni said.

"And what will you do?" he asked.

"Smooth over your entry to our little group. But I should do this without a tail."

Jake agreed with a shrug. He had to trust that she knew what she was doing.

Toni walked off down the narrow lane, her hips mesmerizing Jake.

"She is a pretty woman," the Italian girl said.

"Your English is quite good," he said, laying on the German accent.

"So is yours. Come with me. I'm cooking a *Polpo*."

"What?"

She seemed to be searching for the right word. "Octopus?"

"Right. *Krake* in German."

"Okay." She turned and walked across the street, and Jake was right behind her, his new leather bag over his shoulder.

He was led into Maria's apartment on the second floor and it seemed similar to Toni's across the street. Only Maria had a small bedroom off to one side. When he looked into her bedroom, he couldn't help noticing a large crucifix prominently displayed above the head of her bed.

Jake could smell the octopus simmering in a large pot on the small stove top, steam rising up to a fan drawing it outside.

"Smells great," Jake said.

She didn't respond. Instead, she lifted the lid from the pot and lifted the octopus with a set of tongs. Then she turned and smiled at Jake.

"You like?"

"I don't know," he said. "I've never had it."

Maria raised her thin brows. "Seriously? You will like."

He sat in the attached living room and watched her cook angel-haired pasta. Then she prepared the octopus by slicing pieces and sautéing them in olive oil, garlic, salt and pepper. She set the octopus atop the pasta. It was a simple dish but very tasty.

When they were done, they sat together in the living room area sipping sambuca—a drink that Jake had come to like in the past few years.

"How do you know Toni?" Jake asked her.

"We are neighbors." She hesitated and then continued, "She can be very intense. About a week ago a man tried to hurt me on the street. She, how you say. . .kicked the shit out of him."

"Really."

Maria nodded with approval. "How do you know Toni?"

Now he had to delay, since the two of them had not discussed their relationship yet. He went with an old standby. Something close to reality. "We met not too long ago. But we are just friends."

"No. . ." She shoved a fist into the palm on her other hand while she smiled.

Jake swished his head vehemently side to side.

"But I saw how you looked at her."

"Just friends," Jake reiterated.

"So, then we can have sex," she said.

"I thought you were inactive for a couple more days."

"If you don't like that, we can do other things. And, I'm almost done."

Jake wasn't sure if she meant for a price, or gratis. "We should probably just stay friends," he said.

"You don't like how I look?"

"No, you are very pretty."

"It would be free."

This was taking hospitality to a new level. Jake wondered if Toni knew Maria would do this for him. Maria was a beautiful girl. It would be hard to say no, and he wasn't sure he wanted to anyway.

"I'll tell you what," Jake said, "let's go out and get some drinks. Then we'll see how things go."

"*Magnifico.*"

24

Toni sat with six other people affiliated with the Red Brigades at a pizzeria a few blocks from the apartment building used by the leftist group. They had just finished eating and were now sipping red wine from the house oak barrel. Everyone knew not to discuss business in public, so there wasn't much she could do at this time other than get the faction leader, Sergio Aldo, pliable on enough wine.

Sergio was a thin man just like the other Italians in the faction, but he had an intangible charisma. He also had boyish good looks, which he used to his advantage often. Toni thought he could have been a model for Armani suits, but she also knew that Sergio's appearance was a façade to a troubled soul. She had seen the man turn on one of his followers for doing almost nothing at all.

Shortly, Sergio suggested they all go to their apartment. They paid and wandered out into the street, which was dark now, with a chill in the air. The others walked ahead while

Toni pulled Sergio aside and slowed down somewhat to gain a little distance.

"What is the plan?" she asked in Italian. In fact, she had not spoken English at all in front of any of them.

"Don't worry," Sergio said. "Everything will be clear soon."

She wasn't exactly worried. But she did have to answer to her boss in Rome eventually. His patience wasn't endless.

"I am not worried," she assured him. "I am hoping to take some action soon for the cause."

Sergio smiled from the side of his mouth. "I like your enthusiasm, but we could use some more money first."

"Why?"

"To buy more explosives."

Perfect timing. That's what she had heard from the others. "What if we could cut our risk? Instead of robbing a bank, what if we could get the explosives free."

He grabbed her arm and stopped her, his gaze intense. "How can you do that?"

"I know a guy."

"Italian?"

"No. Austrian. A former Army officer."

"An old boyfriend?"

She knew that Sergio had a jealous streak, even though Toni had never dated the man or even had a one-night stand with him. She needed to tread lightly.

"No," Toni said. She pulled on him to walk so the others would not suspect anything. "He's just a friend. He might be gay."

"Do you trust him?"

"Absolutely."

"But an army officer. . ." Sergio swished his hand under his chin.

"But he hates his government," she said. "He hates every government. We can trust him."

"How does he still have access to what we need?"

"He helped run a munitions depot in Austria. He still has contacts there. Look at it this way. He takes all the risk in Austria, and transfers it to us in Italy."

Sergio looked skeptical. "What kind of explosives? And what does he want?"

"Semtex. He wants nothing from us."

"That's hard to believe."

"He is a true believer. He is working in Austria to establish his own faction. He has supplied the Baader-Meinhof Gang in the past. Until he gets established, I think he should work with us."

Her Italian friend was thinking it over. Finally, he said, "I would have to meet him."

That's exactly what she hoped he would say. "He would like to meet you as well. He is in Naples now."

Sergio stopped again. "Bring him by tonight."

They were now in front of the Red Brigades apartment building.

"Bring him here? What time?"

"Ten."

She checked her watch. "All right. I will go get him."

The two of them kissed on each cheek and then Toni turned and walked down the narrow lane. This wasn't good, she thought. Sergio didn't trust her. Otherwise, he would have set up a later date. Maybe. Perhaps she was being paranoid.

25

Jake and Maria were having a great discussion when there was a light knock on her door. She went and looked out the peep and opened her door immediately, hugging Toni and kissing her on both cheeks.

Toni came in to the living room and assessed the scene. "I need to take him off your hands for a while, Maria."

Maria pouted. "We were having such a good time. He brought me out for drinks. Are you sure you two are not together?"

"Positive," Toni said definitively.

"Hey, don't sound so disgusted by that prospect," Jake said, keeping his accent active.

Maria grasped both of Toni's arms and spoke to her in Italian, occasionally glancing to Jake. Toni responded and then smiled at Maria.

Then Toni shifted her head toward the door. "I won't keep him past midnight," she said to Maria in English.

Maria smiled and said, "I'll be waiting."

Once Toni and Jake got to the street, Jake noticed that Maria's friends were already out and looking for work.

Shifting his duffle bag of new clothes over his shoulder into a better position, Jake asked, "Where to?"

"Come with me."

She escorted Jake across the street to her apartment, her eyes scanning the narrow street for anyone out of the ordinary, or anyone from the Red Brigades.

Once they were safely inside, Jake set his bag on the floor and plopped down on the sofa. "You don't look happy," he said.

Toni crossed her arms over her chest. "I'm not. Did you sleep with Maria?"

"That's what this is about? What did Maria say to you?"

Shrugging, Toni said, "She wants to sleep with you tonight."

Jake guessed that much from Maria's body language. "So, is that a problem?"

"No." She hesitated. "It doesn't matter. Sergio wants to meet you tonight at ten."

Jake shifted his weight to the edge of the sofa. "He's making sure you don't have time to get your story straight."

"That's what I thought." Toni paced back and forth in the small room.

"It doesn't matter," Jake said. "We just need to coordinate how we know each other and what you told him already." But deep down he had a feeling it was a trap.

They spent a while coordinating their story before heading out to the meeting. Still stuck in Jake's mind was the preparation Toni made for the mission. She kept one gun, a small 9mm auto, tucked at the small of her back. An identical handgun was slid down her right boot that came nearly to her knee. Inside her left boot was a straight diver's knife with a double-edged blade. He was mesmerized by her level of expertise. Well, that and her incredible body accentuated by her tight black slacks, her skin-tight gray sweater, and her long leather jacket. He could only imagine what kind of weapons she had stored inside that goat skin coat. And the boots. He was a sucker for women in high boots.

"Are you ready?" she asked him.

He drew his only weapon out quickly and said, "I guess so. But I feel a little inadequate."

Her eyes scanned his body. "I doubt that's the case."

"I meant the gun."

"So did I. Your gun holds more rounds than both of mine combined."

They left and got out to the street, which was now much more active with creatures of the night—pimps and johns and hookers and drunks. They had not walked a block before a man tried to sell them hashish. Toni told him to contort himself sexually.

Once they got to the Red Brigades faction apartment building, Toni walked in like she owned the place. Jake followed her and when someone tried to stop him, he twisted the man's hand back and brought the guy to his knees.

The faithful drew guns and pointed them at Jake.

Toni shook her head and put her hands on her hips. She said something in Italian and the guns went back into holsters. Then she said to Jake, "Let him go."

Jake did as she said, but he kept his back to the wall.

Sergio came forward and Toni introduced him to Jake. The two men shook hands. Then the Italian faction leader shifted his head toward the kitchen area. Jake and Toni followed the man and they all stopped to look inside a big cardboard box. Inside was a stack of plastic explosives, along with detonators and a crude timer.

This was a test, Jake thought. They needed to see what he knew.

Sergio said something in Italian and Jake simply shrugged.

"He doesn't speak Italian," Toni said in English.

"Why not?" Sergio asked.

"My school teachers would tell you I barely speak German," Jake said with a smile.

That lightened the mood. Sergio smiled and then pointed to the box. "How much damage can this do?"

Jake looked at the plastic explosives, noting that it was not even Semtex, a higher grade with more power. Then he decided to play down the impact.

"Not enough," Jake said. "I can get you ten times that amount of Semtex."

"You didn't answer my question?" Sergio reiterated. His disposition changed quickly from curious to annoyed.

Jake looked again. "It depends on your target. If it's soft like in Berlin with the bombing there recently, you can rip through a lot of bodies. Assuming you pack a bunch of metal around the explosives. I would use ball bearings and heavy nails that rip flesh and bone. Now, if you want to place this under a car, say next to a full tank of gas, you can still make a huge impact. In that case I would also fill tanks of gas in the trunk. The gas might not do that much damage, but it will scare the shit out of people. If you want to blow a bank vault, it should be enough for most in this city. But, of course, there are problems with those kinds of explosions."

"Such as?" Sergio asked.

"They've been known to destroy a bunch of money in the process," Jake explained. "Plus, the noise will have every law enforcement officer in the city come for a visit."

"Toni says you can get much more," Sergio said. "How long will that take?"

"A week."

Sergio shook his head. "That's too long."

"It's in an ordnance locker in a secure facility on an Austrian army base," Jake explained.

Glancing out to the others in the room, who seemed to be content with drinking and smoking pot, Sergio cast his gaze back at Jake and Toni. "We go tonight."

"To Austria?" Jake asked.

"No," Sergio said, a smile changing to resolve, crossing his face. "We'll use what we have tonight and use what you get us for something bigger in a few weeks."

Great, Jake thought. "What's the target?"

Sergio's gaze became even more intense now. "The American USO."

Toni interjected. "Is that wise? This takes planning."

"Why?" Jake asked. "You put the bomb in a duffle bag, walk in and set it down somewhere. Get up to go to the bathroom, but instead go out the door. A couple minutes later. . .boom. But you should have some shrapnel."

Sergio laughed. "Good point." He opened a lower kitchen cabinet and pulled out another box.

Jake looked inside and found it filled with various nails, screws, nuts and bolts. "This will work. Do you have someone in mind to set the bomb in place?"

Sergio poked his finger into Jake's chest. "Yes, I do. You."

That's what Jake thought the terrorist bastard might say.

26

Jake and Toni were picked up out front by one of the faction members driving an older black BMW. Sergio got into the front passenger seat and Jake and Toni got in the back, with the bomb in a satchel between them. A second car, an early 80s four-door olive drab Fiat, pulled up behind them and three more of the Red Brigade members piled in to that sputtering little car.

The BMW pulled away and the Fiat waited a moment before following.

"Will there be enough people at the USO at this hour?" Jake asked.

Sergio turned and looked back at him. "Of course. We have been watching the place for weeks. The American aircraft carrier is in the harbor. They must take boats from the pier near the USO back to their ship. The last boats go back at one in the morning. The drunks hang out at the USO and wait for the last boats."

Toni gave Jake a concerned look. But there was no way they could communicate.

Jake simply smiled at her and nodded slightly. He had an idea how to get out of this mess, but somehow he needed to get his plan to Toni. He gazed back and saw that the Fiat was keeping back a distance. Jake guessed they might not want to be too close to the bomb.

Turning back, Jake lifted the bomb and scooted to the middle of the back seat, placing the satchel on the seat by the door. Then Jake moved in close to Toni, put his left hand behind her neck and pulled her in for a passionate kiss. At first she thought to pull back, but then she went with it, becoming quite enthusiastic.

Pulling away slightly, Jake kept his peripheral gaze at the front of the car. He could see the driver looking at them. So Jake kissed her again. Then he nuzzled her neck and whispered gently in her ear what he had planned. She acknowledged him with a lift of her chin, as if he had just said something endearing.

"I love you, too," Toni said, perhaps loud enough for the others to hear.

Jake got back to his seat, placing the satchel bomb on his lap. He looked inside, checking out the construction again in the subdued lighting, with flashes from street lights illuminating the bomb. It was a simple configuration with a detonation timer made from a battery-operated clock radio. There were no fail-safes. They were coming upon a large park ahead.

"Pull over," Jake said.

Sergio turned. "We are not there yet."

"I need to set the timer so all I have to do is hit one button and get out," he said.

"Do it there," Sergio said.

"If we hit a bump and my finger triggers the timer, we all go boom."

Reluctantly, Sergio told his driver to pull over to the curb. The BMW slowed and came to a stop alongside the curb. Jake saw that the trailing Fiat did the same thing, only they kept their distance again.

With one coordinated move, Jake and Toni both pulled their guns and aimed them at the men in the front seat.

"Get out," Toni said. Then she said something in Italian more harshly.

"You are both dead," Sergio said.

"Get the hell out or I'll detonate this bomb right now," Jake said, his left hand inside the satchel.

The driver looked to his boss for direction.

"All right," Jake said. "Here's a better idea. We'll get out."

Toni got out her door, but kept her gun aimed at Sergio's head. "Come on," she said.

Jake shook his head. "Sergio goes first."

The Red Brigades leader looked pissed. But he reluctantly got out onto the sidewalk with Toni.

Glancing back, Jake saw that the others from the Fiat had also gotten out of their car, looking concerned and confused.

"You speak English?" Jake asked the driver.

"Yes, a little."

"Good. Drive."

The driver looked at his boss on the sidewalk, who couldn't help him now.

"Come on. Punch it."

Now the driver popped the clutch and hit the gas, lurching them forward quickly. Jake holstered his gun, set the satchel at his feet, opened his door, and then hurled his body out to the pavement, hitting the surface on his right side and then rolling several times before coming to a stop. He raised his head just in time to see the car explode in a ball of fire, the entire chassis rising five feet in the air in the conflagration.

Jake was stunned but he got up and rushed back toward Toni, his gun drawn and pointed ahead toward the Red Brigades members. Luckily, Toni was standing between the men in the Fiat and Sergio. But the men had all pulled their weapons and were moving in on Toni's location.

Aiming his gun toward the terrorists, Jake vectored down the road toward the Fiat and the three men and the woman.

Toni disarmed Sergio, taking the man's gun and throwing it to the grassy area of the park.

"You are dead," Sergio said.

Those from the Fiat started shooting at Jake. He returned fire as he kept moving, knowing that most people couldn't hit a moving target. He hit the driver first, dropping him to the pavement.

Toni turned for just a second, but it was too long. Sergio ran across the grass. She shot once. Not at Sergio, but in his direction. She needed this man alive.

Now that Toni was away from Sergio, the three remaining at the Fiat started shooting at her as well.

Jake opened fire on the three remaining as he walked in a direct line now across the road. He ran out of bullets and quickly replaced the empty magazine with a full new one.

Sirens were going off in all directions in response to the car blowing up and the gunfire.

Toni dropped another man, but only hit him in the leg.

The three Red Brigades members jumped into the Fiat and the driver hit the gas, pulled a U-turn, and powered up away from Jake and Toni.

Jake emptied the new magazine on the Fiat as it sped away.

Once they were gone, Jake ran back to Toni, changing out his final full magazine in his gun. "Are you alright?"

"Yes, but I should be asking you that, after jumping from that car. Damn it!"

"What? We saved lives tonight."

She shook her head. "I know. But Sergio got away. And I'm burned with them."

The sirens were getting closer.

Jake let out a heavy breath. "Let's go. I'm not ending up trying to explain this to the Italian police."

Toni agreed. The two of them ran off into the park, the sounds of sirens intensifying over their shoulders as the police closed in.

27

A few blocks away Jake and Toni found a taxi. They were now heading quickly back to her apartment. Jake felt the side of his leather jacket and realized it was in pretty bad shape after hitting the pavement. Luckily, he had jumped before the car got going too fast.

"What if he's waiting at your apartment for you?" Jake asked Toni.

She moved her head closer to Jake and whispered. "Then we either kill him or bring him in." Toni leaned forward and said something to the driver in Italian.

The driver nodded and smiled.

"What was that?" Jake asked.

Before she could answer, the driver pulled over to the curb and Toni jumped out. She found a pay phone and shoved some coins in. Her call was quick, lasting less than thirty seconds. Then she got back to the taxi and got in the back seat again with Jake.

"You called in their apartment?" he asked.

She smiled and nodded.

"Awesome."

They got to Toni's apartment and they had the driver wait for them. Once they got into the dark corridor, each of them pulled their guns and expected to find Sergio and his people waiting. But Jake guessed Sergio would have had to regroup at either the apartment or some other pre-determined location. That would take time.

Inside, Toni went to her closet and shoved her clothes into a bag. Next, she removed a small panel from inside the closet and pulled out a smaller bag, which she put in the larger bag with her clothes. Then she looked around, making sure she had everything important.

Jake found the bag and clothes Toni had helped him buy earlier in the day.

Together, they hurried out of there and down the stairs to the waiting car.

He grabbed her bag and shoved it in the back seat, sticking his on top of hers. Then he ran around the back of the taxi and was about to get in when he saw the Fiat approaching from the rear.

Jake pulled his gun.

A woman screamed and Jake looked up at Maria, hanging out her second-floor window. "Get down," he yelled, at both Maria and Toni as he jumped into the car and lowered his window.

Then Toni yelled at the taxi driver to get going just as the first bullets started flying, a couple hitting the back window.

The taxi driver jammed the gas down hard.

Both Jake and Toni leaned out their windows and returned fire, hitting the windshield and the front grill of the Fiat.

Now the taxi driver did what most taxi drivers did in Naples—he drove like a maniac through the streets. Jake guessed the guy knew these streets better than most. The driver kept turning right and left to avoid the shots, the entire time yelling something in Italian.

Eventually the Italian police took up the chase behind the Fiat and Jake knew it was only a matter of time before they would set up a road block.

Soon they reached the waterfront, and the taxi driver turned toward the north out of town.

"Where does this road go?" Jake asked Toni.

"It will lead to a larger road that could connect to the autostrada heading north to Rome."

That won't work, Jake reasoned. They needed to get out of town, but not by taxi.

Jake looked back and saw that two police cars were now right on the tail of the slower Fiat. Then the first police car rammed into the back end of the Fiat, sending it hurtling to the left and into an abutment along the sea, where it flipped in the air and landed on its roof on the rocky shoreline. Both of the police cars stopped at the accident.

"Tell the driver to slow down," Jake said.

Toni tapped the driver and spoke to him in Italian. The driver did as he was told, slowing to a reasonable pace that most Italian taxi drivers never understood.

Jake and Toni finally sat low in the back seat, the Fiat accident fading in the distance behind them.

"What now?" Toni asked Jake.

"Have the driver bring us to the west train station."

She gave the driver instructions and he agreed with a nod.

"Do you think our friend was in that car?" Toni asked.

"I don't see how they could have found him fast enough to get to your apartment."

"I agree."

"You know the man," Jake said. "Where would he go now?"

Toni racked her brain in deep thought. Finally, she said, "I think I have an idea."

"Where?"

She leaned in and whispered in his ear. "San Remo."

Just a few minutes later and the taxi driver dropped them off at the Naples Cavalleggeri d'Aosta train station, which was part of the city metro system, along with a station that would get them out of the city.

They paid the driver and the taxi got the hell out of there in a hurry.

Once inside, they paid cash for a one-way ticket to Rome. From there they could buy another ticket to their final destination.

While they waited for their train for fifteen minutes, Toni took the time to make a phone call at a pay phone. When she was done, she came back and sat next to Jake.

"What's up?" Jake asked.

"I checked with a friend in the Carabinieri," she said. "He talked with the Polizia and I got the names of those in the Fiat. Sergio wasn't one of them."

"So, he's on the run."

"Yep. When we get to Rome we should check in with the Agency."

Jake considered that for a moment. "The Agency might pull us off the case, leaving his capture to the police or to Interpol." He didn't mention the fact that the blond Russian had somehow found him on the train from Rome to Naples. Was there a leak at the Rome station? Or did the Russian simply follow Jake's contact and get lucky?

Toni nodded agreement. "Right. But they don't have his name or his possible whereabouts. I do."

"All right. We'll tell them without telling them everything."

"I think I'm gonna like you," she said.

The feeling was mutual. Jake knew that he was in the relationship business as much as the intelligence game. The Agency was a massive bureaucracy with many moving parts. He had left the Air Force because he didn't feel like he could make a positive impact at his level. Nor could he wait for his level to get higher. Now he had a feeling he was like a frog in a pot of water increasing in temperature.

He looked up at the clock and realized their train would be leaving soon. "Let's go."

28

San Remo, Italy
Italian Riviera

The two of them had traveled all night by train, stopping only for a short while in Rome. Neither of them had slept well on the train, but they had snuggled together in their own first-class car like a young married couple. It felt good to Jake to finally feel normal.

Then they had checked in early to a hotel on the beach in San Remo and regrouped, trying their best to get some sleep before that evening.

Finally, as the sun set on the aquamarine Mediterranean, Jake and Toni prepared for the evening, checking weapons and making sure they had everything they needed.

"Are you sure Sergio will be here?" Jake asked.

"Pretty sure. The man likes to think he's mysterious and intriguing. But deep down he's just a spoiled rich kid from San Remo."

"Who can we expect to run into at his place?"

Toni considered that. "I don't know. He told me he had a small villa off the main house. His parents own one of the largest flower growing businesses in Europe. But I can't imagine them having much security."

"What's the plan, then?"

She shoved her handgun into the holster at the small of her back and slung her leather coat over her shoulders. "We go up there and take a look. If he's there, we bring him in. If he isn't there, we wait and see if he shows up."

"Sounds like a plan." They had gotten a map of the city at the hotel desk and Toni had found the address for Sergio's family in the phone book. "Are you sure your intel is correct?"

Toni laughed. "Positive. Sergio bragged to me about how much money his family had, but he did so only in private, trying to get me in bed."

"Did it work?" Jake asked.

"Hell no. And if the others in the Red Brigades knew his parents were rich, they wouldn't have followed Sergio to a coffee shop, let alone incite them to violence."

They left and found their rental car, a new black Alfa Romeo GTV-6, parked on the street a block from the hotel.

"Let me drive," Jake said.

"No way. This is the same car I have in Rome."

"Nice. The Agency must be paying you much more than me."

She shook her head and got behind the wheel.

Now she drove them from the beach area into the hills overlooking the city. From up there Jake was sure he could see all the way to Monaco. Since this was December the flower fields were dormant, but Jake remembered driving through this area in June and it was a spectacle of the color wheel.

Toni parked the car on a curve pull-off and they sat with the windows open, the cool night air seeping in.

Jake took out a pair of binoculars he had bought in San Remo that afternoon. He looked through the binoculars and said, "This is a really nice area. It would be great to come back here in the summer."

"Is that a date?" she asked.

He turned to her. "Would you say yes to a date?"

She shrugged. "Maybe. You saved me from getting shot last night."

Jake looked through the binoculars again. "Did I?"

"You know you did. But you never mentioned it. Why not?"

"You would have done the same for me."

"Are you sure? You barely know me."

"I know you enough."

"Okay, but I think I know you also," she said. "You're the screw them and leave them guy."

"Well, as you know, the Agency doesn't actually lend itself to long-term relationships."

"That's like sex for you isn't it?"

He looked at her critically. "What?"

"The adrenaline rush you get from this job."

Jake ignored her as he checked out the villa up the hill from their position. Maybe she was right, but he wouldn't admit that to her. "Here we go," he said. "Lights just came on. One guy in the living room."

"Is it Sergio? Let me see." She took the binoculars and nearly ripped Jake's head off with the strap. Toni looked for a while and then said, "It's got to be him." She handed the binoculars back to Jake.

Their plan was to leave the car where it was and hike up through the dead flower fields. Quietly they put the windows up, got out, and gently closed the doors.

It was perhaps two hundred meters from the car to the compound above. They could bypass the main house completely and vector directly to the guest villa to the left.

When they reached the top of the hill, they came to a retaining wall—something they couldn't really see from their position on the road, since the wall was covered with overgrown vines and ivy.

Jake signaled that they should go around to the left. Toni nodded agreement. The sound of a water feature nearly drowned out the music of U2 blaring from inside the villa. But as they rounded the corner to the left and made their way toward the villa, the water was no longer audible. Only the sound of Bono screeching out *Sunday Bloody Sunday*.

The wall got lower as they found their way closer to the villa and the terrain leveled off. Now lower bushes helped hide their approach. Jake could finally see the backyard area, which included a large pool, a hot tub, and the waterfall flowing into the far corner of the pool.

Toni stopped when they saw a dark figure dancing in the living room. "That's him," she mouthed to Jake.

Both of them drew their guns. The plan was for Toni to go around to the front of the house, while Jake would wait and enter through the slider by the pool. They had to take Sergio alive. Toni was sure he had information about other Red Brigades factions in Italy, along with possible affiliated groups in other European countries. That was one of the reasons Jake's boss had sent him to Italy in the first place.

She took off now and made her way along the side of the house.

Jake moved to the corner of the villa, with a view of the back slider and the front of the structure.

The song changed to the second tune, but Sergio must not have liked that. He skipped to the song *New Year's Day* and started singing along with U2's Bono.

Then something unexpected happened. Jake heard another voice coming from the sliding glass door, which was open a couple of feet. Then a third voice joined in. Damn it. He had no way of warning Toni. If he ran around to tell her, he might be too late. She was planning on simply knocking on the front door if it wasn't unlocked.

The music continued, but the bad sing-a-long ended abruptly. That was followed by yelling in Italian.

Crap! Jake needed to move now. He rushed toward the sliding glass door.

29

By the time Jake got to the slider, the first shot broke through the U2 song. Toni must have come through the front door.

Jake moved now with purpose, his feet slipping methodically toward the inside.

More shots rang out.

Searching for a target, Jake needed to make damn sure he was firing only at the bad guys and not Toni. But he also wanted to take Sergio alive. They needed his intel.

As Jake rounded the opening in the door, a man crouched inside behind a chair saw him and turned to fire. But Jake was quicker, hitting the man in the chest with two shots. When the two other men in the room turned to shoot Jake, he dove to his right. Bullets shattered the glass from the sliders and the windows next to it, the shards raining down onto Jake's back.

Rolling farther away from the opening, Jake felt the glass penetrate some of his exposed skin.

More shots blended with the U2 song. Jake's ears rang from the blasts. Then a flurry of shots from both Toni and the men echoed through the night.

By now Jake had recovered, getting to his feet but remaining crouched along the edge of the door opening, the wall his only cover.

Silence for a moment. Only the sound of U2 as the track switched to *Like a Song....*

The pounding of the opening of the song sounded to Jake like someone was at the door. Then Bono started to sing.

Toni and the men started to exchange fire again, when suddenly a figure came rushing outside.

Jake aimed low and shot twice. The first bullet seemed to miss, but the second one dropped the man to the pavement in front of the swimming pool, the guy's gun bouncing harmlessly into the water.

Taking a closer look, Jake had just shot Sergio in the ass. The man rolled around holding his butt and screaming in Italian.

Just as quickly as the shots had started, they stopped now.

Only U2 blared into the night blocking the ringing in Jake's ears.

"Coming out," Toni yelled from the front of the house.

Sergio continued to scream like a baby about being shot in the rear end.

Toni stepped through the living room and aimed her gun at the stereo, shooting once to shut up the music. "I hate that song," she said.

They both holstered their guns as they closed in on Sergio.

Crouching down to take a look at Sergio's wound, Toni said, "That's gotta hurt." She looked up at Jake. "You think he needs a doctor?"

"I don't know," Jake said. "It looks like a clean through and through—both cheeks."

Sergio looked up at Toni and said in English, "Please. You must be Carabinieri. You must bring me to the hospital."

Toni shook her head and hurried into the villa, making a quick phone call.

By the time Toni returned they could hear sirens in the distance. There was no way Jake wanted to explain this to the local Polizia or the Carabinieri.

"Let's get him out of here," Toni said.

Sergio screamed as Toni and Jake pulled him to his feet.

"Quit being a baby," Toni said. "Now you know why I didn't sleep with you."

They hauled Sergio down the side of the hill toward their car; a couple of Polizia cars whizzed by below as they got closer to the Alfa Romeo.

Once they got to the car, Toni opened the hatchback and pointed to Sergio. "Get in."

"I'm not riding in there," Sergio protested.

"Well, you're not riding inside the car," she said. "I didn't take out the insurance."

Sergio turned and looked at his butt. "I think the bleeding has stopped."

Jake grabbed the man by the shirt and his belt and shoved the guy into the back end, under the cover. Then he slammed the hatchback down.

"All right," Jake said. "Now what?"

Toni rounded the car to the driver's side. "Now we get this asshole to our people for interrogation."

"Shouldn't we do it?"

She shook her head. "No, we need to hang low. The Polizia will be looking for shooters. The Agency will send a plane to pick him up in Nice. They'll be there within an hour."

They drove up to Autostrada 8 and entered westbound toward Monaco and Nice, France. It was about 60 kilometers to the Nice Cote D'Azur Airport. Toni made the drive in 30 minutes, passing through Monaco and the French border without even stopping.

Periodically on the drive Jake could hear Sergio pounding on the back of the rear seats.

Toni handed over Sergio to the crew on the small jet in the private area of the Cote D'Azur Airport. The two of them stood and watched the jet taxi and take off into the night sky.

"Who will do the interrogation?" Jake asked.

"Our people in Rome. If I do it now, I might cut the guy's nuts off."

Jake raised his brows. Then he said, "We need to turn in this car."

"And get back to our hotel."

"Yeah, I've gotta get my camera and those new clothes you helped me buy."

She smiled. "I was thinking more about my clothes." Toni looked him over. "Look at you. Your leather jacket is ruined. And your pants. Didn't your mother ever tell you not to roll around in broken glass?"

"Sure did," Jake said. "But she also said not to get shot."

"Good point. No problem. San Remo has some good stores. I'll find you a new leather jacket."

They dropped the rental car off at the airport and took a taxi back to their hotel in San Remo.

30

The next morning, Jake woke up early and went to the hotel balcony wearing nothing but a smile. He looked back into the room and saw the naked body of Toni Contardo sprawled out on their bed. Despite how tired they had been after the firefight the night before, they found time to make love. Twice.

It had started with Toni picking glass out of Jake's skin. As it turned out, none of his cuts were deep. But soon she had ripped his clothes off him and they hurried through their first sexual encounter. Then, following a shower together, they had taken their time for their second round.

He glanced out to the beautiful ocean below, hoping that this moment would never end. Jake had a feeling this was just the beginning of a long, passionate relationship. At least he hoped so.

"Come back to bed, Jake."

Turning to her, he smiled and admired her perfect body. How could he say no to her? Jake slowly walked back to bed, sliding in with Toni. He kissed her on the forehead and then lowered himself to kiss her passionately on the lips.

Rome, Italy

A couple of days had passed since Jake and Toni had called in their progress in San Remo. As Toni thought, Sergio was talking like a little kid who had just gotten caught with his hand in the cookie jar. Based on the man's intel, the Agency, along with law enforcement in a number of European countries, had made raids, rounding up a bunch of terrorists.

Jake had been secretly brought into the American Embassy, where he and Toni briefed the Agency station chief on their successful mission. But as he and Toni had agreed to prior to their de-briefing, Jake didn't tell them everything—including their sexual encounter, which was officially not authorized.

Once they were done, Jake and Toni were alone in the secure briefing room. He would travel back to Germany by train that evening.

"What do you have planned now?" Toni asked.

"That's classified." At first Jake kept a straight face, but that turned into a smirk.

"Asshole."

Jake shrugged. "I've got something in the works. Maybe we can use your help someday."

She moved in closer to Jake, placing her hand on his arm. "I hope so. If not, maybe we can meet on leave."

"That sounds great," he said. "I've gotta get going."

Toni nodded. "Do you need a ride to the train station?"

"No. I'll take a taxi."

She walked Jake down to the main lobby outside the security checkpoint. They hugged briefly and then kissed each other on both cheeks.

"You have my number," she said. "Don't be afraid to use it."

"The lines go both ways," Jake said, "and you have my number also."

"I know."

Jake picked up his bag and slung it over his shoulder. Then he turned and walked out of the embassy, fighting the urge to look back at Toni.

He got to the sidewalk and found his taxi waiting for him a block from the embassy. Jake threw his bag into the back seat and was about to get in, when he did glance back.

Instead of seeing Toni, he saw a tall man with blond hair approaching.

Jake drew his gun just as he saw the man pulling a silenced automatic pistol from inside his jacket. But Jake was two bullets faster than the KGB officer, striking the man in his right shoulder with one bullet. The second bullet must have gone wide. The man dropped his gun and it landed a few feet from his outstretched hand. Jake could have simply put a couple of rounds in the man's chest and followed that up with a tap to his face. But something deep inside him spared the possible KGB officer.

Moving in closer to the man, Jake holstered his gun and stooped down to the man's head. The Soviet man's eyes were still lively, but he was obviously in pain. Jake's bullet must have shattered the man's shoulder socket.

"You should have gone back to Moscow," Jake said.

"You killed my brother," the KGB officer said, blood running down the man's arm.

Jake lowered his voice and said, "That's right. He tried to kill me, and my aim was better."

Casually, without saying another word, Jake went back to his taxi, got in the back seat, and nodded his head for the driver to pull away.

He turned back and saw two marines rushing to subdue the KGB officer. Jake knew that the man would be patched up and sent back to Moscow. More than likely the man wasn't even sanctioned to kill Jake, and that's why Jake had decided to spare the man.

31

Now

The Gulfstream jet cruised slowly along the Norwegian coast on final approach to the Bergen airport.

Sirena said, "Maybe you should have killed the KGB officer back in the day."

"It didn't seem right at the time," Jake said.

"And you think this man had something to do with Hildur's death?"

"Maybe," Jake said. "He had a photo of me with Hildur in Iceland, so the KGB must have believed that I was involved with Alexi Sokolov's death."

"Why wait so long to get revenge?" she asked.

"I can't say. The KGB kept great control of its officers. The current SVR is not as restrictive. But retirement often brings reflection. Maybe he now sees his revenge as his lifelong mission."

"What does this former KGB officer have to do with the son of the dead Stasi assassin?" she asked.

"I honestly don't know. But Vasily Sokolov might be involved, so it's worth a quick talk with the man."

The jet banked left and lowered its landing gear. Soon, they were on the ground and taxiing toward the private operations building.

The flight attendant swiveled in her chair and said to them, "You have a car and driver waiting for you outside the terminal. How long will we be here?"

Jake glanced at Sirena and then back to the woman in the front of the aircraft. "Let's assume one night. We'll need just one bag." The two of them had become accustomed to packing clothes from each into each bag, allowing for them to travel light.

The Gulfstream stopped and shut down. As the flight attendant lowered the ladder, Jake stood up and took Sirena into his arms, giving her a deserved hug.

"What's this for?" Sirena asked.

"I don't know. I just felt like it."

"I'll allow it," she whispered.

Then they left the jet and found their smaller bag and went to the ops building. They found the black BMW waiting out front, the driver standing against the trunk. He was a prototypical Norwegian—a younger man with blond hair cropped short. He was a taller man, slim and not very muscular.

"I am Edgar Borg," the man said, reaching out his hand to Jake.

Jake and Sirena shook the man's hand and then got into the back of the car, their bag on the seat between them.

Edgar got behind the wheel and glanced back in the rearview mirror. "Where are we going?"

Sirena took this question. She gave the man an address from her phone and then followed their progress on a map function.

"Bergen is about seventeen kilometers north," Edgar said. "About a twenty-minute drive."

While they cruised toward the city, Jake dug around in the bag and pulled out their tiny comm units. He put his into his right ear and then connected to his SAT phone, before tapping in his contact in Portugal.

Jake whispered, "Comm check."

"Loud and clear, Boss," came the familiar voice of Sancho Eneko.

Jake handed Sirena her comm and she took less than a minute to connect with the two of them.

"Check," she said.

Giving her a thumbs up and a smile, Jake leaned back in his chair and watched as they headed toward Bergen. He had been to Norway a number of times, but this was his first trip to Bergen. In fact, years ago he had conducted an operation in the Arctic region of Svalbard.

Twenty minutes later, the driver pulled up the hill overlooking the Bergen harbor and parked in front of an older timber house painted bright red.

Jake opened his door and before getting out said to the driver, "Hang here. We'll need a hotel soon."

The driver nodded understanding.

Coming around to Sirena's side at the sidewalk, he said to her, "Let me take the lead."

"Fine with me," she said. "You have history."

As they walked toward the house, Jake unzipped his jacket for easy access to his gun. He didn't expect trouble, but the man did try to kill him the last two times they had met.

An elegant woman in her mid to late fifties answered the door.

"Good evening," Jake said. "Do you speak English?"

"Of course," the woman said. "How may I help you?"

"I'm looking for an old associate of mine," Jake said. "A man named Vasily Sokolov."

"Vasily is my husband," the woman said. "Did you do business with his import export company?"

"Yes," Jake said. "In Germany and other parts of Europe. I'm in town for just today and hoped to stop in and say hello."

She blinked her eyes and seemed to be tearing up. "I'm afraid Vasily is sick. I don't know if he will take visitors."

"I'll just be a minute," Jake said.

Sirena chimed in. "Could we bother you for a glass of water or tea?"

The woman looked beyond them and saw the BMW and driver waiting out front.

"Tea would be wonderful," the Norwegian woman said.

"I'll help," Sirena said.

She let them into their house as if they were old friends, explaining to Jake that her husband was out in the back courtyard getting fresh air.

Sirena and the lady of the house went into the kitchen, while Jake vectored straight through the house, through French doors, and onto the courtyard.

The last time Jake had seen Vasily Sokolov was when he had shot the man in Rome in December of 1986. At that time, the man was a hulking figure in his prime—perhaps mid-thirties. Now, the man before him, sitting in a wheel chair, was perhaps half the size. His muscles had atrophied and his thick blond hair was now falling out and gray. Vasily had obviously been fighting cancer and cancer was kicking the old Russian's ass.

"Vasily," Jake said.

The man barely turned his head to look at Jake. But his eyes looked glazed-over and cloudy.

"Do I know you?" Vasily asked in English with a heavy Russian accent.

"It depends," Jake said. "I heard Vasily Sokolov had a scar on his right shoulder."

The old Russian pulled his shirt away, showing Jake a scar on his right shoulder. "This one?"

"You got that in the import export business," Jake said, smiling.

The man tried to focus his eyes on Jake. "Who are you?"

"The man who gave you that scar," Jake said.

"You don't say," Vasily said. "Then how did you do it?"

Jake quickly explained what led up to that fateful day outside the U.S. Embassy in Rome.

Vasily shook his head. "You killed my brother and now you have come to kill me. But I'm afraid that cancer has beat you to the punch."

"If I had wanted to kill you, I would have done it that day in Rome."

"I suppose you are correct," Vasily said. "At the time, we did not know much about you. We just assumed you were a new cowboy with the CIA. We had no idea you would become the man known as the Shadow Warrior. No idea you would become a legend in your own time. You are the famous Jake Adams."

"I left the Agency a long time ago," Jake said.

"I know. We followed your career for quite some time. Moscow wanted to recruit you. I didn't believe that would ever be possible. But you are alive today because you decided to leave the CIA."

"What's he talking about?" Sancho asked in Jake's ear.

Jake ignored his ear and said, "I have come for a specific reason."

The man stared at Jake with his cloudy eyes. "You want forgiveness for killing my brother?"

"Would I get it?" Jake asked. "Never mind. I will tell you that Alexi followed me in Iceland and tried to kill me. He shot a number of times before I pulled the trigger. It was me or him."

Vasily nodded his head slightly. "At least he died with honor. Not like this."

"He didn't suffer," Jake said.

"We assumed his body went over the waterfall."

"It did. But only after he was already dead. Do you know that he was part of a group of hardliners within your government who wanted Gorbachev dead?"

Vasily laughed. "A lot of people wanted that man killed. He was responsible for the collapse of the great Soviet Union."

Jake turned a patio chair and took a seat across from the Russian. "Tell me how you found me in Rome."

"KGB had eyes and ears everywhere back then," Vasily said. "I was angry at what happened to my brother. The hardliners in the KGB were also not happy. I don't know for sure how we found out about your location. I just know there was an intercept in Bonn connecting you with what happened in Iceland. Along with the fact that you would be going to Rome and meet with a particular man. I simply sat on that man and he led me to you."

That was kind of what Jake had thought at the time, but he never got the full story.

"After our encounter on the train, how long did you have to wait in Rome for me to return?"

"The whole time. I was working alone, outside the KGB establishment. They thought I was on holiday leave."

"How did you explain getting shot outside the U.S. Embassy?" Jake asked.

Vasily shrugged his narrow shoulders and said, "I was forced to tell the truth. They almost kicked me out of the KGB. Instead, I was sent to crappy assignments for a while until I could redeem myself."

"I've got most of those assignments, Boss," Sancho said.

"Okay," Jake said. "What can you tell me about the Stasi assassin sent to kill Gorbachev or Reagan at the Iceland summit?"

"It was definitely Gorbachev," Vasily said. "The KGB admired Reagan. He was strong man. Like a bull."

"And the Stasi man?"

Vasily smiled. "They called him The Wolf. But you know that. We assumed you killed him also."

Jake didn't confirm or deny that. Instead, he said, "Well, the Stasi man's son tried to kill me."

"Then I guess he is dead."

"Why do you say that?"

"Because you are not the man you were back then," the Russian said. "If I had to guess, I would say you no longer shoot people in the shoulder and let them live to fight another day."

"I was justified to put a bullet in your head," Jake said. "Or to hit you center mass with a few bullets."

"I know. Part of me wishes you had. I would do it now myself if my wife had not hidden my guns."

"She really thinks you were in the import export business?"

"It was not a big lie for me," Vasily said. "In the last part of my career with the new SVR, I was set up as a businessman. You understand."

Yes, Jake did. But there was one more thing he needed to know from this man. "Did you have anything to do with the death of a former police woman in Iceland recently?"

"Was this the woman you worked with back during the Iceland summit?" Vasily asked.

"Yes. You had the photograph of us together."

"She is dead?"

"Yes."

"I had nothing to do with that. In fact, we were ordered specifically by the old KGB to leave her alone. She was not to blame for anything that happened to my brother. Are you saying that the son of The Wolf killed her?"

"Afraid so."

Something was churning in the mind of the old Russian intelligence officer. Jake could tell he wanted to say something.

"What?" Jake asked.

"You suspect this man in Iceland was not working alone," the Russian said.

"Yes."

"You have good instincts."

Jake had been thinking about this case on the flight from Montana to Iceland, during his time there, and on the short flight to Norway. Nothing was adding up. "Tell me what you know."

"You first."

After a short hesitation, Jake said, "Your brother was working with a young KGB officer in Iceland. What's his name?"

In his ear, Sancho said, "Boss, we have that man's name."

Jake ignored Sancho and waited for Vasily to confirm what he already knew.

"What the hell," Vasily said. "I have nothing to lose now. That man was Anton Grishin."

"Is he still alive?"

"Of course. He is perhaps fifty-six. Retired from SVR recently."

"That confirms what we know," Sancho said in Jake's ear.

Jake said, "What do you know about Anton Grishin?"

Vasily swished his head side to side and said, "Our paths crossed a few times over the years. I was older and always of higher rank. Then I did not hear from him for years. Until two weeks ago. He surprised me with a visit while I was receiving chemo."

"Wasn't that strange?"

"Almost as strange as you showing up here."

"What did he want?"

The Russian let out a deep breath and finally said, "He asked me if I ever got a resolution for my brother."

"And you said?"

"I said I was resolved with what happened to him."

"He's involved with this," Jake surmised.

"He said the old KGB would not let him avenge my brother's death. Nor would the new SVR. Moscow did not want to dredge up the past. Neither did I."

"But that didn't satisfy him."

"Obviously not."

With a calm in the conversation, Sancho said to Jake, "Boss, we know where to find this Anton Grishin."

Jake already knew this. But he said, "What can you tell me about Grishin?"

"Not much," Vasily said. "I know that he married a German woman. She is a former BND officer. Anton now lives in Germany with this younger woman."

Finally, Sirena broke in to the comm and said, "We didn't know this."

"Where in Germany?" Jake asked.

"Berlin. Are you going to kill him?"

Jake raised his hand and said, "I just want to talk with him."

"He is not much for small talk," Vasily said.

"We'll see." Jake got up to leave. Before departing, he reached out to shake the hand of his former adversary. "I'm sorry that I shot you."

"I was angry. I would have killed you. You did what you had to do."

The two of them finally shook hands, but much of the former strength had already departed the old Cold Warrior's body. As Jake walked out through the house, he saw that Sirena and the Norwegian woman were drinking tea and sitting in the living room. Sirena set her cup down and met Jake at the front door. She hugged the Norwegian woman and then followed Jake out to the BMW.

"Interesting conversation," Sirena said.

"About what I suspected," Jake said. "The old Russian is a shell of his former self."

"I meant my conversation with his wife," Sirena said. "When the Russian came to visit two weeks ago, he was here with his German wife. Both of them were very rude."

"This is my surprised face," Jake said. "Let's get a hotel and a meal."

Sancho said in both of their ears, "Oh, get the whale. I hear it's great."

"I've had it," Jake said to Sancho. "Focus, young man. I need you to dig into a few names for me."

"Anton Grishin," Sancho said. "I've already started digging on him. Who else?"

Jake thought about those he had encounter around the same time as the Iceland and Italy operations. Right after both of those missions he had considered a link to what happened in Germany. Everything seemed to lead to the fall of the old Soviet Union and the Berlin Wall. Much of this was linked to Reagan's introduction of the Ground-launched Cruise Missiles and the Pershing II missiles into Europe.

"I'll text you a couple of names," Jake said. "I'll need you to get the spellings right."

Before getting into the BMW, they both shut down their comms.

Sirena asked the driver, "Any recommendations on a hotel?"

"Without a doubt. You should stay at the Valhalla Hotel. It's right on the harbor. My girlfriend works there. She can get you a sea view. It's like you are on a cruise liner."

Jake said, "Not sure I want to go to Valhalla yet."

The driver looked back through the rearview mirror. "Trust me. It is the best hotel in Bergen."

"Okay," Jake said. "Drive on." Then he pulled out his SAT phone and typed in a few names for Sancho to dig into.

•

She had pulled her hair down and tied it back into a ponytail since leaving Iceland. She had also changed clothes, putting on dark athletic shoes for mobility. Although it had taken her people a while to track down the American, they had finally done so, tracking the private jet to Bergen. But Jake Adams and his whore had a long head-start. She was now playing catch-up.

She had tried to dismiss the possibility of Adams coming to Bergen for a specific purpose. Unfortunately, she had a feeling Adams did nothing for no reason. He was here in Norway to gather intel. She would prove this in a moment.

As she got out of the taxi, she told the driver to wait for her to return. She wouldn't be long.

Standing on the curb outside the small house, she tapped her comm and said, "Are we sure there was no report of foreign contact?"

"That is correct, Tatiana," came the reply in her ear.

Finally, her contacts had refrained from using her official rank in case of intercept. Progress, she thought.

"This will be personal," she said.

"Understood."

She turned off her comm and walked to the front door, where an older woman escorted her to a back courtyard. Tatiana almost gasped when she saw the formerly-vigorous man sitting hunched over in a wheel chair. He was a shell of the man he had been in her youth, when he was one of the most accomplished officers in the new SVR. She could only imagine how he had been during the height of the Cold War in the old KGB. Well, she had seen photos of Vasily from that era.

She came over and pulled up a patio chair in front of Vasily, waiting for him to come clean.

"Now you come to visit me?" Vasily asked. "When I am dying."

"You did not report a visit from a foreign officer," she said with her official voice.

He released a disgusted breath of air from his hairy nostrils. "Adams? He has not been in the game for a long time."

"What did he want?" she asked.

"World peace." Vasily gave himself a slight chuckle.

"This is serious."

"Hmm. Do you come here as a colonel or as my relative?"

"I take no pleasure either way," she demurred.

He shot her a serious glare with grit teeth. "You have a gun. If you ever had any love for me, you would put a bullet in my head."

"I can't do that, Vasily."

"What if I told you that I told Jake Adams everything he wanted to know," the dying Russian said. "Then you would be forced to shut me up."

"Is this true?"

Vasily hung his head low to his chest, as if the weight of his skull could no longer be held upright. Then, with considerable difficulty, he swayed his head side to side. "Even in my current state, I could not give away my former position."

She figured this much. Vasily Sokolov was nothing if not an honorable former officer of the KGB and SVR. Yet, she also sympathized with his position. It was hard to see him in such obvious pain. Humans were the cruelest of animals. When a dog became ill and could no longer perform simple tasks, humans found it in their hearts to put them down. A simple shot at the veterinarian's office.

"What can you tell me?" Tatiana asked.

Finally, Vasily said, "Adams asked about Anton Grishin."

She tried not to respond with shock or acknowledgement. "The name sounds familiar."

"It should," Vasily said. "Anton was a young KGB officer working in Iceland with Alexi."

She raised her chin and said, "The man found tied up in the hotel room."

"That is right. The man who should have been watching the back of my brother. Instead, my brother is killed and thrown over a waterfall."

"Did this Jake Adams say he killed my. . .Alexi?" she asked.

"In self-defense," Vasily said. "Alexi was dead by the time Adams threw him over the waterfall."

"So he says," Tatiana said derisively.

"He had no reason to lie to me, Tatiana. I will tell you now that Anton Grishin came here recently with his German wife. If you want a foreign contact, she is a former BND officer. What is her name?" Vasily tapped the side of his head as if to conjure the words. Finally, he said, "Katja Meyer."

"What did the two of them want from you?" she asked.

"Like everyone, they wanted information. They talked about a former East German Stasi officer code named The

Wolf. My understanding is this Wolf was killed by Adams at the same time as my brother, though."

Tatiana knew much about that mission, but more was still classified than public knowledge within the SVR. She guessed she knew everything Vasily knew by now. There was no more to learn from a dying former intel officer.

She got up to leave, but Vasily grasped her arm with as much strength as he could muster. "Please, Tatiana. Help out a dying old man."

Tatiana was about to pull away from Vasily, when she thought of a potential outcome for him. She reached into her left front pants pocket and came out with a small plastic bag with one capsule inside. She slipped this into Vasily's shaking, shriveled hand.

"Do not take this until tomorrow," she said. "I do not want your wife to think I gave this to you."

"I understand," he forced out of his chapped lips. "Thank you."

"Good bye," she said.

"Good bye, Tatiana."

She wandered back through the house and into the waiting taxi, trying her best not to cry. If God existed, how could he allow something like that to take a proud man? It made no sense.

The taxi driver asked her where she wanted to go.

"To the airport," Tatiana said.

32

Jake and Sirena checked into the Valhalla and he immediately decided that their driver had not led them astray. The place was special—from the lobby to the room on the fourth floor they had gotten on the water.

Although Jake knew it should have been dark by now, he also realized that they were still quite far north. Darkness wouldn't come until sometime after midnight, he was sure. But the sun had drifted down low enough to put the city of Bergen under an ethereal spell of spectacular colors and tones.

Jake opened the windows wide and let in the sea breeze. Then he took off his leather jacket and threw it onto a chair at the edge of the window.

Sirena came up behind him and wrapped her arms around his chest. "This is beautiful."

"I didn't think I could like Norway this much," he said.

"You said you were in an operation here in the past."

"Yeah, but that's not a proud time in my past."

"Anna?" she asked.

"Yes. But I was also drinking like a sailor with an endless supply of money. I didn't distinguish myself appropriately."

She twisted him around to face her. "We can't linger on our past. We both did things we're not proud of, I'm sure."

"The chickens are coming home to roost on some of these things," Jake said.

"What do you mean?"

"Hildur died because of my actions decades ago," Jake said. "When you're in the moment, you don't consider the long-term consequences of your actions."

"There's no way to predict aberrant behavior."

He kissed her quickly on the lips and then put her head against his chest. "Maybe. But what if our actions now are dooming our future?"

She lifted her head to focus on his eyes. "You don't believe that."

"I don't know. Maybe I've been in this game too long. I'm jaded."

"Are you thinking of Iceland or here?"

He pulled away from her and paced the edge of the room in front of the window. Finally, he turned to her and said, "You didn't know Vasily Sokolov back in the day. The man was a beast. He stood tall like a bear. And that might have been his problem. His brother Alexi was older and wiser. He blended in much better to his surroundings."

"Yet, you still made both of them as KGB."

"What if I did the right thing with Alexi, but the wrong thing with Vasily?"

"You think you should have killed Vasily in Italy?"

"He did try to kill me."

"You showed constraint. Compassion. After all, you had just killed his brother."

"I hesitated. I didn't shoot to kill."

She put her hands on his forearms and rubbed him gently. "Trust me, that's not the Jake Adams I know. You always do the right thing. You kill when you have no other choice. People make their own destiny."

"You heard my conversation with Vasily," Jake said.

"Yes. Why?"

"Something about him disturbed me."

"I only saw him from a distance," Sirena said. "He was obviously dying."

"But it wasn't that." Jake thought with purpose now. "He wasn't like other old KGB officers I've known."

"How so?"

"I haven't been able to discern entirely," Jake said. "It's just that he seemed too quick to give up the name Anton Grishin."

"But you already knew that name."

"True. But he didn't know that I knew."

"Good point. What else?"

"He wasn't overly surprised to see me. Nor was he that surprised to hear about Hildur's death. Or the death of The Wolf's son in Iceland."

Sirena considered this carefully. "What are you saying?"

"I'm saying we need to proceed with caution."

"We always do," she reminded him.

His SAT phone buzzed, so he pulled it from his pocket to view the text. "Sancho," Jake said. "He's got some information already on one of the names I gave him."

"Seriously? I hope you're paying him enough."

"Trust me. We pay him a lot of money. Most of it is tax free, going into his bank in Andorra."

"What does he say?"

"He doesn't have much yet. But I think there's a link to what's happening now. First, I need to explain a mission in Germany. This happened a couple of months after leaving Italy. Four or five months after Iceland. I'll explain and you see if it makes sense to you. . . ."

33

Bonn, West Germany
February 1987

Jake Adams came from the U.S. Embassy visiting the CIA deputy station chief, found his green rental Volkswagen Golf, and turned over the engine and waited for it to heat up. Although it was not as cold here as his home in Munich, the air seemed much crisper this afternoon.

He had gotten his new orders and wasn't sure what he thought. His contact was an unpleasant man whom Jake didn't trust. But, after working for more than four years as an Air Force officer and a few more now in the Agency, he knew he didn't have the luxury to pick his assignments. They were what they were.

Jake pulled out and eventually turned onto Autobahn 565 south, which would bring him to Autobahn 61. He glanced up at his rearview mirror and saw the older dark blue BMW. The car had pulled out from a side street near the embassy and was now following him onto the autobahn.

Jake looked at himself in the mirror for a second, unsure if his mind was playing tricks on him. His brown eyes looked tired. His hair was a lot longer than he had kept it in the military. And his face seemed to always have a three-day growth of beard. He got the big picture, but the simple things in life he sometimes forgot—like shaving.

He jammed the pedal to the floor and started switching through the gears to enter the autobahn, bringing the little VW engine whining to life. Now he wished he had gotten a faster car.

Despite the BMWs age, it had no problem keeping up with him. Moments later and he slowed just enough to make the interchange onto Autobahn 61. Luckily, at this time in the afternoon on a Sunday the traffic was light.

Once he got on to Autobahn 61 heading south toward Koblenz, Jake picked up speed again, redlining the engine with the fifth gear and his foot against the firewall.

The BMW was still there. It looked like a man driving and a woman in the passenger seat. They could be KGB, he reasoned. They liked to pick low-hanging fruit, hanging out in front of U.S. embassies and following anyone who could be a foreign intelligence officer. His Agency did the same thing. It was a game of cat and mouse. But he had to be sure. He couldn't let these people follow him.

He slowed somewhat as he entered the outskirts of Koblenz. Then he remembered a rest stop ahead near the Mosel River.

Glancing behind him, he passed a transport truck at the last minute. Then just after he got in front of the truck, he jammed the wheel to the right and hit the brakes to slow down on the rest-stop ramp.

Checking his mirror, he saw that the BMW had gotten stuck behind the truck for a moment, but was able to make the same turn and get off at the rest stop. All right, now he knew. It had to be KGB.

He slowed more, but instead of coming to a stop at the rest area, he crept alongside a large truck that was ready to enter the autobahn. Jake quickly cut in front of the truck and hit his brakes, bringing the truck behind him to a complete stop and blocking the entry ramp. Then Jake smashed the gas and powered through the gears again, picking up speed. He kept his eyes on the mirror.

But instead of continuing on Autobahn 61 as planned, he got off on the first exit and connected with Highway 327, the main north south road that would eventually pass by Wueschheim Air Station and Hahn Air Base.

Even though that was where he would eventually end up tomorrow, he got off of 327 as soon as possible, heading east toward Simmern.

Glancing back through his mirror again, he knew he had lost the BMW. But he wasn't satisfied. Now he needed to know how the KGB had picked up on him. What did they know? Or were they just fishing?

34

Rhineland-Pfalz, West Germany

Jake had checked into a gasthaus on the outskirts of Simmern a few hours ago. Then he plopped down on his bed to think about his current assignment.

He had recently completed critical missions in Iceland and Italy, when his boss in Bonn redirected him to the Hunsrück region of West Germany, some 115 kilometers west of Frankfurt. The Hunsrück was an area of rolling hills and farmland between the Mosel and Rhine Rivers. An area of plush contrast, speckled with quaint villages with tall church spires and houses connected together like a herd of bovines being circled by lions.

This was a coming home of sorts for Jake, since he had been stationed in the area as an Air Force officer with a tactical intelligence squadron a few years past. Most of his squadron dealt with crypto linguistic intercept, with language experts in German, Polish, Czech and Russian. His job had involved more hands-on human intelligence. He had also been there a few months back trying to cover a massive nuclear weapons protest by some one hundred thousand people at Wueschheim Air Station. A lot of people were pissed off at the deployment of Ground-Launched Cruise Missiles by the U.S. Air Force. The introduction of the GLCM to Europe was a game changer, and the Soviets were not happy either.

Now, as a field operative with the CIA, Jake was charged with trying to infiltrate the Baader-Meinhof Gang, an ultra-left-wing terrorist group more broadly known as the Red Army Faction or RAF. As an Air Force intelligence officer, he had been assigned to observe this group a couple of years ago near Ramstein Air Base in West Germany. They were mostly a bunch of pot smoking radicals in dire need of a shower, Jake remembered. But occasionally they pulled off some major terrorist activities. The German Polizei and the BND, the Federal Intelligence Service of Germany, had been playing Whack-a-Mole with these idiots for more than 15 years.

Although both Andreas Baader and Ulrike Meinhof were both dead, for some reason their names were still associated with the RAF. Probably because of conspiracy theories associate with their 'suicides' while in federal custody.

Jake sat in a back booth at his gasthaus sipping a beer, waiting for his BND contact. He was in the small bar area, where smoke had stained everything a light tan, and the air was foul now with a cloud of cigarette plumes.

When his contact came through the front door and said "*Guten Abend*," a few patrons answered him. Gunter Schecht lumbered in like a bear, a cigarette hanging from the right side of his strong jaw. He lifted his chin when he saw Jake in the back booth. The two of them had worked together briefly in Munich a few months ago while Jake was setting up his communications company. Gunter was one of the only members of German intelligence who knew Jake's real name. Others knew him as Austrian Jacob Konrad.

Gunter took a seat across from Jake. But before he spoke, he lifted his thumb to the bartender, meaning to get him a large beer. In the rural areas of West Germany gasthauses were one-beer joints. This one was exclusively Kirner Pils. It was either drink that beer, Jagermeister, or schnapps.

"Good to see you again, Jake," Gunter said in German.

"And you too," Jake responded. "What's the plan?" He sipped on his beer.

"Truthfully?" Gunter looked over his shoulder and saw that the nearest to them was at the bar. "I say we round up all of those assholes, line them up, and shoot them. Bury their corpses in the forest."

Jake had heard that Gunter was old school and brutal, but he had no idea the man would have made a great Gestapo officer. "Okay. But short of that."

"You Americans have no balls for dealing with the radical element," Gunter said, taking in a deep breath of his cigarette. Then he pulled out another fresh Camel and lit one from the other. He crushed the butt into the ash tray and hesitated for a moment while the bartender brought him a beer. Gunter took a hearty drink of his beer and continued. "They're expecting hundreds of 'peace' protesters at Wueschheim tomorrow. They're already starting to arrive, camping out in fields by the American air station. Nothing like October, though."

"And you have intel that the RAF will be part of that demonstration?" Jake asked.

"That is correct. The RAF is being funded in part by the Stasi."

The Ministry for State Security, or Stasi, was the secret police and intelligence agency of the German Democratic Republic (GDR). Last October Jake had tracked down one of those East German butchers in Iceland, and he wasn't keen on the idea of going up against them again so soon. Yet, he knew that was a major part of his job for the Agency in Germany.

"Are you sure Stasi has anything to do with the RAF?" Jake asked. "I mean, most of the RAF are a bunch of anarchists."

"Right, but they're also Marxist-Leninist assholes," Gunter reminded Jake.

True. So, the Stasi and the RAF had that in common. "How do I get in?" Jake asked.

"We have an agent we've been working for a while already in the gang."

"Then why do you need me?"

"You're the right age. You've got the right look. Your background story as a former Austrian Army officer could be helpful."

Jake looked over Gunter Schecht and figured he was probably right. Gunter was mid-forties going on retirement. The RAF would never accept him. "You know my Austrian persona is totally bogus."

"Not anymore. Our organization has planted a doctored image of you along with your background into the official Austrian Army records."

Wonderful. "All right. I'm guessing you disgraced me in some way."

"Just like you have been telling others recently," Gunter said, taking in a deep inhale of cigarette smoke and slowly exhaling it to the side of his mouth. He had a smartass smirk on his face.

Jake shrugged. "Great. How do I make the approach on your agent?"

"No need. She's over my right shoulder at the end of the bar."

His eyes shifting to that location, Jake studied the woman nursing her beer. She was a mousy looking waif with dirty blonde hair barely touching her shoulders. The woman kept shifting her eyes their way, obviously not adept at subtle observation. Or at least pretending not to be.

"She's not a BND officer," Jake said.

Gunter tamped out his cigarette in the ashtray and then drank down the last of his beer. "Not quite. She's a former Polizei officer who got in a little trouble."

Jake let himself look at the woman again. "What kind of trouble? She looks like one of those peacenik assholes who hasn't discovered deodorant."

"Let's just say she has an addictive personality."

"I'm not working with a junkie," Jake said with considerable edge.

"That wasn't her vice," Gunter assured Jake. "She barely drinks. She's a recovering nymphomaniac."

"Now you're just fucking with me, Gunter. Her? She doesn't look the type."

Gunter got up to leave. But he hesitated. "She's also a kleptomaniac. So watch your stuff." He smiled at Jake and left the gasthaus.

Seconds later and the woman at the bar picked up her beer and took the seat Gunter had just left. She introduced herself as Nina Kirsch, reaching her hand across the table.

Jake shook her hand, which was warm and firm, something unexpected. He talked with her through another beer, gleaning all kinds of information from her without giving her anything but a few tidbits of his Austrian persona.

"I heard you were in the Austrian Army," Nina said.

"I heard you were a nymphomaniac," Jake said.

"Did he say I was trying to recover?"

"He did." Then he felt her foot between his legs. "I feel it's a struggle for you."

She finally smiled and took back her foot. "Gunter was messing with you."

"And the kleptomaniac part?" he asked.

"I'm still working on that. I'm thinking right now about stealing this beer mug."

Jake discovered her anew, close up. If she wore makeup, she would be much more appealing, he thought. Perhaps that was her defense mechanism to keep assholes away. That and her ratty jeans that might have been dipped in acid and her bulky sweater, which revealed bulges in the right places, but also one in the wrong place. Instead of girly shoes, she wore Converse high tops.

"We need to discuss plans for tomorrow," Jake said.

"Not here." She shifted her head and Jake followed her. Instead of going outside, though, they went upstairs toward the second-floor gasthaus rooms.

Without saying a word, she unlocked a door and opened it for Jake. Turns out she was staying across the hall from Jake. It wasn't a coincidence, he guessed.

Once they got into her room, she quickly stripped down to her bra and panties, revealing a much nicer body than he had suspected was hiding behind those frumpy clothes. But she also revealed a specially designed gun holster with a small pistol under her left arm.

She put her hands out to her sides and turned slowly around. "As you see," she said in English. "I have nothing to hide."

Nothing to hide or be ashamed of, he thought. "And this disgraced Polizei story?"

"My persona," she said. "And it was not easy. I actually had to sit through a thirty-day rehab session with some of the sickest sexual deviants in Germany. Oh, the stories they told. There are some nasty people out there, Jake."

He knew that. "So, you are with German intelligence?"

She reached her hand out again and said, "Nina Krause."

"I suspect everything you told me was total bullshit, then," he said.

"More or less the same bullshit that you told me," she assured him.

"Walther PPK?"

"That's right. And you?"

He reached inside his leather jacket and retrieved his new handgun. "CZ-75. A little hard to conceal, but a nice piece."

"You know we don't like Czechoslovakia," she said.

"That's politics," Jake said. "I don't deal in that. Besides, it's a damn fine weapon. Very reliable." He shoved the gun back into its holster under his left arm.

They shook hands again, but he felt strange trying to keep from observing her healthy nakedness. Moments later she put her clothes back on and the two of them discussed how they would approach the protest in the morning. Others from the Red Army Faction were not expected to meet until around 8 a.m. in the small town of Kastellaun just a few kilometers from Wueschheim Air Station.

"We have a meeting tonight here in Simmern," Nina said.

"With who?"

"A former member of the RAF," she said.

"Where?"

"A disco."

"Great." He hated the European discos, with their heavy beat that would knock loose fillings and the strobe lights that could put average folks into an epileptic coma.

35

Simmern, West Germany

Jake and Nina walked toward the downtown region in the darkness. The disco was about a kilometer from their gasthaus. He would be the first to admit that disco was not his scene. They might be great pick-up places, or places to pick up something—like the clap.

They were in more of a residential area, with the disco coming up on their left ahead some two hundred meters. Jake could already hear the heavy techno beat.

"I feel like I might lose a little hearing tonight," Jake said. "Who are we meeting?"

"Simmern was not a random location," she said. "My contact lives here. He's a bit of a sleazy character. He sells drugs to a network of people, who sell them to the American military and the German students."

"Maybe we should just put a bullet in his head," Jake said.

"Not a good idea," she said. "He is. . .what do they say? A useful idiot. He informs to our Polizei and to our organization."

This was an aspect of the Agency that Jake didn't like. They were associated with too many dipshits and assholes.

"What do you hope to learn from him?" he asked.

"It's not what I hope to learn," Nina said. "I need him to keep his mouth shut. He thinks I'm Polizei, and if he outs me to the RAF, I will be dead."

"Jesus," Jake said. "You need to get him off the street."

"I know. But my boss won't let that happen. He sourced the man to me."

"Gunter?"

She nodded her head, and then stopped, her hand outstretched to Jake's arm. "You need to pretend to be my boyfriend. Or at least a good friend."

"This is moving way too fast," Jake said. "I barely met you." He held back a wry smile.

"Good." She turned and walked again.

Jake paid their cover at the door, and they walked slowly into the dark cavern of debauchery, where the music went from absurd to obnoxiously intolerant. They stood along a back wall to let their eyes adjust to the black lights, strobe light, and spinning mirror balls. The place smelled like stale beer and pot. His feet might have been permanently stuck to the concrete floor.

Nina nodded her head at a couple of tables along the opposite wall with four men and three women sitting on a curved bench against the wall. The two of them weaved their way through the crowd, trying to keep from getting drinks spilled on them.

She closed in and asked the largest of the men where she could find her contact, having to scream above the music. He looked like he didn't hear her, so she moved in closer and asked again. Now, as Nina leaned in, the man grabbed her ass.

Jake moved in and the other three men stood up just as Nina shoved her knee into the large man's face.

The closest man took a wild swing at Jake, but he simply sidestepped the punch and kicked the man in the right knee, buckling him to the sticky floor. Then Jake snapped a kick to the man's face.

Now Jake moved in closer, blocked a couple of strike attempts, and struck the second man in the nose with a quick punch. The man's nose exploded with blood and he collapsed back onto the lounge seat behind him.

The last man, seeing his odds go quickly from four against two to two against one, decided to put his hands up in surrender, backing away from the area.

Nina grabbed Jake's arm and pulled him out through the crowd. Instead of going out the front door, they rushed toward the back exit.

Once outside, Jake's adrenaline still high, he scanned the area for any potential threat.

"He said my contact was out here," Nina said.

"Why?"

"I don't know. He said he went out with a woman about fifteen minutes ago."

Jake wandered down the back alley, lit only by a single street light about fifty meters away, back in the direction of their own gasthaus. Now they were behind a three-story apartment building with a small grassy area behind it. He wasn't sure at the time what made him see what he saw, but his instincts kicked in and he moved into the grass toward a large pine. He saw the boots first. Then he pulled back some branches and the street light shone on the body of a man.

Nina gasped behind him.

"Is this your guy?" Jake asked.

The man had blood all over his clothes and his face, where a bullet had obviously struck right between the man's eyes.

Nina nodded and then collapsed into Jake's arms, her body trembling.

"We need to get out of here," Jake whispered. "We'll call the Polizei from a pay phone." He wrapped his left arm around her, keeping his right arm free in case he needed to pull his gun, and escorted her back toward the brighter lights of the main streets.

36

Kastellaun, West Germany

Jake and Nina ate breakfast and drank coffee in the gasthaus before taking off in his car to the meeting in Kastellaun. It was about six-thirty, so darkness was still hanging over the Hunsrück. He would never get sick of driving the narrow country roads in Germany, through meticulously-maintained fields of grass and crops and perfectly-groomed alpine forests.

Nina had been a mess after finding the man dead outside the disco the night before. Jake had called it in anonymously to the Polizei from a phone outside a small store. But a good night sleep seemed to do wonders to her disposition. They still had not discussed who might have shot her contact, though. With drug dealers the list could be long, he knew.

"Who are we meeting again?" Jake asked, as he fiddled with the radio, trying to get the station he used to listen to when he worked in the area with the Air Force. He knew, but he just wanted to hear the same answer. He wasn't entirely sure that he trusted Nina.

"A faction leader named Holgar Engel and his girlfriend, Etta Frei."

Jake glanced into the rearview mirror and noticed a car hanging back quite a distance. It was a dark blue BMW. But it was probably nothing. Could it have been the same car that had chased him on the autobahn the day before? Not likely. BMWs in Germany were like Fords in Michigan.

Soon they crossed through the small town of Wueschheim and then came to Highway 327, turned right, and headed toward Kastellaun. Shortly they passed a small field filled with large crosses left over from the protests in October. A mass of people had built camps, pitching tents and make-shift coverings, with only a few people wandering about this early in the morning. Just down the road from the crosses sat the GLCM site at Wueschheim Air Station. Jake laughed when he considered the crosses, which came from a group of secularist pacifists who were more closely aligned with the Soviet Union than the Americans.

Now Jake downshifted as he cruised into the town of Kastellaun.

"There used to be a good pizzeria here," Jake said.

Nina didn't answer. She was obviously concentrating on something else. Perhaps the death of her contact the night before. His death could actually turn out to be a blessing, and that might have been part of her internal calculus.

"Everything all right?"

"What? Yeah. Pull over in the town center."

Jake found a spot alongside the curb and parked. Then he watched as the BMW that had been following him passed by and continued through the town. Damn it. A man was driving and a woman sat in the passenger seat. It was them.

"There they are," she said. "You ready?"

"Yep. Let's do it."

"Remember. German."

"I know."

They got out and met the man and woman on the sidewalk. Holgar Engel was a tall man with broad shoulders. His hair was nearly black and covered his ears. He was wearing jeans and Doc Martins. Strangely enough, he wore a frayed olive drab German Army jacket with the flag still intact on his left shoulder. Probably from his conscription days, which would have been at least fifteen years past, since Engel was about thirty-five.

His girlfriend, Etta Frei, was a foot shorter than her man. Her hair was platinum blonde, cut short, and spiked up a couple of inches. She was dressed much like Nina, with acid-stained jeans, a sweater and a puffy down jacket. Jake wondered if she was also armed under all those bulky clothes.

Introductions were brief, since everyone but Jake knew each other.

"Nina never mentioned a cousin from Austria," Holgar said.

"Our mothers are sisters," Jake said. "And the two of them have been fighting since sixty-eight."

Nina hit Jake in the arm. "We don't talk about that."

"I can't help it if your mother holds a grudge," Jake said.

"Settle down," Holgar said. "You are family. Nothing is more important than that."

Wow, Jake thought. A family-loving terrorist. He checked his watch and said, "Should we get going?"

Holgar lifted his chin. "Absolutely. We should drive separate, though. It will look better with more cars. Why don't you come with me, Jake? Let Nina drive that car. Then we can get to know each other better."

Jake handed his keys to Nina and said, "It's a rental. So don't crash it."

She hit him again. Then Etta got into Jake's Golf with Nina.

Moving down the street with Holgar, Jake said nothing for a while. He had a feeling this was a test. They got into a nearly new white Audi 100. Somebody had some money, Jake thought.

Now they drove slowly out of town back toward Wueschheim Air Station.

"Nina says you were in the Austrian Army," Holgar said.

"Unfortunately," Jake said. "We didn't like each other, though."

"What did you do in the army?"

Yep, this was a test. "As little as possible."

Holgar laughed. "No, I mean what was your specialty?"

"I was an ordnance officer with a mountain infantry regiment."

"Impressive. I'm afraid I was a lowly corporal in a training unit."

"It wasn't that impressive," Jake assured the man. "It was mostly like a supply officer keeping track of explosives. I hated it."

"Nina said you had some problems in the army."

"The army was my problem," Jake said. "I just wanted to climb mountains."

"She said something about that. That they think you are dead."

Jake hung his head low and swished it side to side. "Nina should keep her damn mouth shut." He turned to the driver and added, "Can I trust you?"

"Of course."

By now they had reached the outer area of the American Air Station, with the crosses and the tents. Holgar turned left and drove slowly, since the road was full of protesters walking from the camp toward the front gate.

Jake continued, "I was a captain in the Austrian Army. Four years ago, while climbing Mont Blanc in France, I decided to die. Not in reality, of course. I was married to a controlling bitch, who was a pain in my ass. More than the army, in fact."

"So, you just walked away?" Holgar asked.

"Why not?"

Holgar found a spot behind a line of cars that had pulled over to the side of the road, and he shut down the engine. Jake looked back and saw that Nina had pulled in behind them.

"Do you know what we do?" Holgar asked.

"I think so," Jake said. "You want these imperialistic Americans to get the hell out of Europe."

"That's right."

"That sounds good to me. As far as I'm concerned, we should get rid of all of these weapons of mass destruction." It was so easy to play into the sentiments of the misguided.

Holgar smiled. "My sentiments exactly."

Together now, the four of them walked down the narrow country road alongside the faithful rabble-rousers. Soon they came upon a group of media and cameras. Jake couldn't let them catch his image. His cover in Germany depended on his anonymity.

Jake tugged on Holgar and whispered, "I'm still wanted in Austria for a few things. We need to avoid the media."

The RAF faction leader nodded agreement. "Same here."

The four of them drifted around the media by skirting outside the main group of protesters alongside the ditch. Finally, they came to the main gate entrance to Wueschheim Air Station, where a mass of people linked arms together across the road. Beyond them, Air Force security police personnel held tight with their M-16s across their chest. Behind them were a couple of armored personnel carriers with gunners high on top manning automatic weapons.

Jake looked farther down the road toward the interior of the nuclear weapons compound and he could see two more groups of security police airmen with imposing-looking 40mm automatic cannons that could take out a group of protesters this large with a single salvo. He smiled inside, knowing his old colleagues in the Air Force were prepared.

Holgar checked his watch and looked concerned.

"What's the matter?" Jake asked. Then he looked at his 'cousin' Nina and Etta, but they were busy observing the circus-like atmosphere.

"Where are the other military workers?" Holgar asked. "It's Monday morning. They should be coming in to work by now."

Jake shrugged. "Maybe it's a holiday." But he knew it wasn't. The wing commander had probably initiated a recall notice telling the personnel to either stay home or to delay coming to work until further notice. Wueschheim Air Station was an operational base only. It was serviced, the same as his intelligence unit had been, by Hahn Air Base. That's where the dormitories and base housing were located. But Jake also knew that most of the airmen lived off base in various communities from the Mosel to the west to as far away as Morbach to the south and Simmern to the north.

"Perhaps," Holgar said.

Holgar gazed at the perimeter wall and had to realize it would take a tank to penetrate that. Atop the cement wall was a thick line of razor wire and cameras at intervals to cover the entire perimeter. Even if the wall could be breeched, a rapid deployment force would be on them in seconds. Of course, Holgar and his friends didn't know this, but Jake did. He also knew about the motion sensors.

Jake glanced back down the wall toward where their car was parked, and a number of protestors had spray cans out writing various peace slogans. Some made no sense to Jake. But logic was never a sane concept for some.

While Jake observed Holgar and his girlfriend, he tried to discern what they had planned. It was obvious they weren't here to protest the deployment of nuclear weapons, although that was probably a major goal of the Red Army Faction. In reality, they wanted the nukes out, but more importantly, they wanted all Americans off of German soil.

Within a half an hour, Holgar shifted his head toward the road where they had left their car. As Jake guessed, they were simply here for recon. But what did Holgar and his people have planned? That's what Jake would have to discover.

37

This time Jake and Nina got into his VW Golf and followed the Audi with Holgar and Etta. They were planning to drive to the small town of Hahn, just out the back gate of Hahn Air Base, to get a cup of coffee. Apparently protesting was rough work and needed rewarding with foamy Italian java and strudel.

"What did you think?" Nina asked Jake once they were alone and slowly driving out to the main road, Highway 327.

"I think this was simply a recon mission," he said. He turned on his blinker and waited behind Holgar's Audi.

"That's what I thought."

"You have no idea what these people are planning?"

"Afraid not. But I've only been with them for a short while. They might not trust me yet."

"Well then they sure as hell don't trust me," he concluded.

"But they can vet you soon enough," she said.

That was true. But he had no idea how well the BND officer, Gunter Schecht, had planted his cover story. There was something about that man that made Jake's hair stand up on his neck. The man wasn't quite right. Yet, he had one way to make sure his story stuck.

When they got to the restaurant in Hahn, Jake parked across the lot from the Audi.

"How do you normally contact Holgar?" Jake asked.

"He has a beeper service," she said. "I call a number and the service sends the number to his beeper. He calls that number, which must always be a public telephone."

The U.S. military in Germany used a similar service, but theirs flowed through the government phone system. He had been required to carry a beeper while stationed there as an Air Force officer. But the system was only used for non-classified and non-OPSEC communications.

"All right," Jake said. "Let's do coffee with some terrorists."

The four of them went into the restaurant and sat down in a back-corner booth. Jake didn't even look at a menu.

Leaning toward Nina, Jake said, "Could you order me a cappuccino and apple strudel? I have to go to the bathroom."

"Sure," Nina said.

Jake went back toward the bathroom, but instead slipped into an enclosed phone booth. He put in a few Marks and punched in a long number. When a woman came on the line, he gave his code name and hung up. He opened the door a crack and peered around the corner. All clear. Just as the phone rang, he closed the door and picked up. He rushed his instructions and then hung up.

He barely got out of the phone booth when Holgar came around the corner, a suspicious smirk on his face.

"Everything all right?" Holgar asked.

"Of course." Jake smiled at the man. "I just needed to relieve myself of my morning coffee. Time to refill."

Jake left the man and went back to their booth.

•

After the Austrian rounded the corner, Holgar continued on to the restroom. But instead of going to the bathroom, he too got into the phone booth.

Holgar put in some Marks and dialed a Frankfurt number.

When a man answered, Holgar said, "Yeah, this is Holgar. I need you to look up a man for me. Name is Jacob Konrad. He's an Austrian. A former captain in their army."

"What are you thinking?" the man on the other end asked.

"I don't know. Something isn't right. Do a quick background check and then beep me."

"Yes, sir."

Holgar hung up and left the phone booth. He started back to the restaurant area, but then stopped and decided he really did need to take a piss.

•

Jake sipped his cappuccino after devouring his hot apple strudel with vanilla ice cream on top. The coffee wasn't comparable to what he got recently in Italy, but it was still better than anything in America.

Jake noticed that Holgar seemed distanced after returning from the restroom. He needed to do something to smooth over his entry into this faction.

Checking his watch, Jake said, "Well, this has been fun. But I should probably get going." He nudged Nina with his right elbow. "I can only take so much time with my cousin."

Holgar looked confused. "I thought you would be staying with Nina for a while."

Jake shrugged. "I don't know. I need to consider what to do with my life." There. He left an opening.

Nina put her hand on Jake's arm. "I'm sorry, Jacob. I have not been very nice to you since you arrived."

Etta finally chimed in. "You should set him up with one of our friends in Frankfurt."

Shaking his head vehemently, Jake said, "No way. I just got rid of my wife. I don't need another woman."

"Perhaps a man, then," Holgar said with a smile.

With one quick move, Jake pulled his CZ-75 pistol from inside his jacket and pointed it at Holgar's face. The terrorist was surprised, shifting back into his seat on the booth.

"I meant nothing by that," Holgar said. "It was a joke. Put the gun away."

Changing his disposition from obviously disturbed to humorously indifferent, Jake slowly slid his gun back into the holster under his left arm. He liked playing crazy.

"That was a joke as well," Jake said. Then he turned to Nina. "I'm sorry, cousin. Maybe we should hang out for a few more days."

"Good," Nina said. "We can talk about what you can do next with your life. Many of us were lost for a while, but now we see a way forward."

Jake leaned in and gave Nina a hug. Then he kissed her on the forehead.

Holgar paid for their coffee and sweets and they left the restaurant. Out in the parking lot he said, "Why don't you go with us to the Mosel this morning, Jake?"

Glancing at Nina first, Jake turned and said, "What do you have going on there?"

Smiling, Holgar said, "You will see. Come on. I'll drive."

38

Bernkastel-Kues, West Germany

They drove slowly from Hahn toward the Mosel River. Jake had spent a lot of time along this wine region, from Koblenz to Trier, during his time stationed in Germany. Mosel Rieslings were his favorite white wines.

The road from the Hunsrück to the Mosel River went from high forest and fields down switch back curves through forests, until they would eventually reach steep hills filled exclusively with grape vines.

"Your cousin must have told you about our little group," Holgar said to Jake, without looking his way or taking his eye off the road. Jake was in the front passenger seat again, while Nina and Etta gabbed in the back seat.

"Not much," Jake said, which was not really a lie. The two of them had discussed mostly their mission going forward, not what she had learned about the Red Army Faction.

"Let's just say we are nationalists," Holgar admitted.

So were the NAZIs, Jake thought. But where the NAZIs were nationalist socialists, Jake knew that the RAF were Marxist-Leninist communists. A distinction without much of a difference as far as Jake was concerned. Yet, he needed Holgar to continue talking.

"I understand. But I'm Austrian."

"You are Germanic people," Holgar corrected.

"Absolutely." Jake looked back at Nina, and added, "We are literally cousins." While he was looking at Nina, he noticed a dark blue BMW on their tail. But it was hanging way back. Instinctively he felt the gun under his arm as he turned back to the front.

"That's what I'm saying, Jake," Holgar said. "We must remain one people. The last world war is over. There is no reason for the Americans to still remain here."

Now Jake needed to play devil's advocate. "Some would say that the Americans are not so much an occupying force as a deterrence to Soviet aggression."

Holgar laughed. "Do you believe that?"

"I said some would say that," Jake reminded the man.

"And you?"

"I believe the Soviets will collapse under their own weight."

"Really? Why do you say that?"

"All great empires eventually overextend their reach. Think about the Mongols, the Vikings, the Romans, the

Ottoman. They tried to expand their reach and spent too much money. They couldn't even feed their own people."

"You are a student of history," Holgar declared.

"University. Before my service in the military. And a bit on my own." True for his real life as well as his Austrian persona.

"You didn't mention Hitler," Holgar said. "Is that because he was Austrian?"

"Perhaps. Hitler's problem. . ." Jake hesitated to make sure he had the proper reason for his audience. "Was that he spent too much time killing Jews and not enough time killing his real enemy, the British and Americans."

Holgar now turned for a bit too long to stare at Jake, forgetting about the winding road. Then he turned back to his driving and said, "I say that all the time, Jake. We are very much alike."

Yeah, they should become best friends, Jake mocked in his head.

Shortly they entered the town of Bernkastel-Kues on the east bank of the Mosel River. Holgar pulled through town and turned back, parking diagonally along the river, with a small park along the water where Jake knew people fed the ducks, geese and swans. But today was a little cold, and most children were in school. Consequently, nobody was in the park area.

Jake tried to keep his eyes open for the blue BMW, but it must have parked elsewhere. How in the hell had they found them?

"What are we doing in Bernkastel?" Jake asked.

Holgar didn't answer. Instead, he got out and leaned back toward the women in the back seat. "Why don't the two of you hang out at the shops downtown for about a half hour."

Etta looked confused. "Give us at least an hour."

"Forty-five minutes," Holgar compromised.

They all got out and Jake watched the two women wander toward the small downtown shops. Bernkastel was so small that there was no way the two women could possibly get lost. The downtown area was a quaint little square with half-timbered houses. It was one of Jake's favorite places in Europe.

Jake and Holgar wandered down toward the river, through the damp grass along the edge.

Holgar stopped at the bank of the river. "Did you notice the blue BMW following us?" he asked.

"Yes. Are they friends of yours?"

"I was going to ask you the same thing."

Jake turned his back to the river, his eyes scanning the city streets for the BMW. "They're no friends of mine." The truth.

"Then they must be the Polizei," Holgar surmised.

Think bigger, dude, Jake thought. "You might be right. Have you done something to deserve their scrutiny?"

Holgar shrugged. "Of course. But maybe they are looking for a former Austrian army officer who has deserted."

"Not likely," Jake said. "My time was almost up anyway. I could have just gotten out."

The RAF man turned to Jake with more scrutiny. "Really? There's nothing you need to tell me?"

Perfect opportunity, Jake thought. Now he could bring it on home. "Well, perhaps. I was in charge of certain ordnance that might have come up a little short on inventory."

"What kind are we talking about?"

"I'm not sure I should mention it to you. We just met."

"I am friends with your cousin, Nina. That makes us friends."

Okay, that was perfectly logical. "A few grenades." Jake shrugged innocently and smiled. "Maybe a little Semtex."

"Plastic explosives?" Holgar asked. "You have balls the size of footballs."

Jake guessed he was talking about soccer balls. He hunched his shoulders. "You never know when these things could come in handy."

"I understand. Do you still have this Semtex?"

"Of course." Jake hesitated again. "Why do you ask?"

Before Holgar could answer, an older gentleman walked up to them cautiously. He reminded Jake of some character actor right out of central casting for a heavy. Then Jake noticed a couple of other security types hanging back near the parking lot. Crap.

39

Jake was getting pretty good at discerning the origin of accents. When he was introduced to the older man, he knew immediately that he was not who he said he was, considering a slight Russian slur mixed among certain German words. Well, Jake had a slight advantage with this discovery. The man Holgar introduced as Nikolaus Verner, Niko for short, was in actuality Nikolai, Niko, Volkov. Jake had been briefed on the man a couple of months back, but he thought that Volkov, an experienced KGB officer, was working mostly in the Berlin area.

Shaking Niko's hand, Jake kept things simple, only giving brief statements. Volkov was a trained officer and might have been briefed on Jake as well. But that wasn't likely, since he had not been involved with many major operations in Germany. Jake was still establishing a deep cover in the Munich area under his Austrian persona, so he had a feeling the KGB wouldn't have much of a file on him yet. Well, that was true until his involvement in Iceland recently, and he couldn't forget the blue BMW that had followed him leaving the U.S. embassy in Bonn. Was that the same car?

"Holgar mentioned that you might want to join his merry gang," Niko said to Jake.

"I have not given it much thought," Jake said. "After all, we just met."

Niko lifted his strong jaw and gazed out at the passing river, which was swollen from recent rains. "It is good to be cautious. But we have heard about your recent problems with the Austrian army."

Jake hesitated long enough to consider two things had happened that morning. First, his cover, thanks to the Agency and the German BND, had held up to scrutiny. And second, Holgar had made a call at the restaurant in Hahn as well. This was an interesting development. The Agency believed that the Red Army Faction had a relationship with the East German Stasi, but now Jake had connected the dots to the KGB as well.

"I was not suited to the military," Jake explained.

"At some point we must all follow orders, Mister Konrad," Niko said, his Russian even more pronounced now.

"True. But I would much rather work for myself."

Niko let out a little grunt, as if he didn't understand the concept of independence. Then he said, "Let me speak with Holgar for a moment." He waved his hand, dismissing Jake.

That was fine with Jake. He wandered a respectable distance away, studying the two security types hanging back by the parking lot. Yeah, they reeked of KGB as well. Looking beyond those two men, across the main street that ran parallel to the Mosel River, Jake finally caught a glimpse of another woman standing on a corner smoking a cigarette. Although Jake had only gotten a brief look at the woman as they drove by that morning in Kastellaun, he would bet his life that she had been the passenger in the BMW.

"Jake," Holgar called to him.

Jake turned and looked. Holgar waved him back. Jake had a feeling the two men had been exchanging notes. He didn't say anything when he met again with Holgar and the Russian. But he did have his hands in the pockets of his leather jacket. His right pocket was false, so Jake could reach across and grab his gun if needed.

Niko considered Jake with much more interest now. Perhaps scrutiny, Jake thought.

"My friend tells me you acquired something from the Austrian army before. . ." Niko hesitated. "Before going private. How much of the gray stuff do you have? And is it for sale?"

Jake delayed his answer. If the KGB was truly in with the Red Army Faction, they could easily transfer all the C-4 or Semtex they wanted to Holgar and his crew. Why would they need him?

Finally, Jake said, "I have a little more than ten kilos. And Semtex is generally red."

The Soviet man smiled. "I didn't know that."

Yes, he did. But Jake passed the test.

"How much for the entire amount?" Holgar asked.

"I wasn't planning on selling it," Jake said.

"Plans can change," Niko said.

Having already considered this possibility, Jake had come up with a way to ingratiate himself with these people. "Maybe I want to use it myself. That's why I took it."

"For what purpose?" Holgar asked.

Jake shrugged. "Maybe a bank. Maybe just a statement against the Austrian government."

"Why a bank?" Niko asked.

"That's where they keep the money," Jake said with a smirk. "With more money I can get more Semtex."

"Through your old military contacts?" Niko asked.

"Yes. But before it even gets to Austria. I have a contact at the Czech factory where it is produced."

Now Jake had them, he thought. Both men seemed to be anxious to work with him.

"What if you skip the bank?" Niko asked. "Let's say I can get you all the money you need. How much Semtex can you get me?"

Jake smiled. "How much do you need?"

•

Nina and Etta were wandering through various shops, buying the occasional trinkets like tourists. But Nina needed to maintain her cover, so when she was sure that only Etta was watching, she would pocket items like a deviant teenager. But then she saw the blonde woman wandering about in the town square. Unfortunately, she had been assigned to track this woman a couple of years ago in Berlin. Since then, Nina had completely changed her appearance, so it was possible that the KGB officer would not recognize her.

Finding a rack of wool knit hats with strings down the ear flaps, Nina tried on a black one with a German flag on the front. She looked at herself in a small mirror, keeping the KGB officer in view behind her.

"That looks good on you," Etta said. Then she moved in closer to Nina and whispered, "It's good to show German pride."

Nina took off the hat and checked the price. "Yes, but twenty Marks?"

Etta took the hat and said, "I'll buy it for you." Then she went to the old woman at the cash register, who had been scrutinizing them carefully since the moment they entered the store.

While Etta paid for the hat, Nina stood behind a rack of post cards pretending to choose one, but really keeping the KGB officer in view. What was she doing here? Nina didn't believe in coincidences.

•

Jake and Holgar, finished talking with Niko, wandered downtown to look for the women. But Jake watched as only one of the men standing guard for Niko got in the car with his boss. Jake had a feeling the other would end up behind the wheel of a dark blue BMW with a blonde woman at his side.

It was getting close to lunchtime, and Jake's stomach was beginning to growl.

"Do you know of any good places to eat here?" Jake asked. He had been here many times, but he didn't want Holgar to know that fact.

"There's a pizzeria in the main square," Holgar said. "Very good pizza."

"Sounds good."

40

They ate a slow lunch at the pizzeria. Nina kept casting her gaze at Jake, wanting to convey something to him. But with the others around, she couldn't come out with what she wanted to say.

After lunch they piled into Holgar's Audi and drove back up to the Hunsrück region, where they dropped off Jake and Nina at his car outside the restaurant in Hahn.

Jake agreed to meet with Holgar in the morning to solidify their plans. He had a feeling that Holgar was going to do a much deeper background check on him.

Now, with Jake behind the wheel of his rental VW Golf and Nina in the passenger seat next to him, Jake started the engine and let the car warm up while the both of them waved goodbye to the departing Holgar and Etta.

Finally, once the Audi had pulled out of the parking lot, Nina let out a burst of air and said, "My God, Jake. What in the hell just happened?"

"I'm not sure," he said. Should he bring up the KGB to her? He wasn't sure he trusted her completely. But she was obviously distressed over something. "What's wrong?"

Nina shook her head and finally turned toward Jake. "When we were shopping downtown, I saw a woman from my past."

"From Hamburg?" Jake remembered her say she grew up there the night before.

"No. From a mission in Berlin," she said.

"Don't tell me it's a blonde woman. About as tall as me."

"How did you know?"

"I think she's KGB," Jake said.

"She is. But how. . ."

"We met her boss down by the Mosel," he said. "A man named Nicolai Volkov. But he's going by the name Nikolaus Verner, a German. But his German is flawed at best. He goes by the name Niko."

"We were briefed on him a couple months back," she said. "But we thought he was working mostly in Berlin."

"Not anymore. Now he's trying to fund the Red Army Faction."

"Well, we've suspected the Stasi of doing the same thing. So it makes sense. What do they want from you?"

Jake laughed and shook his head. "My ten kilos of Semtex."

"You have ten kilos of Semtex?"

"Not exactly. But it makes for a nice story. Even better, I told them I have a contact at the factory in Czechoslovakia."

"Must be nice."

"If it were true, yes." Jake put the Golf in reverse and pulled back out of his parking space. Then he jammed the stick into first and pulled out toward the main highway.

"Now what?" she asked.

He stopped at the crossroad and waited for a couple of cars to pass. Then he turned left onto the main road and drove slowly to the north.

"Now," Jake said, "we call in our information. I take it you report directly to Gunter Schecht."

"Unfortunately. Why?"

"You don't like the man?"

"The feeling is quite mutual."

"I've had limited contact with the guy in the past few years, but I don't trust him." He looked at Nina for a response. She was biting her lower lip.

"You have good instincts, Jake. What do we do?"

That was the problem. There was no good solution. Even though Jake suspected that Gunter had somehow put the KGB onto them, he wasn't sure why he would do so. And if Gunter did that, then why was the KGB officer willing to work with Jake? He had to at least suspect that Jake was with the Agency. After all, Jake had come out of the U.S. embassy in Bonn, a mistake he didn't plan on making again in the future. It wasn't like an Austrian citizen would have a reason to go to an American embassy.

Finally, Jake said, "This is a tough one. Do you believe that Gunter has sold us out?"

She shook her head. "I don't think he would go that far. But he could be working this Niko from another angle and not telling us."

"You might be right." Jake told her about the blue BMW that followed him from Bonn, and how he had lost it. But then it showed up again in the morning following them to Wueschheim.

"So, you have to question either side of the equation," she said. "Why do you assume it came from our side?"

Good point. "Because only one person knows I'm undercover here. And I trust him."

"But the KGB followed you," she said.

"Yes, but Gunter knew I was going to our embassy."

"He also knew about the meeting at the gasthaus in Simmern. Why not just pick up your tail there?"

"As you know, the Soviets work on redundancy theory. My guess is that Niko and his partner were waiting at the gasthaus, while the other two picked up my tail in Bonn. More than likely, they were testing my skill to see if I could pick up on their tail, and once I caught on, to see if I could shake them."

"Then we're screwed," she said. "If they know about you then they probably know about me."

Jake couldn't argue with that logic.

He turned around the car, making sure he had not been tailed by the KGB, and headed back to Hahn Air Base, getting through the gate security with a fake military I.D. that matched his rental car agreement. Once on base, he drove to the local Air Force Office of Special Investigations detachment. It took the OSI nearly fifteen minutes to verify his Agency identity and to vet Nina as a BND officer.

Jake needed secure communications without going to the base command post, which would have been much more intrusive to his investigation.

But his next request required nearly an hour wait.

41

Hahn Air Base, West Germany

Jake was able to make a secure phone call to his boss in Bonn, explaining his current situation. Then Nina called her boss, Gunter Schecht, saying Jake was in as a potential arms supplier to the Red Army Faction. Ever since the RAF bombed Ramstein Air Base in 1981, security on European military facilities had seen an increase in vigilance. They were still not up to what Jake would consider ideal, but they had gotten better, with pop up barriers and other measures.

Soon the base and wing commanders from Hahn Air Base and the wing commander from Wueschheim Air Station showed up in the secure briefing room. Nina sat in a chair in the far corner, while Jake stood near the head of the large conference table.

Once everyone settled into their chairs, Jake said, "Sorry to call this meeting on such short notice, but we have a grave situation with security—especially on Wueschheim. We would have briefed you there, but I assume there are still a lot of protesters outside the gate."

"A bunch of God damn rabble," a colonel said, the Wueschheim wing commander. "If they try to storm the gate, my people are ready to open fire."

"I understand, colonel," Jake said. "Let's hope it doesn't get to a situation like that. We're trying to cut the RAF off at the source."

The Hahn wing commander pointed at Jake and said, "You look familiar. Weren't you Air Force?"

Jake shook his head. "You must be mistaken. You know who I work for. Now let's get back on track. You need to worry about your own back door." He pulled his fake military I.D. from his pocket and slid it across to the wing commander. "I just came through your ops gate with that fake I.D." Now, officially, they had no way of knowing it was fake, since it was an actually military I.D. But he needed the Hahn people to focus.

The wing commander handed it to the base commander, who officially had control of base security.

Then the base commander shook his head and said, "This looks like a good I.D." He slid it back to Jake across the table.

Jake continued. "Now, I have it on good authority that the Red Army Faction will attempt to strike Wueschheim soon."

This revelation made the Wueschheim colonel sit up straight in his chair. "What kind of authority?"

"My authority," Jake said. He gazed across the room and saw that Nina had a smirk on her face. "I have infiltrated a faction, along with our BND counterparts. I am set to provide this group with a number of kilos of Semtex."

The colonels looked like they had just seen a UFO land on their flight line.

The Wueschheim colonel said, "What in the hell do they intend to accomplish by that?"

"As you all remember," Jake said, "the Red Army Faction was responsible for the nineteen eighty-one car bombing at Ramstein."

"Of course, I remember it," the Wueschheim colonel said. "I was stationed at the headquarters that day and was injured in that attack. But no car like that will get onto Wueschheim."

"They don't need to get inside," Jake said. "They're just looking for a statement. I was outside your front gate this morning with one of the faction leaders and his associate. Right in the middle of the protests. Cars were still allowed to drive down that road. A driver could have dropped the car off out front, walked away, and let the car kill a bunch of protesters. Also, you don't have pop up barriers. If they get a driver willing to commit suicide, he or she could ram the gate and detonate the bomb."

The Wueschheim colonel didn't respond.

The base commander for Hahn said, "Our barriers have been approved for construction. But they won't be in place for a while."

Jake said, "You need to consider every vendor who comes on base as well. You have civilians working in dining facilities and other retail outlets. I suggest you build a parking lot outside the base and make these people walk through the gate. I'm not here to give you every suggestion for improvement of security. We can do that later if you like. But we need to concentrate on the current threat." He gazed sternly at every one of the colonels in attendance.

Finally, when the silence in the room could no longer be ignored, the Wueschheim colonel leaned his thick arms onto the conference table and said, "All right. What is your plan?"

Time to bring it on home, Jake thought. And they wouldn't like this part.

"The Red Army Faction is being funded by the KGB," Jake said.

The colonels mumbled indistinguishably around the table.

Jake continued, "How do I know? Because I just made a deal with one of them for the Semtex. There are at least four of them roaming around the Hunsrück."

"Holy hell," the wing commander complained. "That's a damn infestation."

"You have to know that Moscow is very concerned about the GLCM and Pershing II deployment," Jake said. "My counterparts in BND and the Agency are also working the Army Pershing angle. But for some reason the RAF seems intent on striking the GLCM site."

"We had over a hundred thousand assholes protesting outside Wueschheim last October," the Wueschheim wing commander said.

"I know," Jake said. "I was one of them. I worked the crowd for any potential threat. But now we have actual intelligence of a future strike."

"Why don't you just round up those RAF dirtbags and haul them in?" the Hahn wing commander asked.

Jake gazed across at Nina and then back to the military officers. "It's more complicated than that. Especially now that the KGB is involved. These people are only in the planning stages right now. We could pull the leader in and interrogate him. But the RAF is organized in such a way that one faction doesn't know diddly squat about another faction. That's how they stay alive. And the only thing the German government can do to the KGB officers is have them deported back to the Soviet Union. Then these officers will simply get a new assignment in Korea or Japan or some other location."

"This is insane," one of the officers mumbled.

Yes, it was, Jake agreed. But it was the nature of the spy game.

"What is your plan?" the Wueschheim wing commander asked.

"First, I need you to increase security without officially changing the Threat Con," Jake said. "And I'm gonna stop these assholes."

42

Kirchberg, West Germany

By the time Jake and Nina left Hahn Air Base it was late afternoon. Jake checked in to an old favorite gasthaus with cash and they settled into a second-story room with a feather bed. Actually, it was two single beds pushed together, a common choice in Germany.

Kirchberg was a small town on a hill with a prominent Catholic church with a tall bell tower, steeple and spire visible from kilometers away in all directions.

Both of them plopped down side by side on the bed, their eyes concentrating on the high ceiling, where old timber beams crossed at intersecting angles.

Jake needed answers, and he guessed Nina might need to get something off her chest.

"Tell me about the murder of your contact last night," Jake said.

She let out a heavy sigh. "What do you want to know?"

He had been considering the prospect of that man's death since the long walk home after finding his body behind the disco. "You said that Gunter put you in contact with the guy."

"That's right," she said. "One of Gunter's friends in the Polizei was using the guy as an informant."

"How was the guy related to Holgar?"

"Not at all. He was Etta's second cousin. And I felt like crap all day while I was with her not being able to let her know."

"My guess is that the word didn't get out yet about his death," Jake said. "Why is that?" He glanced sideways for a reaction.

She shrugged.

"Maybe someone pulled his identification."

"Perhaps," she agreed. "But I'm sure the Polizei would have asked those in the disco if they knew the dead man. And also, the Polizei knew the man. He had been arrested many times."

"Okay. So, the Polizei was holding back on the identification."

"It seems so."

Now came the tough part. "Who would want your contact dead?"

She let out a frustrating puff of air. "Just about everybody."

"What about those four men we got in a scuffle with in the disco?"

"No, they were friends of his who depended on the man for their drugs."

Jake had a thought. "Are you sure the big guy said your contact left with a woman?"

"Positive."

"Could that have been Etta?"

She turned to her side to stare directly at Jake. "Are you serious? You think Etta had something to do with her cousin's death?"

"I'm just asking the question," Jake said. He needed to redirect. "All right. Let's say Etta brought her cousin outside to talk and she got him to admit that he was working with the Polizei. Maybe he didn't mention your name. But still, it could have gotten him killed by Holgar."

"I don't know. It's a stretch. My money might be on our KGB friends. Maybe that tall blonde got him to go outside."

Jake was thinking the same thing, and that would have been his next question. "Good point. But why would the KGB want him dead?"

"Because he was working with the German Polizei and the BND."

That theory had merit, assuming they no longer had a need for the man. "He could have been working both sides."

Nina turned onto her back again. "I didn't think about that."

And now the toughest theory, which Jake left for last. "What about Gunter Schecht?"

Her face contorted with that question. "What about Gunter?"

"Maybe he was protecting your cover and had a friend of his lure the man out to the alley."

"You have a nefarious mind, Jake."

"You were thinking it as well," he said.

After a long hesitation, she finally said, "It crossed my mind."

"Does he run with any women who might do this for him?"

She laughed. "He has every prostitute and stripper in southern Germany in his little black book. And he has something on every one of them that he could exploit."

Jake had a feeling that wasn't hyperbole. Although Gunter had no personal attributes to make the women swoon over him, he more than likely had enough money to make things happen.

There was a long lull in their conversation as they both simply stared at the ceiling.

Then she said, "Would you like to have sex with me?"

He was about to answer when there was a quiet knock on the door. Jake instinctively drew his gun from the holster and jumped to his feet. There was no peep in the door, and no security chain either. He glanced back at Nina, who also had her gun out now and had moved toward the bathroom.

His gun pointed at the door entrance, Jake said, *"Das Zimmer ist nicht frei."*

"Open the door," came a man's voice. It was Gunter Schecht.

Jake unlocked the door but kept his gun pointed at the entrance point. Then he quickly opened the door, saw that it was in fact Gunter. He pulled the man inside and locked the door after him.

"Are you paranoid?" Gunter asked. He strut around the room like he was paying for the place, his eyes scanning until they concentrated on Nina. "I told you she was a nymphomaniac, Jake. I guess you like that kind."

Nina put her gun back in its holster. "If that were true, I would have slept with even you. But I have not."

But she was about to sleep with Jake, he thought. "What are you doing here, Gunter? And how did you find us?"

Gunter laughed and then he concentrated on Jake's gun. "Is that a CZ-75? Don't you know that Czechoslovakia is still our enemy?"

Putting his gun in the holster under his arm, Jake said, "I thought using a Glock would be too much on point for my cover. Now answer my question. How did you find us?"

"Superior German intelligence." Gunter sat on the edge of the bed and felt the soft white down cover.

Jake shook his head. "Seriously."

Gunter glared at Jake. Finally, he said, "You used to rave about the schnitzel here."

He wasn't buying it. "And?"

"And this is my fifth stop," Gunter admitted.

The two of them had spent a few days earlier in the year chasing down an East German defector with ties to the area, whom they wanted to interrogate for intel. In the process they had crawled across the Hunsrück like drunks looking for the last beer on earth.

"What are you doing here, Gunter?" Nina inquired.

"Your drug-dealing contact showed up late last night with a new hole in his head," Gunter said, his hand still very interested in the thread count on the bed.

Jake and Nina shared a glance, but Jake shook his head ever so slightly.

"What does that have to do with breaking cover?" Jake asked.

Lifting his right hand from the down cover and pointing directly at Nina, Gunter said, "She's burned. And if she's burned, then you are too, Jake."

Nina found a chair in the corner of the room. "How?"

"We have a certain Soviet operative under surveillance," Gunter said. "We intercepted a call and both of your names came up. Well, your cover names. The KGB has sanctioned your removal."

She sat forward on her chair. "We have a meeting tonight in Longkamp."

"I know," Gunter said. "You two need to make that meeting."

"It's a trap," Jake said. "But we know it's a trap."

Gunter got up from the bed. "Exactly. I have to run down a few things with the local Polizei, but I'll be back in two hours. We can grab something to eat downstairs before we head out to the. . .trap." He smiled and left the room.

Jake locked the door behind Gunter and he turned to Nina. "Now what?"

Nina stood and started to strip off her clothes. "Now we have sex."

How could Jake say no to that?

43

Longkamp, West Germany

The small town of Longkamp sat on a hill surrounded by fields of grass used to feed horses, cattle and swine that were held indoors in Germany like minimum security prisoners. It was a quaint town like most others in the Hunsrück region of Rhineland-Pfalz, with a standard church dominating the skyline of half-timbered one to three-story buildings. But what concerned Jake the most about the town was its access and outlets. Longkamp was right off of Highway 50, which wound down to the Mosel and Bernkastel-Kues to the west. Highway 50 also connected to Highway 327, which ran north to Autobahn 61, which connected to Frankfurt in a hurry and points north just as fast. Drive to the south and one could eventually link up to either Autobahn 62 or Autobahn 1, which led to Luxembourg and France. Even a half-assed driver could be out of Germany within an hour. Of course, Jake knew that this analysis could hold true for damn near every small town in western Germany, which hugged the countries of France, Luxembourg and Belgium in this area. The roads in this region were like the red lines in the eyes of a drunk man.

After a rather interesting encounter with Nina in their gasthaus, the two of them looked over a map and then went downstairs to eat their evening meal with Gunter Schecht. Jake was sure that Gunter knew that he and Nina had been intimate, and he didn't give a shit. They both had the right to some private time. Some pleasure.

Once they finished their dinner, Gunter came up to their room and briefed them on how he had also coordinated their coming activities with the regional counter terrorism branch of the German Polizei. This highly trained unit would hold a backup position in Morbach to the south and just outside of Hahn Air Base to the north. This unit would be backed up by patrol Polizei down in Bernkastel-Kues to the west and would eventually close off every escape route on the gray roads leading from Longkamp.

Gunter also gave Jake and Nina radios, which Jake refused to wear. It was still not clear if Nina had been burned by her contact, so she agreed to be wired. After all, the faction had been working with her for much longer and might still trust her. Either way, Jake wouldn't trust any of them with his life, and that included Gunter Schecht. Jake wasn't certain that Gunter hadn't put a bullet in the man's head behind the disco. Why? Gut feeling.

Now, with darkness a shroud over the Hunsrück, Jake sat in the driver's seat of his VW Golf, with Nina in the passenger seat next to him. He looked into his rearview mirror and smiled.

He started his car and then drove slowly out of town toward Highway 50, which intersected the town. Construction was starting soon to bypass the city center of a bunch of these little Hunsrück towns, which would make transportation connections much quicker between there and Frankfurt and other German cities. Progress, Jake thought, but also might do to them what the American freeway system had done to cities bypassed by the freeway system, shifting commerce toward the major highway and away from city centers.

"Are they there?" Nina asked Jake.

"Yes." The dark blue BMW was holding back, but not too far. Somehow the KGB had found them again and that was disturbing. Yet, it also gave them an opportunity to kill two birds with one stone, he thought.

Jake bypassed Hahn Air Base, driving through Sohren and connecting up where 50 joined with Highway 327. Then he drove south down the spine of the Hunsrück, the KGB car still on their tail. He wasn't worried so much about who he knew about, but more those ahead who might be out to kill him. How many people would Holgar have with him?

Soon Jake came to the junction in the road which turned right toward the Mosel River. He was quite familiar with Longkamp, since he had attended a number of military functions in a gasthaus there during his Air Force days.

Slowing somewhat to make their eight p.m. meeting time a few minutes early, Jake asked, "Are you ready for this?"

Nina pulled out her Walther PPK and checked it over one last time. Then she felt the extra magazines in her pocket. Jake also had two extra magazines, so he was confident with his 45 rounds of 9mm.

"I'm ready," she said.

But Jake could tell she was not. She had to be thinking about her contact and the bullet hole between his eyes, the blood everywhere.

He downshifted and then put his hand on hers. "Everything will be fine," he assured her.

When he turned toward the downtown area of Longkamp, he could see the headlights from the KGB car behind them. But where were the others? Waiting, he guessed.

Longkamp was dead. Jake drove slowly into town, seeing the main gasthaus ahead on the left. He planned to turn around and park about a block away, facing his vehicle with an easy escape to the main highway he had just been on. As he made a quick U-turn, he saw the headlights of the dark BMW pull onto the curb a couple blocks ahead in front of a large three-story house, its lights going off immediately.

Jake turned his lights off but left the engine running. "Anything you want to say before you turn on your wire?"

She unbuckled her seat belt, leaned over, and kissed Jake on the cheek. "Thank you?"

"For what?"

"Working with me on this case." She paused to select her words. "I still don't trust Gunter."

Jake didn't either. But they really had no other choice at this point. "Trust me and I'll trust you."

She nodded. Then she reached under her sweater and found the on/off switch. She flipped on her wire and straightened her clothes over it. Then she did a comm check, but she had no way of knowing if those listening could hear her. She had no ear piece.

"Dark blue BMW with KGB followed us from Kirchberg," Nina said into the mic. "Male and female officers."

Glancing into the rearview mirror, Jake saw a thick man step out of the gasthaus, put on a fedora, and light a cigarette. That was their signal that she was being heard and recorded.

He shut down the engine and pulled his keys from the ignition. "Let's go," Jake said.

Jake went around to the back of his car and popped the hatchback. He was supposed to bring 10 kilos of Semtex to the meeting in the park a couple of blocks away, but instead he had filled a black duffle bag with about 20 pounds of bricks he had knocked from a wall in Kirchberg and wrapped in newspaper and plastic bags.

Hoisting the bag out of the trunk area, Jake slung the strap over his shoulders and shifted toward his back. He still wanted to be able to pull his gun if needed.

Then he slammed the hatchback and locked the car. Jake met Nina on the sidewalk and they headed down toward the park, which was a block past the main gasthaus in Longkamp.

•

Gunter had gotten to Longkamp long before anyone else, as far as he knew, and parked on the north end of town. He had placed the Polizei counter terrorism unit in a non-descript Bundespost Van on the east end of the park, knowing Jake and Nina would be entering from the west side. Then he went to the gasthaus and got a beer, waiting for the others to arrive.

Once he gave Jake and Nina the signal that he could hear their communications by putting on his hat and lighting a cigarette, he wandered down the sidewalk like a local taking a stroll after dinner.

Although he couldn't see Jake and Nina trailing him at least a hundred meters behind him, he could hear their footfalls through his ear piece. Then the footsteps stopped for a couple of seconds while Jake told Nina he needed to tie his shoe. Smart move, Gunter thought, since Jake mentioned after walking again that the two KGB officers were across the street posing as a couple, walking arm-in-arm.

When Gunter got to the next intersection, he crossed the street and caught both couples through his peripheral vision, well back from him. Now he used the cover of trees and darkness to pick up his pace and disappear into a cluster of pines.

44

Jake and Nina crossed the street once they got to the park, and they stepped from the cobblestone sidewalk onto the damp grass of the park. He had driven by this park many times and knew that it ran two blocks toward the east. Beyond that was another little side road. Past that was an open field, which led to an alpine forest with a small creek.

The park was so dark that Jake could barely see the opposite side. But then he finally noticed a car and a couple of figures moving toward him. In the center of the park was a small monument and fountain. He could hear water dripping as he approached.

Once he got to the fountain, Jake set the heavy bag onto a wooden park bench and stretched some life into his shoulders. Then for two reasons he put his hands in the pockets of his leather jacket. First, it was chilly out. But more importantly, he could easily grasp and draw his 9mm handgun through the pocket. But now he needed to show he was comfortable with the meeting, so he pulled his hands out and unzipped his leather jacket. Now he could still pull his gun.

"Remember," Jake whispered to Nina. "We need to be close enough to him to have his voice register on the mic."

"I know."

Jake recalled the plan they had worked out with Gunter at the gasthaus, and he guessed by now that the BND officer was somewhere in the trees to his left. He naturally turned toward Nina, glancing over her shoulders at the sidewalk where the KGB officers had been following them. But they were nowhere to be seen. And then there was the other guy, Niko, the Soviet officer pretending to be a German, along with his shadow. Where were they?

As Jake turned around again, he did so in a way to cover all three hundred sixty degrees, trying to discern where the others were.

By now Holgar and Etta were a short distance away, moving from the grass to the cobbled area around the fountain.

"You found it," Holgar said, his hands spread out to his side.

Jake wasn't sure if the man was doing that to show he wasn't armed, or if it was a grand gesture of his importance.

Holgar moved closer and reached out his hand for Jake to shake, which he did. Jake noticed Etta, much like Nina, had her hands shoved in her coat pocket. Etta was shaking and seemed to be more than cold. She was scared.

"Is that it?" Holgar said, shifting his head and gaze toward Jake's duffle bag.

"What?" Jake asked. He needed to make the man say it.

"The product," Holgar said.

This guy was smarter than Jake thought. But he held firm.

Finally, Holgar said, "The Semtex. That's ten kilos? It looks like much less."

"It's very dense," Jake said. "And a little goes a long way, especially when you combine it with a conflagrant."

Holgar nodded and smiled. "Perhaps petrol and a gel mixture?"

"That would work," Jake agreed. Now he needed to get to the crux of his mission. "What's the target?"

Without knowing he was doing so, Holgar's eyes shifted around the perimeter of the park. He was looking for something. Perhaps help.

"It's a legitimate question," Jake said, "considering I will be providing the Semtex. I should know how it's planned to be used."

"Does the gun dealer need to know that from his customers?"

"If it's an assassin, yes," Jake reasoned.

"You might have a point. If we were buying this from you. But you said we could have this first batch. Then we'll talk about your future acquisitions."

Now Jake needed to change the deal. This only worked if the man purchased the Semtex. "I could use some walking around money," Jake said. Through his peripheral view he could see Nina shift nervously.

"If you're one of us we can make that happen," Holgar said. "What do you need?"

"What do you have on you?" Jake had heard from Nina that the man carried thousands of Marks, paying for everything in cash.

Holgar reached into his jacket and it took every muscle in Jake's body to keep from drawing his CZ-75. But instead of a gun, the man pulled out a stack of cash. "What about two thousand Marks."

"It looks like more than that," Jake said.

"Well, you can't wipe me out. I'm not the Deutsche Bank."

"Make it three thousand and we have a deal."

The German counted off the bills and then handed them to Jake, who accepted them and went to put them into an inside jacket pocket. That's when the shit hit the fan. Jake had barely put the money away when both Holgar and Etta drew their weapons. Jake pulled his hand out with his gun in his hand at the same time. Nina was the only one who didn't have a gun drawn, perhaps to maintain the possibility of her cover.

"You're gonna shoot me for three thousand Marks?" Jake asked.

"No. I'm going to shoot you for lying to me," Holgar explained.

Jake considered simply pulling the trigger. He was justified. But he was also curious. "Explain yourself."

"Put the gun down, Holgar," Nina said. "He's my cousin."

Holgar laughed. "Your only cousins live in northern Germany. A small town outside of Hamburg."

Nina said nothing.

Now Jake wondered how much Holgar knew about him.

"That's crazy," Jake said. But then he realized that the Germans were nothing if not thorough when it came to familial recordkeeping. Somehow Holgar had gotten access to these records. But how did he find out her real identity?

Holgar continued, "Which brings me to you. Who are you? That's the question we have all been asking since you showed up with Nina."

"I'm the man with the Semtex," Jake said. "What more do you need to know?"

The German let out a little grunt. "A drug dealer is not the most reliable source. But once in a while they get things right."

So, Jake thought, the team of Holgar and Etta had lured the drug dealer outside the disco and put a bullet in his head. But he couldn't let Holgar know that he knew. "I don't understand," Jake said. He kept his eyes on Holgar, trying to see when the man might pull the trigger. Those who didn't know much about gun safety almost always kept their finger right on the trigger. Others who have been trained properly know to keep the trigger finger along the outside of the trigger guard and to only put it on the trigger when ready to fire. Holgar had been trained by someone, since his finger was not directly on the trigger.

The next couple of seconds were a massive cluster of chaos.

45

Jake first heard movement to the north of the park, followed by a single shot. Then there were a couple of blasts from the south side of the park. Jake turned just in time to see a couple of more flashes of light from the south.

Then Jake turned his attention back at Holgar, who now had his finger on the trigger and didn't seem to know how to respond.

More shots came from the south and Jake returned fire in that direction, firing five times.

Now Holgar turned and ran to the park bench, grasped the heavy bag with what he thought contained Semtex, and then hurried across the park toward his car.

Nina and Etta looked at each other for a moment and then Etta's gun fired, hitting Nina somewhere. Nina hit the ground, but returned fire, hitting Etta with at least two bullets.

Meanwhile there was another gun fight going on in the area where Gunter should have been.

Jake rushed to Nina. "Are you alright?"

"It's just my left arm," she said. "Go get Holgar."

More shots came from the south. Jake turned and saw that Holgar had gotten a decent head start on him, but he was laboring with the heavy bag. He ran after the German.

If the man made it to his car, Jake would be screwed. His own car was on the far side of the park and three blocks up past the gasthaus.

Holgar got closer to his car and Jake gained on him. He was now within 9mm range. When Holgar fumbled to pull his keys from his pockets, Jake took the opportunity to fire. But not at Holgar. Instead, he shot out the front and back tires of the car.

Instead of pulling his keys, Holgar turned and fired at Jake, but Jake dove to the ground. He aimed and almost pulled the trigger. No. He needed this man alive for interrogation. Jake shot, but instead of hitting flesh and bones, he hit metal and windows right next to Holgar, which made the man drop the heavy bag of bricks.

Then Holgar rushed around the outside of the car and headed toward the open field.

Jake jumped to his feet and took up the chase.

•

Despite her gunshot wound to her arm, Nina crawled to see if she could help Etta. Shots still rang out from the south side of the park. And now she could hear gunfire from

Jake and Holgar. She hoped Jake would remember to try to take Holgar alive. They needed his possible intel.

Etta lay on her back, her eyes lifeless and staring off to the night sky.

Nina checked for a pulse. If she had one, Nina could not feel it. But she herself had a hard time feeling anything in her left arm, and her right hand still held her gun.

When she heard movement behind her, Nina rolled to her side and aimed her gun at the approaching figure. Her finger came to the trigger but for some reason she stopped. It was Gunter, she realized.

By now the gunfire had stopped all around her. Nina's breathing was labored, her adrenaline starting to settle down.

"Did Jake get Holgar?" Nina asked Gunter.

Gunter holstered his gun and got to his knees next to her. "I don't know. I was occupied with at least one shooter."

"What about the others over there?" she asked, her attention on the direction of the main gunfire toward her.

"The Polizei are after both of those groups," Gunter said. He pulled out a handkerchief and tied it around Nina's gunshot wound on her left biceps. "They are tightening the cordon as we speak."

"I'm fine," she said. "Go help Jake."

"Are you sure?"

"Positive."

Gunter nodded agreement, stumbled to his feet, and moved off toward Jake and Holgar.

•

Jake chased Holgar across the damp grassy field toward the woods in the distance. Once he reached the woods, the surface became slippery, since the sun had not melted the last dusting of snow. He slid down the side of the hill toward the sound of a small creek at the bottom of the gorge.

He hesitated long enough to hear his opponent crashing through the woods ahead of him. In the darkness, it was almost impossible to see much of anything. But Jake pushed forward methodically, listening and then moving faster toward his prey.

When Jake heard a tumbling, like the noise a deer makes when it's shot and falls to a heap down the side of a mountain, he stopped to pinpoint the location. Then he put his gun forward and stepped lightly toward that noise.

Moments later Jake came to a spot where the ground was disturbed alongside a steep crevice. By now his eyes could see much better, since they had adjusted to the darkness and he had not hurt that vision by firing his gun.

Trying his best not to fall, Jake made his way down the snowy hillside.

Silence. Jake froze. His heart was pumping fast and his ears rang from the gunfire.

"Come on, Jake," Holgar yelled. "It doesn't have to be this way."

Jake moved to his right and leaned behind a large pine. "You killed the drug dealer," he answered.

Holgar laughed. "He was what's wrong with this country. He poisoned our youth with drugs. A man like that deserved to die."

"Maybe. But that wasn't your call. And that's not why you killed him."

"Be reasonable."

"I might let you go if you tell me the truth," Jake lied.

"I'm guessing you must be Polizei also," Holgar said.

"Also?"

"You and that bitch, Nina. Or whatever her name really is."

"Nina is not Polizei," Jake said truthfully.

"Right."

"It's the truth." Jake hesitated and then said, "I'm coming down."

"I will shoot you."

No, he wouldn't, Jake knew. The man had either lost his gun or run out of bullets.

Jake made his way down the hill and pointed his gun at Holgar, who had found his way across the small creek and was leaning against the other bank. He just hoped the man didn't have a second weapon.

"I think my ankle is broken," Holgar said.

"Where is your gun?"

"I don't know. I lost it on the fall down that hill."

Moving cautiously closer, Jake finally got to the man and checked him for a weapon. He had nothing else on him. Not even a knife. When Jake patted the man's right ankle, Holgar winced in pain. Yeah, it was probably broken.

Jake holstered his gun and sat on the bank of the creek next to the terrorist.

"Tell me something, Jake," Holgar said, "what was in that bag of yours?"

"About ten kilos of bricks."

"Figures. So, I was right. You are Polizei."

"No, you're wrong about that."

"But were you ever in the Austrian army?"

"Not everything I ever say is false or the entire truth. It's somewhere in the gray area."

"Good to know. What happens now?"

"Now, you tell me everything you know about the Red Army Faction."

"You know more than you probably think."

Jake saw the flash of light almost at the same time that he heard the sound of gunfire. He had his gun out within a couple of seconds to return fire.

"Stay here," Jake whispered to Holgar.

"No way."

Switching his gun from his right to his left hand, Jake twisted his body on top of the German and punched him as hard as he could in the mouth. He heard bone crush and he hoped like hell it wasn't his hand. But Holgar collapsed back to the river bank, unconscious.

46

Moving through the woods like a hunter stalking his prey, Jake stopped for a second behind a large tree. Here the darkness was nearly complete. He could hear whispering, so there had to be at least two people, he thought. But were these misguided Polizei officers or someone else?

Jake didn't have to wait long to find out. As the two targets got closer, the two of them could be heard speaking Russian. KGB. But which ones?

He glanced down at his gun and tried to remember how many rounds he had fired. Quietly he pressed the magazine release and slid the magazine from the handle. Then he found a full one in his pocket and gently, softly slid that into place, clicking and locking it into the handle.

Hearing the crunch of footfalls getting closer around the left side of the tree, Jake readied himself. Then he heard another twig crack to the right side and he knew he was in trouble. Pick one target, Jake.

Aiming toward the last sound, Jake waited for another misstep by the KGB. But he was hesitant to fire unless he was sure of his target.

Jake had an idea. He turned his head to throw his voice. Then he yelled "Nikolai Volkov."

The shots came almost instantly after he yelled the KGB officer's name. Jake fired five shots at the flash of light from the man's gun.

More shots came from the right side, striking the tree in front of Jake. He shoved his back against the tree.

Now more shots came his way. But that was followed up by shots from another direction. Who was that?

With the gunfire coming from two other people, Jake took that opportunity to round the tree to the left and work his way across the hill toward the next large tree in the forest.

Just as he was about to reach the safety of the tree, he tripped over a log and crashed to the forest floor. Luckily, he still had his gun, but now he crawled as bullets flew in his direction.

But Jake was able to reach the tree. He rested to control his breathing and made sure his gun barrel had not been blocked when he fell. It was fine. He cycled a round back into the chamber.

One of the men yelled something in Russian, but there was no response.

Then Jake heard a brusque voice echo through the forest. This time it was German, and the words were meant for him. It was Gunter, who had to be the other shooter. He was targeting himself for the Russian to fire. He kept on yelling, talking nonsense.

When the Russian started firing on Gunter's position, Jake took that as an opportunity to empty his magazine on the Soviet officer's location. Gunter also seemed to be giving the KGB every bullet in his gun.

Out of bullets, the slide racked back, Jake found his last full magazine and replaced the old one with the new one. Then he found the used magazine and counted out the number of bullets left in that one. Only three. He added the one he had just taken from the chamber while he checked his barrel. So, he had 15 rounds plus four more. He would have to be more careful with his shooting.

Silence. Nothing moved.

Could he dare let Gunter know where he was? He had to, just in case, so Gunter wouldn't shoot at him.

"Are you all right up there?" Jake asked in German.

"Pristine," Gunter said. "I think you hit your target."

"There were two of them," Jake said.

"I know. I was playing with them earlier. Then they were gone, and now I know where they went."

"Moving in," Jake said. "Don't shoot."

"Stay put," Gunter ordered. "I have a flashlight."

Moments after saying this, the light shone and swept the hillside. Now Jake could see the German BND officer stop and look down. That was the position of the first man Jake had encountered. Then Gunter moved toward the second position. He stopped there for a moment and then rushed down the side of the hill, slipping and sliding his way toward Jake.

Gunter shone the light on Jake's face, then toward the ground, and said, "They're both dead. You got the first one and I think we both got the second one. Where is Holgar?"

"Right down there," Jake said.

Gunter pointed his light onto the body of the Red Army Faction leader. "Is he dead?"

"No. He's taking a nap. I think he can provide us some intel."

"I agree."

"We're still missing two KGB officers," Jake said. "Which ones are dead?"

"A blonde woman and a big man with short hair."

"Those were the two who have been tailing me since I left the embassy in Bonn," Jake said.

The two of them wandered over to Holgar, who was still knocked out. Gunter got on his radio and told the Polizei his position and condition.

"We're still missing two KGB officers," Jake warned. "Including Nikolai, Niko, Volkov."

Gunter shook his head and sat on the ground next to the German terrorist. "Our people might catch them on the way out of town. But it won't matter. The German government will just expel them."

"Right. And they'll show up in some other European country next week."

"That's the way the game is played, Jake."

He was beginning to understand that, but it didn't make him happy about the prospect. He had a feeling the Soviet Union would treat him much worse if he was caught doing some nefarious crap in that country.

"How is your officer, Nina?"

"She took a bullet to her left arm, but she will be fine."

"And the other woman, Etta?"

Gunter shook his head.

"Well let's keep that info from Holgar," Jake said. "We can use her as leverage during our interrogation."

"We should take the lead with that," Gunter declared.

"I don't think so."

"This is German soil."

"True. But they were planning on bombing Wueschheim Air Station. That's American property."

"I'll tell you what, Jake. Let's let someone higher up the food chain make this call."

Jake couldn't argue with that.

Moments later and the woods were filled with Polizei officers shining lights everywhere. Before leaving, Jake made sure they slapped the cuffs on Holgar and followed them as they hauled the man back up the hill to Longkamp.

By now medical personnel were on the scene of the park where the first shoot-out occurred. Nina had already gotten a bandage on her left arm, but would have to eventually go to the hospital in Simmern for additional care. Based on normal activity, the Germans would probably keep her there for a week.

"Are you alright?" Jake asked Nina.

She nodded her head, but she seemed reticent.

Jake knew why. "She was going to shoot you."

"I know," Nina agreed. "What happened out there?"

"The KGB happened."

"Which ones?"

"Our tail," he said. "The big guy and the blonde."

"Just before you came, I heard that the Polizei caught the other two down the hill on the way to Bernkastel."

"It won't matter," he said. "They'll be on a plane to Moscow by morning."

"That's what I was thinking. What now?"

"Now, we fight over Holgar. Hopefully we make it a joint interrogation. I think he knows more than he was willing to let on to you or even his girlfriend, Etta."

"You might be right."

Jake put his hand on her shoulder. "Come on. I'll drive you to the *Krankenhaus* in Simmern."

•

It was two in the morning before Jake got through the emergency room, the procedure to stitch up Nina's arm, and then back to their gasthaus in Kirchberg. They should have both been dead on their feet, but for some reason, perhaps the adrenaline, neither of them could sleep.

As Jake suspected, word had gotten back to him that the Russian KGB officer, Nikolai Volkov, had been escorted to a plane in Frankfurt and deported to Moscow. Jake guessed the man would simply change his name again and show up elsewhere. Men like Volkov were like cockroaches.

Nina found some little bottles of alcohol in the tiny refrigerator. She threw Jake a whiskey and kept a vodka for herself. They both opened them, ticked them together, said *Prosit*, and sucked down the contents. Then they found two more and repeated.

When they were done with all the bottles in the mini-bar, Jake slowly undressed her, being careful with her arm. Then they crawled under the soft white down duvet and made love anew.

47

Now
Berlin, Germany

Jake and Sirena flew in the company jet from Bergen, Norway to Berlin the next afternoon. They had learned much more about Anton Grishin and his German girlfriend since the day before. Part of this intel had come from their man Sancho, but Jake had also worked his contacts to get some more info from direct sources. Jake had arranged for an old friend to meet them at the airport.

Once they landed at Berlin Tegel International Airport, a BMW SUV was waiting for them on the sidewalk out front. Jake barely recognized Nina Krause when she got out and rounded the BMW. Back in the day, she had been a slim woman—almost too slim. But now age had added a few pounds to her frame. Some would say she looked much better. Healthier. She had obviously dyed her hair blonde now. One thing had not changed, though. She had a smile for Jake.

They hugged like the old friends they were, and then Jake introduced Nina to Sirena. The two women shook hands and then turned that into a quick kiss on the cheek.

"So," Nina said. "You are the woman to finally settle this man down." Her English had improved to a near-flawless level.

"Well, I'm not sure about that," Sirena said. "He's still chasing ghosts from his past all over Europe."

Jake shook his head and then put both of their bags in the back end of the SUV.

Sirena got into the back seat and Jake went to the front passenger side.

Nina got behind the wheel, buckled up, and then pulled out slowly before picking up speed.

"You dredged up some old names last night," Nina said. "Remember Holgar Engel? Thanks to you, he did twenty years in prison."

"Can you ever rehabilitate a Red Army Faction member?" Jake asked.

"I don't know about that," Nina said. "But the week before he was to be released, he was murdered in prison."

"I never heard about that," Jake admitted. "What can you tell me about Katja Meyer?"

"She's a piece of work," Nina said. "As far as I'm concerned, she should be in prison. Instead, the BND first suspended her with pay. Then they switched that to suspension without pay. Finally, they let her resign instead of face prosecution."

"What did she do?" Sirena asked from the back seat.

Nina glanced back at Sirena and then again to the road ahead as they passed through a sparsely-populated suburb of Berlin. "First, you must know that her ancestry is Russian. Well, technically it's German or Prussian. Her grandfather was stuck behind the Iron Curtain after World War Two. In the Baltic region. Her father was born in Tallinn. Katja was also born there, but they came to Berlin after the Soviet Union collapsed. Just after the Berlin Wall came down. Many ethnic Germans were allowed back into our country at that time. Katja grew up speaking German and Russian. Because of her language skills, she was recruited by the BND."

By now they had reached the western area of Berlin, near the famous Charlottenburg Palace. For Jake, Berlin was like a third home to him. Feelings of familiarity and nostalgia rushed through his body.

"What got her booted from BND?" Jake asked.

"That happened a couple years ago," Nina said. "She was working opposite her SVR counterparts. In very deep. Turns out her SVR contact was in even deeper. If you know what I mean." She had a wide smile on her face.

"Not good," Sirena said. "Did she transfer any intel?"

"We think so," Nina said.

"I thought you were retired," Jake said.

"I am. Five years now."

"I thought you would have moved back to Hamburg," Jake said.

"I had a daughter," Nina said. "She lives here in Berlin. She has two children. A boy and a girl."

"Oma Nina," Jake said. "I don't see a ring. Are you still married?"

Nina shook her head. "I have never been married. My daughter was a gift from God. I call her my reunification girl."

"Born in Nineteen-Ninety?" Jake asked.

"Yes. Three years after our mission together. Her father was also BND, but he was killed in an autobahn accident before my daughter was born."

"I'm sorry," Jake said.

Nina nodded and turned from the outer ring autobahn onto a side street. From this location, Jake could see the downtown area of Berlin. Occasionally, he could look down a wide street and see the Brandenburg Gate in the distance.

"Where are we going?" Jake asked.

The German woman smiled and turned down a narrow road, which led to the back side of a three-story stone building.

"Here we are," Nina said. She turned into the center of a two-car garage. "I have a guest room for the two of you."

"This isn't necessary," Sirena said, leaning forward. "We can get a hotel."

Nina shut down the engine and turned to face Sirena. "Nobody knows about me and Jake having worked together."

She wasn't entirely correct, Jake thought. "What about Nikolai Volkov?"

A confused look on her face, Nina said, "You don't think he could be involved. I thought he was dead."

"Do you have a beer?" Jake asked.

"Always," Nina said.

The three of them got out. Jake pulled their bags from the back end, slung them over his shoulders, and followed their host into her house.

The first level of the house was traditionally set up as a kitchen, dining room and living room facing the road out front. Jake set their bags down and took a seat in the living room on a tan leather sofa.

Nina came in carrying three bottles of beer. She handed them out and said, "*Prosit.*" Then she took a seat in a leather chair across from Jake and Sirena. "Volkov?"

"Nikolai Volkov and Anton Grishin worked together for their last assignments here in Berlin," Jake said.

"Which means that they both also know Katja Meyer," Nina surmised.

"That's right," Jake said. "But, perhaps more importantly, the Russians also knew another former BND officer."

Jake noticed Sirena looked confused now.

"Who?" Sirena asked.

"The man I was just forced to kill in Iceland," Jake said.

"Son of the old Stasi officer, The Wolf?" Nina asked. "You told me about him the last time our paths crossed."

"Right," Jake said. "I was no longer with the Agency. Working out of Innsbruck, Austria."

Nina shifted her glance at Sirena and said, "It was a security conference. Strictly professional. Jake was a speaker."

"Nina was there under a fake persona," Jake said. "Tracking a potential security threat from a German company doing business with a company in Iraq."

"Anyway," Nina said. "Is there any indication Katja Meyer worked with this man you killed?"

"I don't know," Jake said. "Maybe you can ask your old BND contacts. The man's death in Iceland must have raised some flags in your old agency. Someone must be looking into his background."

"Maybe," Nina said. "It depends on the nature of the man's dismissal from the BND. We only track the good ones."

Jake thought about his daughter's mother, Alexandra, who had retired and was living with Jake in Calabria, Italy, before she was killed. The BND didn't do much to investigate her death. Part of that was Jake's fault, though. He was sure to make those responsible for her death to pay.

"What's the plan?" Nina asked.

Jake sipped his beer, his eyes tempered on his old friend. "For you? Nothing but intel. We'll take care of the rest."

"I take it you haven't been to Berlin in a while," Nina said. "Things have changed here a lot over the years."

"I know," Jake said. "I've been here a lot over the years."

"It is said that Berlin has more retired spies than any other place on earth," Nina said.

Sirena finally broke in. "That's a lot of bored people looking for relevancy."

"That's a nice way to put it," Nina said. "We are so used to high drama in far-off locations. It's difficult to settle down and watch football."

Smiling, Sirena said, "Which is why you want to help."

"Absolutely," Nina said.

"All right," Jake said. "Tonight we drink beer and talk. Tomorrow we take action."

Nina nodded agreement. "Tell me about the old spy in Bergen, Norway."

"He's dying," Jake said. "But he isn't dead yet. He's a lying bastard." Then Jake explained how he guessed the Russian was part of this entire ruse to take out Jake and anyone else involved during those old days of the Cold War. Another good reason to keep Nina close, Jake thought. She could be the next Hildur.

48

Jake woke the next morning to the sound of six bells ringing in the nearby church tower. He glanced out the window and viewed a dreary scene. It wasn't so much raining as the sky was bleeding slowly across the German capital.

"It's too early, Jake," Sirena said from the bed. "Come back to bed."

"I think we made too much noise last night," he said.

"I half expected Nina to join us."

He shook his head. "That's crazy."

"I saw the way she looked at you." Sirena flipped the covers from her, exposing her naked body.

Yeah, how could Jake say no to that?

They made quiet love and then Jake showered before heading down to the main floor. Sirena was still showering.

Nina was already sipping a cup of coffee, sitting at the large dining room table. She smiled at Jake and said, "I like her." Then she poured Jake a cup of coffee from a carafe.

"Sirena?"

"Yes. She's beautiful. And obviously very smart."

"She is," he agreed, accepting the cup of coffee. "Have you had a chance to think about how to proceed?"

"I think we start with Anton Grishin and Katja Meyer."

"I agree. We know they were in Bergen together meeting with the dying Vasily Sokolov."

"Also," Nina said, "we might have a little more leverage against Katja, since she fell from grace with the BND."

"They had more motive to kill Hildur in Iceland," Jake reminded his old friend.

"And you. After all, you were the one who killed Grishin's father."

"Allegedly," Jake said with a smirk. "This coffee is amazing."

Nina shook her head. "People like Anton Grishin and Vasily Sokolov don't worry about allegations. They simply kill and let God sort out the details."

He wondered if Nina would include Jake in that category as well. Before he could ask, Sirena came into the dining room with her hair wet and curlier than normal. She poured herself a cup of coffee and sat at the dining room table next to Jake.

"Good coffee," Sirena said. Then she turned to Nina and said, "Have you two worked out a plan?"

Jake said, "We think we should start with Anton Grishin and Katja Meyer, since we know they were in Bergen talking with Vasily Sokolov."

"Hmm," Sirena said. "I think we should split up. You two check on Anton and Katja, while I go talk with Nikolai

Volkov. After all, Volkov has never seen me before. He might remember the two of you. Especially if he's involved. He would have gotten recent photos of you."

"I knew she was smart," Nina said. "This makes sense to me."

Jake gave Sirena a concerned look.

"I can surely handle one former KGB and SVR officer," Sirena said. "He won't see me coming."

"All right," Jake said. "But we need to coordinate this simultaneously. And stay on your comm."

Sirena gave Jake a half-assed salute, and he knew exactly what that meant.

•

The three of them spent the rest of the day resting and discussing their actions for that evening. As the sun set on the German capital, the city really started to come to life.

Sirena took the U-Bahn subway to the eastern section of Berlin that used to be under Soviet and Russian control.

Nikolai Volkov was living under a German name three blocks from Alexanderplatz. Before German reunification and the fall of communism, Alex had been a depressing wide-open square with unimpressive buildings. Not that much had changed, other than a general sprucing up and more freedom, Sirena thought. Alex still didn't look German to Sirena.

"I've got you crossing Alexanderplatz," Sancho said into Sirena's comm.

"That's correct," she said without moving her lips much. "Are you sure he's still there?"

"His phone is," Sancho said. "In fact, according to his phone records, he hasn't left Berlin in more than a month."

"And before that?" she asked.

"A short trip to Poland."

"Where?"

"Gdansk."

She stretched her legs as she crossed the wide square toward the eastern entrance.

"Let me know if anything changes," she ordered.

"You got it, Boss," Sancho said.

Sirena walked a couple of blocks to a section of row houses of old Soviet-style apartments. According to her intel, Nikolai Volkov lived on the second story, which was actually the third floor in Germany. The top floor in this case. When she approached the front entrance, which had a security system with a FOB, she had to wait only a few seconds for someone inside the building to exit the building. She thanked the man with a smile and entered the building.

Instead of taking the elevator, Sirena went to the stairs and made her way slowly up the stairwell toward the top level.

"Here we go," Sirena said.

Now, the voice that came through her comm was that of Jake. "Don't underestimate this man."

"He's got to be seventy-five," Sirena said. "I think I can take him."

"He will be armed," Jake said. "He only needs to be strong enough to pull about four pounds on a trigger."

"Roger that," she said. Then she opened the door to the top-level corridor and went out to find the Russian's apartment.

"Should be the third door on the right," Sancho said. "By the way, he's currently watching a soccer match between Hertha Berlin and Leipzig."

"Now you're just showing off," she whispered.

"Just being thorough."

Sirena unzipped her jacket and felt inside for her Glock. She could have drawn her weapon, but decided to hold off for now. Especially after finding out that Nikolai Volkov had not been out of Berlin in a month.

She knocked on the door lightly, trying her best to smile and look less intimidating. That was one advantage she had over men in this business. Guys like Jake had a hard time looking innocuous. This was especially true when encountering older men who had been in the business. They didn't respect women or think they could be dangerous.

Sirena could hear movement inside, along with the sounds of soccer on the man's television. Damn it! She hated when Sancho was this precise.

The door opened slowly and an old man stood before her. The only photo Sirena had viewed of Nikolai Volkov was at least ten years old. The Russian had deteriorated significantly since that time.

She didn't even try Russian. Although she was nearly fluent in that language, she knew that Volkov spoke perfect English.

"I won't even try subterfuge with you," Sirena said. "I know who you really are, and I simply want to ask you a few questions."

"How can I refuse a pretty woman?" Volkov asked. "I was hoping you were here to kill me."

She gave the Russian a stern glare and said, "Not unless you lie to me."

The old KGB officer smiled, showing a few missing teeth. She guessed the Russian retirement system didn't cover dental.

"Please come in," Volkov said.

Out of caution, Sirena went inside but didn't turn her back on the man. It was then that she saw the old intel officer had an ancient Makarov handgun in his right hand.

"You won't need that gun," Sirena assured the man.

"Old habits," he said. Then he set his gun on a table behind the door.

Her eyes scanned the room and she saw that this old KGB and SVR officer wasn't exactly living the high life. This was a modest apartment by Berlin standards. She guessed it was a one-bedroom and one-bath place, with the charm of an old Moscow apartment from the seventies.

"Sorry to disturb your evening," Sirena said. "And your football match."

Volkov shrugged and said, "Leipzig is up two goals with time running out." He hesitated a moment and then asked, "Would you like something to drink?"

"Don't do it," Sancho said in her ear. "This man has been known to poison people in the past."

"No, thank you," she said. "I just have a few quick questions."

"Well, I will have another beer," Volkov said, and then went to the attached kitchen area and opened his small refrigerator.

"No vodka?" She gave him a broad smile.

He shook his head. "Afraid not. My stomach cannot handle vodka anymore. I know. What kind of Russian cannot drink vodka?" He pulled out a German beer and popped the top. Then he poured the beer into a tall glass. He shuffled back into the living room area and asked, "Do you mind if I sit down? My legs are shot."

She stood back as the man groaned to sit in an old chair, raising his legs on an ottoman.

"Now," Volkov said. "What can I do for you?"

"Do you know who I am?" she asked.

He shook his head and said, "If I had a gun to my head, I would guess BND. But you do not look German. So, I know they are hiring more ethnic people. I would have to guess you are a Turk or a Kurd."

"Good guess," Sirena said, playing along with his assumption. There was no way she wanted the Russian to know she was an American and Israeli.

"Is this about an old case? Because my memory is not what it used to be."

She had contemplated how to handle this man. She didn't want to give away too much information. Sirena finally said, "I understand you worked with a man named Anton Grishin."

Volkov didn't react too severely. He simply said, "Years ago, yes. But, as you probably know, I have been out of the game for over a decade."

"Why did you go to Gdansk a month ago?" she asked.

Now the Russian reacted. "Why is German intelligence still tracking my travel?"

"Old officers never really retire," Sirena said.

The man was obviously calculating the math in his head. If Sirena knew about his travel, what else could she know? She was betting on this.

Finally, Volkov said, "My daughter lives in Gdansk. She wants me to move there to be closer to her and my grandchildren."

"There's no record of this in his dossier," Sancho said over Sirena's comm.

"When was the last time you spoke or met with Anton Grishin?" she asked.

Now, the old Russian waited much too long to respond.

"Don't lie or I will know it," Sirena said.

"My guess is that you really want to know about that woman he is with," Volkov said.

"Which woman?"

"You know her. Katja Meyer. She is one of yours. Anton married her."

"She was a traitor to Germany," Sirena said. "If I had my way, she would be in federal prison."

Volkov laughed. "Your prisons are like Russia's country clubs."

Unfortunately, the old Russian was probably correct. She said, "You don't seem to hold Katja Meyer in high esteem."

Volkov tightened his jaw and said, "She is a whore. Anton was a good SVR officer before she came around. He should not have been susceptible to her. We train for that. But sometimes the heart wants what the mind knows it should not have."

"They came to you recently," she said with authority. She needed to try a new tactic.

He drank his beer, but kept his eyes on Sirena. Then he said, "You seem to already know everything I am about to say."

"I know you met," she lied. "But we are not entirely certain what they wanted from you."

Volkov shrugged and drank more beer. Then he cradled his half-empty glass and said, "Anton wanted to know about something from my past."

"The Sokolov brothers?" she asked.

The Russian couldn't hold back his shock now. But he said, "Anton worked with Alexi Sokolov in the old days. They went to Iceland together, but only Anton came back."

She said nothing.

The Russian continued, "They wanted to find Alexi's brother, Vasily."

"Why?" she asked.

"Because we had a mutual encounter with a man who said he was from Austria during that time," Volkov said.

"How was this man significant?" she asked.

"He was very good," the Russian said. "He could have killed Vasily, but for some reason he spared my old friend. He could have killed me here in Germany as well."

"And you told Anton Grishin about this Austrian man?" she asked.

Volkov shook his head. "Eventually we learned he was not Austrian. He was an American named Jake Adams. Code name was the Shadow Warrior."

She tried not to react, and hoped she had been successful. "What about this man?"

"We were told that this man killed a famous Stasi assassin code named The Wolf. Now, there have been many with this code name over the years, but this Stasi man was the original. Very brutal."

"He killed this Stasi man here in Germany?"

"No." The Russian took a long sip of beer. Then he continued, "In Iceland. This Adams man killed the Stasi officer and KGB officer, Alexi Sokolov."

"And you ran across this Jack Adams?"

"Jake Adams," the Russian corrected. "Yes, we crossed paths in Germany in early Nineteen Eighty-Seven."

"I'm confused," Sirena said. "What did Anton Grishin want with this American?"

"Retribution," Volkov said.

"How could you help? After all, you are retired."

"True. But I had this man's history." He tapped the side of his head. "Up here."

"Along with how to find Vasily Sokolov," she said. "Where is this man?"

Volkov shook his head and then drank the last of his beer. "No. I have said more than I should."

"Why did the KGB not kill this Jake Adams long ago?"

"Many tried. But then the Kremlin made him off limits. Don't ask me why."

"And now?"

"Now, this man is probably too old to worry about," Volkov said. "The SVR does not care about him anymore."

Sirena had heard what she needed to hear. She started toward the door.

"Wait," Volkov said. "Are you sure you are not here to kill me?"

"I'm sure," Sirena said.

The old Russian let out a deep breath of air. "Too bad. That is the only honorable way for an old KGB officer to die. I would take my own life, but my grandkids would never forgive me."

Mist seemed to form in the eyes of the old Russian KGB officer as Sirena left the man's apartment.

"You are out?" Sancho asked.

"Yes. Heading down to the stairwell."

"He really wanted you to kill him?"

"No," she said. "He would have pulled his gun on me, forcing the issue. But he didn't. How are Jake and Nina?"

"Just moving in. There was a slight delay. I'll patch you onto their comm."

"Roger that." Then Sirena pushed through the door leading down the stairwell. She couldn't help thinking about the last two old Russian intel officers they had encountered.

Was this the fate of her and Jake? Sitting around waiting to die or be killed?

49

In the former East Berlin side of the capital city, Jake and Nina sat in her BMW SUV, his eyes cast upon a row of townhouses. He had intentionally not listened to the comm feed Sirena was on only a couple of kilometers to the southeast. But he had gotten periodic updates from Sancho saying what Sirena was currently up to. He had a sigh of relief when he heard she had gotten what she could from the former Russian officer and was now heading toward their location. Initially they had planned to go in simultaneously, but their two targets had been out eating dinner at a nearby restaurant. Sancho had come up with a quick fix, though. He had been able to jam the Russian's cell phone and internet, in case he had a reason or inclination to warn Anton Grishin and Katja Meyer.

"Here we go," Nina said. "Coming out of the restaurant."

They were only two blocks from the apartment the unlikely couple shared.

"Go around the block and park with a view of their front entrance," Jake said.

"I just got off the U-Bahn," Sirena said through the comm. "Two blocks out."

Nina pulled out and cut quickly through a narrow street between buildings. She then turned right at the next block, powered forward quickly to circle the large apartment complex, and turned right again. Now she slowed down as she approached the street ahead.

"Turn off your lights," Jake said.

"The running lights will still be on," Nina complained.

"That's fine."

Nina hit the lights and slowly rounded the corner, pulling in behind a row of cars.

"There they are," Nina said. "A block from the entrance. We can beat them to it."

"I've got both of their cell phones tracked," Sancho said over the comm.

"Roger that," Jake said, and then got out onto the sidewalk.

Nina met Jake and took his arm like a couple out for an evening stroll. Now they moved quicker than a stroll to make sure they got to the Russian and German before they entered the building.

"Update?" Jake asked, meaning Sirena.

"Across the street and a block behind the targets," Sirena said.

"Perfect." Jake unzipped his coat for easy access to his Glock. But he tried his best not to look at the couple they approached. Instead, he viewed the area for anything out of the ordinary.

Jake slowed his pace somewhat. He wasn't sure why. But something seemed out of place. It was a gut feeling. Ahead, the Russian was on the right and the German woman on the left. This was tactically flawed, since Jake knew the Russian was right-handed. Unless. Unless he was trying to seem innocuous.

"This might be a trap," Jake said in his comm.

"We knew this was possible," Sirena said. "What are you seeing?"

Nina squeezed down on Jake's arm. "What is it?" she whispered.

"I don't like the van across the street from the entrance," Jake said.

"Heading toward that," Sirena said.

"Keep your eyes on other dangers," Jake demanded.

The dark panel van was parked facing in the wrong direction, giving access to its sliding door toward the front of the apartment building.

Jake's eyes shifted from the van, past their two targets, and toward the front entrance of the building. He thought he saw a flash of movement. Then nothing.

By now they were only about 50 meters away from their targets and closing the distance fast. Jake now kept his eyes on the Russian, his specific target, to make sure he wasn't drawing his weapon.

Jake heard a sliding door and took his view away from the Russian for a split second. When Jake saw the muzzle flashes with the coughing of automatic gunfire, he instinctively pulled his Glock and aimed it toward the couple ahead. Before he understood what was going on, the German woman, Katja Meyer, had hit the pavement like a sack of potatoes.

The Russian aimed at the van as he vectored behind a car. He shot a constant salvo with his gun, still moving for a better shot.

Instead of shooting the Russian, Jake caught a flash to his right, coming from the front of the apartment building. He twisted and took aim, firing five shots as he found a place between two cars.

"What the hell is going on?" Sirena yelled.

"Shoot those in the van," Jake demanded.

Nina was right next to Jake, but she looked confused.

"Take aim at those at the apartment," Jake told Nina. "I'm moving in to the Russian."

Nina nodded understanding. She started shooting to keep those at the entrance at bay, while Jake rushed forward.

The Russian was on his knees between two cars. He twisted his gun toward Jake, but for some reason Jake held his fire.

"You are not with them," the man said in Russian.

"No. Put your gun down and come with us if you want to live."

Now those in the van were having to deal with gunfire from Sirena. Jake could hear guns firing from both sides, along with the distinct sound of bullets striking the metal van.

Finally, the Russian lowered his gun and said, "They killed my Katja."

"I know. But we don't have time for this. Come with us."

The Russian nodded and rushed down the sidewalk toward Nina, who was still firing at the front of the apartment building.

"Let's go," Jake said to Nina.

She got up and ran toward her vehicle, with Jake and the Russian keeping pace.

Over his comm Jake said, "Back out and we'll pick you up on the west side of the complex."

"Copy," Sirena said.

More gunfire filled the night air as Sirena kept up her assault on the van as she moved back.

Nina got behind the wheel and Jake got into the front passenger side. The Russian piled in behind Jake.

Jake turned and aimed his gun at Anton Grishin. "What the hell is going on?"

Nina backed up, cranked the wheel, and then shoved the BMW into drive, lurching them forward along the east side of the apartment complex. Luckily, they had studied the maps of the area earlier in the day, and they had a contingency set up for this possible escape.

"You tell me," the Russian said. "Me and my wife were simply out for a nice dinner. Then someone kills her." Now, the pain of his reality crossed the man's face.

Nina turned left at the end of the building and hit the gas.

"Hurry," Sirena said. "They're coming after me."

"On our way," Jake said. "You should see us by now." Then he turned to Nina and said, "Power down your window and unlock the doors."

Nina hit the switches and her window powered down quickly.

"There she is," Jake yelled.

Sirena was aiming her gun down the street and firing in a slow, steady pace.

Nina screeched the tires to halt only feet from Sirena, who was out of bullets now.

Jake shoved his hand into Nina's chest, forcing her against her seat. Then Jake found his target and started slowly firing at the van, which had pulled out and stopped in the middle of the street.

Sirena piled into the back seat and immediately swapped out a new magazine.

"Go!" Jake yelled.

Nina punched it and the BMW lurched forward quickly. She would need to turn again or end up in Alexanderplatz in a kilometer. On the next block, she cranked the wheel and turned right.

"What the hell is he doing with us?" Sirena asked, pointing her thumb at the Russian.

"Who are you people?" Anton Grishin asked.

Jake turned to view the Russian. "The people who just saved your life."

Grishin seemed to finally recognize Jake. He shoved his body toward Jake and said, "It's you."

Before Jake could say a word, Sirena punched the man in the face and knocked him out.

"What the hell is going on?" Nina asked, her intense eyes gazing into the rearview mirror. "Also, they're on our tail. The van and another car. Looks like a dark Audi."

Jake turned to look back. "Black Audi SUV."

"I can outrun that," Nina said.

"We don't want to outrun them," Jake said. "We need to end this now." He turned to Sirena and asked, "Can you wake him up?"

"I barely touched him," Sirena explained, pulling the Russian into a sitting position.

Through the comm, Sancho said, "Did Sirena deck someone again? Sweet."

Nina got onto a side street heading south and picked up speed.

They had not planned for this contingency, Jake knew. But he was always prepared for the unexpected.

"Sancho," Jake said into his comm. "Map out these crossroads." Jake named two streets.

Seconds later, Sancho said, "It's all under construction. Looks like a huge apartment complex."

"The image could be old," Jake surmised.

"That's what I was thinking," Sancho said. "Hang on a second."

Jake could hear Sancho typing furiously on his keyboard back in Portugal.

Finally, Sancho said, "I was able to pull up some current video feeds in the area. Definitely apartments."

"That used to be warehouses along the Spree River," Jake said.

Nina turned toward Jake for a second and then back to her driving. "What are you thinking?"

Jake shrugged. "Good a place as any to bring the fight to those behind us." He turned back to see the vehicles still on their tail. Then he saw that Sirena had gotten the Russian to wake up. Jake gnashed his teeth and said to the Russian, "Who are these people trying to kill us?"

Anton Grishin rubbed the side of his face and said, "People like me."

"Russian assholes?" Jake filled in. "Why are they trying to kill you?"

Grishin shrugged and shook his head. "We were not sanctioned to kill you."

"Why would they care about me?" Jake asked.

"You tell me," Grishin said.

Suddenly, Jake's mind reeled and he couldn't help think about his son, Karl, who was imbedded deep within the Russian SVR and moving quickly up the chain of command there. Could Karl have authorized a counter operation? Not likely. But he could have made Jake off limits to attack.

Grishin said, "The last thing Moscow wants is a war with America based on past operations. This could be an endless battle. Best to leave the past in the past."

Jake glared at the Russian and said, "You should have done the same, Anton. I could have killed you in Iceland decades ago."

The Russian didn't have an answer for Jake. He simply sunk back against his seat and let out a deep breath.

50

Jake's contact, Sancho, directed them to a flimsy gate that entered a dark construction site with multiple four-story buildings in various phases of construction. Nina was forced to crash her SUV through the metal gate and continue toward a half-constructed building, lit only be sporadic security lights.

Sirena had reached into the back of the SUV, pulling out their identical German-made Heckler & Koch MP5s, with suppressed barrels and retractable butt stocks.

Jake aimed his barrel at the floor and racked a round into the chamber from his thirty-round magazine. Then he flipped the safety off and selected three-round burst.

"Give me a gun," the Russian demanded, just as Nina skidded the SUV to a halt in front of the construction site.

"Shut up and follow me," Jake yelled, and then got out of the SUV. He rounded the back of the SUV and aimed his gun at the approached van. Then he tapped the trigger a couple of times, sending 9mm bullets into the night air and smacking the front of the van.

Sirena and Nina rounded the front of the SUV, collected the Russian, and hauled him into the concrete frame of the new construction.

Halting at the entrance, Sirena turned her weapon on the Audi, firing 30 rounds on full auto, taking out the windshield, tires and side windows.

This shooting gave Jake time to rush toward Sirena and enter the building.

Sirena followed Jake in and quickly replaced her empty magazine with a full one.

"What now?" Sirena asked.

"How many full magazines do we have?" Jake asked.

"Enough to handle these assholes."

The four of them were hunkered down behind the thick concrete walls.

The Russian finally said, "This can't be sanctioned by Moscow."

Jake glanced at Nina, who was on her cell phone. Then he looked at Anton Grishin and said, "Why do you say that?"

"We did nothing to deserve this," Grishin said. "They killed my Katja."

Jake glanced around a corner at the van and Audi outside. Then he said, "You and your people killed an innocent Icelandic police officer, shot the current Iceland National Police Commissioner, and tried to take us out. I can't believe the SVR would allow this."

Without warning, a barrage of gunfire smacked the walls outside, forcing the four of them to get lower to the floor.

Jake switched to semi-auto, plopped prone and shoved the barrel around the edge of the door entrance. Then he looked for movement and let loose a few rounds before backing up again. The response was nearly immediate. A salvo of bullets broke the night air again.

Glancing at Sirena, Jake said, "I can get a better angle upstairs."

She handed Jake another full magazine and mouthed the words, Be Careful.

Jake rushed up the nearby stairway, which was nothing but concrete frame. When he got to the first level, he rounded the corner and slowed his pace toward a nearby open window. Below he could hear gunfire from both sides.

For now, he had the advantage. But as soon as he fired his first shot, they would know his position. He would have to move to another window down the side of the building.

He slowly raised his head up and propped his arm under the barrel on the window ledge. Then he waited for them to fire again.

When the first flashes went off, Jake took aim and fired twice before scooting back behind the wall. Now bullets hit the wall next to the window and some came through, hitting the wall behind Jake.

He hurried down the length of the building, staying far enough back from the edge so those below wouldn't be able to see him. Then he settled next to another open window and waited for them to fire again. As those below fired, Jake quickly raised his rifle and pointed behind the muzzle flash of one and fired three times. He was sure he hit his target.

Jake tapped on his comm and said, "Status, two."

"All good, one," Sirena said. "Three has called in some friends."

Great. That's all they needed was crossfire.

"I think you put two down," Sirena said.

"At least one," Jake acknowledged. Then he got up and moved back to the first window he had shot from. Maybe they wouldn't expect him back there. Or they'd think they had two shooters up high. "Get them to fire."

"Roger that," Sirena said.

Seconds later came slow, sustained firing from below him.

Jake used that distraction to raise his barrel above the window-frame. The first flashes came from the edge of the van. Switching to full auto, Jake held back the trigger and let the bullets fly. He was sure he took out that man. When others trained their fire on Jake, he swished his barrel toward them until his slide jammed back and he was out of bullets.

He shoved his back against the wall and put in his last full magazine. Now he'd need to be sure to choose his targets. He flipped back to semi-auto. At least he still had his Glock with a couple of extra magazines.

"You got at least one more," Sirena said.

"He's da man," Sancho interjected from Portugal.

"How many left?" Jake asked.

"Can't be many," Sirena answered.

"I'm burned here," he said. "Coming down. Got an idea."

Jake backed away from the window entrance and rushed down to the ground level again. He found a spot on the dirty concrete between Sirena and Nina.

"Last mag," Jake said.

Nina said, "We should just wait for my friends from the BND to show up."

Jake unslung his MP5 from his shoulder and handed it to Nina. "That could turn into a cluster fuck."

"I gave them our position and said we were being attacked by the Russian Mafia," Nina said.

"Why did you say that?" Grishin asked.

"They would be less likely to come in knowing those out there are with the Russian SVR," Nina explained.

"She's right," Jake said. "Besides, we have no idea who they are."

Sirena broke in. "I say we kill them all and let God sort them out."

Jake pointed down the corridor in front of him. "I can head down there and vector around them to the side. When I get to the edge of that end of the building, they'll be exposed to me."

Sirena ran that scenario through her mind. Then she said, "That's a long distance to shoot your Glock."

"Fifty feet max," Jake said. "I can close the distance."

"Without cover," Sirena protested.

"Let's just wait for my friends," Nina pled.

"We don't have time for that," Jake said. Then, without waiting, he got up and ran down the corridor.

"Will distract," Sirena said over the comm.

"Roger that," Jake agreed, his breathing heavy.

As Jake rounded the first corridor, heading into another wing of the building, he could hear the near-constant gunfire outside. He took out his Glock and kept it at the side of his right leg.

Now, as he moved through this side of the building, he kept back from the open windows, hugging the far wall. When he reached the end of the building, he quickly looked out the open door on both sides, his gun swishing to each side for a target. Nothing.

He stepped lightly out into the end of the building toward the edge. Just as he was about to round the final corner, a dark figure stepped out.

Simultaneously, Jake and the Russian fired. Both of them hit the ground.

51

In his ear, Jake could hear ringing. Then, echoing in the background, he heard the frantic woman's voice. That voice was accompanied by a calmer male voice issuing directions.

Jake tried to get up, his gun still in his right hand. He finally got to a sitting position and shook his head to attempt to see the scene in front of him. In the background, not in his ear, he could hear the distinct sound of sirens moving in their direction.

"Jake," came the woman's voice again in his ear. "Where are you?"

"He should be just ahead of you," the man said.

Suddenly, Jake felt a presence behind him. He tried to swivel on his butt in the hard-packed dirt, but a sharp pain seeped through his body from somewhere.

"Jake," the woman said again. This time the voice came from outside him.

His eyes adjusted as the woman got closer.

"Jake is hit," the woman said.

Shaking his head again, Jake said, "I'm alright. I took one in the left shoulder."

Sirena got to her knees and put her hand on his leather sleeve.

"Make sure that guy is dead," Jake said.

"Put pressure on this wound," Sirena demanded.

Jake nodded, put his gun down, and held his upper biceps with his right hand.

Sirena went over to the other dark figure laying on the ground about twenty feet away.

"Are you alright?" came the man's voice over his comm. It was Sancho in Portugal.

"What the hell do you think?" Jake asked him.

"I think you aren't getting any younger," Sancho said. "And you're not invincible."

"Is this supposed to be a pep talk?" Jake asked.

"I'm just saying." Then a pause.

Jake saw a flash from Sirena's cell phone.

"Identify," Sirena said, obviously to Sancho.

"On it, boss," Sancho said. In a couple of seconds, he instructed, "I won't need facial recognition for this one. That's SVR Colonel Tatiana Sokolova."

Jake got to his feet and his head swirled. He nearly lost his balance as he made his way to Sirena. "Are you sure?" Jake asked.

"Yes, sir," Sancho confirmed.

When Jake got to Sirena and the fallen woman, Sirena said, "Sit your ass down."

Jake ignored Sirena and said, "Any relation to Alexi and Vasily Sokolov?"

Silence on the other end for a moment, as Jake and Sirena stared at each other.

Finally, Sancho said, "Vasily was her uncle. Alexi was her father."

"Vasily is still alive in Norway," Jake said.

"No, sir," Sancho said reluctantly. "He died this morning in Bergen."

"How?" Jake asked.

"Unknown for sure. Probably the cancer."

Jake suddenly felt weak as the sounds of sirens got even closer. He sat down again and Sirena kneeled down next to Jake.

"Where did I hit her?" Jake asked, his words barely coming from his mouth.

"Looks like three close shots center mass," Sirena said. "Good shooting."

It didn't feel very good, he thought. "I only remember shooting once."

"That happens," she said. Then she pushed on Jake to lay down. "I need to find the exit wound."

She rolled him to his belly and pulled his arm forward. Then she gasped.

"What?" Jake asked, trying to sit up again.

"The bullet went through your arm and vectored into your chest," Sirena said. "We need an ambulance here fast."

Sancho said, "One is with the Polizei. I'll direct them to you."

Jake glanced at Sirena. He had never seen her so concerned. "Did you get all of them?"

"All but one," she said. "He surrendered to Nina, claiming diplomatic immunity."

"He'll just wish he was dead," Jake said.

"Tell them to follow the light," Sirena said. Then she held Jake and said, "Not you. Don't follow the light." She turned on the flashlight on her phone and waved it above her head."

Within seconds, Polizei rushed to them, followed by EMTs.

Jake tried to form words, but his head swirled and he couldn't come up with a single phrase.

"Shut up and lay down," Sirena ordered. Then she placed his head in her lap as the EMTs went to work on him.

Each shot he had taken in the past had been different. Some had hurt more than others. Some he had barely felt, the adrenaline coursing through his body from the bullet strike. But this one was different. There wasn't so much pain as there was a finality to his wound. Was this how it all ended? Had his luck finally run out?

His last memory was an anguished look on Sirena's face, with tears streaking both cheeks. Then there was total darkness.

52

Three days later

When Jake finally opened his eyes, he could see the familiar environment of a hospital room. Could smell the disgusting odors associated with intensive care.

The room itself was rather dark. The only lights were along the edge of the wall, and from the machines monitoring him. He could see the electrical outlets were European. Then he saw some signs in German, and his mind drifted back to his extended stay in an Austrian hospital after he had nearly been killed there years ago.

A stout nurse came in with a smile and saw that Jake was awake. In German she said, "Our special guest is finally awake."

He wasn't sure what she was talking about. "Where am I?" he asked in German.

"The best hospital in Berlin," the nurse said. Then she checked on the monitors and adjusted something on his IV drip. She stopped and said, "I understand you are Austrian. You must be important."

Jake blinked and said, "Why do you say that?"

"You have a number of armed guards," the nurse said. "I can't even tell how many. Perhaps you are a diplomat."

She was fishing, Jake guessed. He said, "I'm just an ordinary average guy."

The nurse patted his right arm and said, "Sure. And I'm the Queen of Prussia." Then she left the room.

Seconds later, a familiar face entered. Sirena had a smile for Jake when she said, "That was one long nap." She came alongside his bed and took his right hand in hers.

"How long?" he asked.

"Three days."

He shrugged. "Not a record." After a brief hesitation, he said, "The nurse said something about guards."

"Nina insisted the BND provide security," Sirena said. "So, you've got a combination of the Polizei, the BND, and even Austrian intelligence."

He gave her a confused look.

Sirena said, "I made sure to show them your Austrian passport. Apparently, you still have some sway there."

Jake shrugged. "At least one country still loves me. When can I get out of here?"

She swished her head side to side. "A few more days."

"I feel fine."

"No way. The magic bullet ripped through your arm, ricocheted off a rib, and planted itself two inches from your spine. The bullet clipped your lung. If it hadn't hit your rib, it could have taken out your heart or aorta. I'd be hauling your body back to Montana right now."

"So, I've got that going for me," he said, trying to smile.

She squeezed his hand. "Maybe it's time."

"For?"

"For an end game that doesn't include you in a pine box."

"You know I want to be cremated," he said.

"No, I don't know that," Sirena said. "We've never discussed it."

"Now you know. I don't want a bunch of critters eating my body."

"While you've been sleeping, I've had time to think about the future. I know we have enough money to retire. What's stopping us?"

She didn't know all of the money he had hidden around the world in various accounts and banks, but Sirena was right. They were set for life. Maybe it was time.

"What have you found out about the Russian woman?" Jake asked.

"A source from the Russian government said she wasn't sanctioned to do anything," Sirena said. "Somehow she got word that a group of former officers here in Germany and Russia were plotting a revenge operation. She had followed the man to Iceland. She was just behind us in Norway. By the way, the Norwegians found a poison in Vasily Sokolov's system. It looks like Tatiana Sokolova gave her uncle the fatal dose out of mercy."

"I wanted to put a bullet in his head," Jake said. "A true warrior should not let cancer take him."

She squeezed his hand again, agreeing with a slight nod of her head.

"What happened to Anton Grishin?" Jake asked. "He was involved with this."

Sirena shook her head. "Nina confirmed this and was ready to call in INTERPOL. But the Russians came in and hauled him off."

"Shit. He would have been better off with INTERPOL."

"I know. Iceland is complaining officially. But they don't have a lot of power against Russia."

"Well, Anton Grishin did try to kill me."

"He did. But he changed his tune when his former Russian colleagues came to kill him and actually killed his German wife."

"What are the Germans saying?"

"The BND?"

"The BND, the Polizei, whatever."

Sirena shrugged. "The son of The Wolf was a disgraced former officer acting on his own. The Germans just want the whole incident to go away."

"Then why all the security?" Jake asked.

"Truthfully, they don't know your true identity," Sirena said. "They think you're a highly decorated Austrian operative. I've overheard them ask the medical staff when you'll be ready to transport."

He smiled. "And who are you to me?"

"I'm your wife," she said proudly.

"How did you explain the shoot-out and the use of our MP5s?"

"Nina made that go away. She's awesome, by the way."

Yeah, she was, he thought. "Any loose ends?"

She shook her head. "As far as we can tell, the man you were forced to kill in Iceland, the son of The Wolf, has no living relatives. The same is true of Tatiana Sokolova. She wasn't married and has no children. Nobody to come after you."

"And the Russian SVR?" he asked.

"Want this to go away. If I had to guess, Anton Grishin is taking a dirt nap somewhere in Siberia. Deep under the permafrost."

"Maybe I should have killed him all those years ago in Iceland," Jake said.

"Do you have any more of these loose ends coming back to bite you in the ass?" she asked.

"Other than the Chinese?" He shook his head. "I got smarter as I aged. Didn't leave many behind."

"That's the Jake I know." Sirena ran her hand affectionately along his forearm.

After a long moment of silence, Jake finally said, "I'll think about a way out."

"It's easy," she said. "You just resign from the Gomez organization."

"But I really like his private jet," Jake said.

"I know. But we won't have to travel as much. When we do, we go first class."

He nodded. "We'll figure it out." This was a lie, of course. He still had one item of unfinished business that needed his immediate attention.

She leaned down and kissed him on the lips.

Then he closed his eyes and went to sleep.

Made in United States
Troutdale, OR
08/25/2024

22294088R10186